SEVEN
UP

Also by Janet Evanovich

Hot Six
High Five
Four to Score
Three to Get Deadly
Two for the Dough
One for the Money

SEVEN UP

Janet Evanovich

Doubleday Large Print Home Library Edition

ST. MARTIN'S PRESS ≈ NEW YORK

ISBN 0-7394-3590-6

**This Large Print Book carries the
Seal of Approval of N.A.V.H.**

ACKNOWLEDGMENTS

Thanks to Amy Lehmkuhl and Vicky Picha for suggesting the title for this book.

SEVEN UP

PROLOGUE

FOR THE BETTER part of my childhood, my professional aspirations were simple—I wanted to be an intergalactic princess. I didn't care much about ruling hordes of space people. Mostly I wanted to wear the cape and the sexy boots and carry a cool weapon.

As it happens, the princess thing didn't work out for me, so I went to college and when I graduated I went to work as a lingerie buyer for a chain store. Then *that* didn't work out, so I blackmailed my bail bondsman cousin into giving me a job as a bounty hunter. Funny how fate steps in. I never did get the cape or the sexy boots, but I *do* finally have a sort of cool weapon. Well okay, it's a little .38 and I keep it in my cookie jar, but it's still a weapon, right?

Back in the days when I was auditioning for princess I had the occasional run-in with the bad kid in the neighborhood. He was two years older than me. His name was Joe Morelli. And he was trouble.

I'm still having those run-ins with Morelli. And he's still trouble . . . but now he's the kind of trouble a woman likes.

He's a cop and his gun is bigger than mine and he doesn't keep it in a cookie jar.

He proposed to me a couple weeks ago during a libido attack. He unsnapped my jeans, hooked a finger into the waistband, and pulled me to him. "About that proposal, Cupcake . . ." he said.

"Which proposal are we talking about?"

"The marriage proposal."

"Are you serious?"

"I'm a desperate man."

That was obvious.

Truth is, I was desperate, too. I was starting to have romantic thoughts about my electric toothbrush. Problem was, I just didn't know if I was ready for *marriage*. Marriage is scary stuff. You have to share a bathroom. What's with that? And what about fantasies? Suppose the intergalactic princess resurfaces and I need to set off on a mission?

Morelli shook his head. "You're thinking again."

"There's a lot to consider."

"Let me hit the high points for you . . . wedding cake, oral sex, plus you can have my credit card."

"I like the wedding cake part."

"You like the other parts, too," Morelli said.

"I need time to think."

"Sure," Morelli said, "take all the time you need. How about thinking upstairs in the bedroom."

His finger was still hooked into my jeans and it was getting warm down there. I inadvertently glanced at the stairs.

Morelli grinned and pulled me closer. "Thinking about the wedding cake?"

"No," I said. "And I'm not thinking about the credit card, either."

ONE

I KNEW SOMETHING bad was going to happen when Vinnie called me into his private office. Vinnie is my boss and my cousin. I read on a bathroom stall door once that Vinnie humps like a ferret. I'm not sure what that means, but it seems reasonable since Vinnie *looks* like a ferret. His ruby pinky ring reminded me of treasures found in Seaside Park arcade claw-machines. He was wearing a black shirt and black tie, his receding black hair was slicked back, casino pit boss–style. His facial expression was tuned to *not happy*.

I looked across the desk at him and tried not to grimace. "Now what?"

"I got a job for you," Vinnie said. "I want you to find that rat fink Eddie DeChooch, and I want you to drag his boney ass back here. He got tagged smuggling a truckload of bootleg cigarettes up from Virginia and he missed his court date."

I rolled my eyes so far into the top of my head I could see hair growing. "I'm not going after Eddie DeChooch. He's old, and he kills people, and he's dating my grandmother."

"He hardly ever kills people anymore," Vinnie said. "He has cataracts. Last time he tried to shoot someone he emptied a clip into an ironing board."

Vinnie owns and operates Vincent Plum Bail Bonds in Trenton, New Jersey. When someone is accused of a crime, Vinnie gives the court a cash bond, the court releases the accused until trial, and Vinnie hopes to God the accused shows up for court. If the accused decides to forgo the pleasure of his court date, Vinnie is out a lot of money unless I can find the accused and bring him back into the system. My name is Stephanie Plum and I'm a bond enforcement officer . . . aka bounty hunter. I took the job when times

were lean and not even the fact that I graduated in the top ninety-eight percent of my
college class could get me a better position.
The economy has since improved, and
there's no good reason why I'm still tracking
down bad guys, except that it annoys my
mother and I don't have to wear panty hose
to work.

"I'd give this to Ranger, but he's out of the
country," Vinnie said. "So that leaves you."

Ranger is a soldier-of-fortune kind of guy
who sometimes works as a bounty hunter.
He's very good . . . at everything. And he's
scary as hell. "What's Ranger doing out of
the country? And what do you mean by out
of the country? Asia? South America? Miami?"

"He's making a pickup for me in Puerto
Rico." Vinnie shoved a file folder across his
desk. "Here's the bond agreement on De-
Chooch and your authorization to capture.
He's worth fifty thousand to me . . . five
thousand to you. Go over to DeChooch's
house and find out why he pulled a no-show
on his hearing yesterday. Connie called and
there was no answer. Christ, he could be
dead on his kitchen floor. Going out with
your grandma's enough to kill anyone."

Vinnie's office is on Hamilton, which at first glance might not seem like the best location for a bail bonds office. Most bail bonds offices are across from the jail. The difference with Vinnie is that many of the people he bonds out are either relatives or neighbors and live just off Hamilton in the Burg. I grew up in the Burg and my parents still live there. It's really a very safe neighborhood, since Burg criminals are always careful to do their crimes elsewhere. Well, okay, Jimmy Curtains once walked Two Toes Garibaldi out of his house in his pajamas and drove him to the landfill . . . but still, the actual whacking didn't take place in the Burg. And the guys they found buried in the basement of the candy store on Ferris Street weren't from the Burg, so you can't really count them as a statistic.

Connie Rosolli looked up when I came out of Vinnie's office. Connie is the office manager. Connie keeps things running while Vinnie is off springing miscreants and/or fornicating with barnyard animals.

Connie had her hair teased up to about three times the size of her head. She was wearing a pink V-neck sweater that molded to boobs that belonged on a much larger woman and a short black knit skirt that would have fit a much smaller woman.

Connie's been with Vinnie since he first started the business. She's stuck it out this long because she puts up with nothing and on exceptionally bad days she helps herself to combat pay from the petty cash.

She did a face scrunch when she saw I had a file in my hand. "You aren't actually going out after Eddie DeChooch, are you?"

"I'm hoping he's dead."

Lula was slouched on the faux leather couch that had been shoved against a wall and served as the holding pen for bondees and their unfortunate relatives. Lula and the couch were almost identical shades of brown, with the exception of Lula's hair, which happened to be cherry red today.

I always feel sort of anemic when I stand next to Lula. I'm a third-generation American of Italian-Hungarian heritage. I have my mother's pale skin and blue eyes and good metabolism, which allows me to eat birthday cake and still (almost always) button the top snap on my Levi's. From my father's side of the family I've inherited a lot of unmanage-able brown hair and a penchant for Italian hand gestures. On my own, on a good day with a ton of mascara and four-inch heels, I can attract some attention. Next to Lula I'm wallpaper.

"I'd offer to help drag his behind back to jail," Lula said. "You could probably use the help of a plus-size woman like me. But it's too bad I don't like when they're dead. Dead creeps me out."

"Well, I don't actually know if he's dead," I said.

"Good enough for me," Lula said. "Sign me up. If he's alive I get to kick some sorry-ass butt, and if he's dead . . . I'm outta there."

Lula talks tough, but the truth is we're both pretty wimpy when it comes to actual butt kicking. Lula was a ho in a former life and is now doing filing for Vinnie. Lula was as good at ho'ing as she is at filing . . . and she's not much good at filing.

"Maybe we should wear vests," I said.

Lula took her purse from a bottom file drawer. "Suit yourself, but I'm not wearing no Kevlar vest. We don't got one big enough and besides it'd ruin my fashion statement."

I was wearing jeans and a T-shirt and didn't have much of a fashion statement to make, so I took a vest from the back room.

"Hold on," Lula said when we got to the curb, "what's this?"

"I bought a new car."

"Well dang, girl, you did good. This here's an excellent car."

It was a black Honda CR-V, and the payments were killing me. I'd had to make a choice between eating and looking cool. And looking cool had won out. Well hell, there's a price for everything, right?

"Where we going?" Lula asked, settling in next to me. "Where's this dude live?"

"We're going to the Burg. Eddie De-Chooch lives three blocks from my parents' house."

"He really dating your grandma?"

"She ran into him at a viewing two weeks ago at Stiva's Funeral Home, and they went out for pizza after."

"Think they did the nasty?"

I almost ran the car up on the sidewalk. "No! Yuck!"

"Just asking," Lula said.

DeChooch lives in a small brick duplex. Seventy-something Angela Marguchi and her ninety-something mother live in one half of the house, and DeChooch lives in the other. I parked in front of the DeChooch half, and Lula and I walked to the door. I was wearing the vest, and Lula was wearing a stretchy animal-print top and yellow stretch pants. Lula is a big woman and tends to test the limits of Lycra.

"You go ahead and see if he's dead," Lula said. "And then if it turns out he's not dead, you let me know and I'll come kick his ass."

"Yeah, right."

"Hunh," she said, lower lip stuck out. "You think I couldn't kick his ass?"

"You might want to stand to the side of the door," I said. "Just in case."

"Good idea," Lula said, stepping aside. "I'm not afraid or anything, but I'd hate to get bloodstains on this top."

I rang the bell and waited for an answer. I rang a second time. "Mr. DeChooch?" I yelled.

Angela Marguchi stuck her head out her door. She was half a foot shorter than me, white-haired and bird-boned, a cigarette rammed between thin lips, eyes narrowed from smoke and age. "What's all this racket?"

"I'm looking for Eddie."

She looked more closely and her mood brightened when she recognized me. "Stephanie Plum. Goodness, haven't seen you in a while. I heard you were pregnant by that vice cop, Joe Morelli."

"A vicious rumor."

"What about DeChooch," Lula asked Angela. "He been around?"

"He's in his house," Angela said. "He never goes anywhere anymore. He's depressed. Won't talk or nothing."

"He's not answering his door."

"He don't answer his phone, either. Just go in. He leaves the door unlocked. Says he's waiting for someone to come shoot him and put him out of his misery."

"Well, that isn't us," Lula said. " 'Course if he was willing to pay for it I might know someone . . ."

I carefully opened Eddie's door and stepped into the foyer. "Mr. DeChooch?"

"Go away."

The voice came from the living room to my right. The shades were drawn and the room was dark. I squinted in the direction of the voice.

"It's Stephanie Plum, Mr. DeChooch. You missed your court date. Vinnie is worried about you."

"I'm not going to court," DeChooch said. "I'm not going anywhere."

I moved farther into the room and spotted him sitting in a chair in the corner. He was a wiry little guy with white rumpled hair. He was wearing an undershirt and boxer shorts and black socks with black shoes.

"What's with the shoes?" Lula asked.

DeChooch looked down. "My feet got cold."

"How about if you finish getting dressed and we take you to reschedule," I said.

"What are you, hard of hearing? I told you, I'm not going anywhere. Look at me. I'm in a depression."

"Maybe you're in a depression on account of you haven't got any pants on," Lula said. "Sure would make *me* feel happier if I didn't have to worry about seeing your Mr. Geezer hanging out of your boxer shorts."

"You don't know nothing," DeChooch said. "You don't know what it's like to be old and not to be able to do anything right anymore."

"Yeah, I wouldn't know about that," Lula said.

What Lula and I knew about was being

young and not doing anything right. Lula and I *never* did anything right.

"What's that you're wearing?" DeChooch asked me. "Christ, is that a bulletproof vest? See, now that's so fucking insulting. That's like saying I'm not smart enough to shoot you in the head."

"She just figured since you took out that ironing board it wouldn't hurt to be careful," Lula said.

"The ironing board! That's all I hear about. A man makes one mistake and that's all anybody ever talks about." He made a dismissive hand gesture. "Ah hell, who am I trying to kid. I'm a has-been. You know what I got arrested for? I got arrested for smuggling cigarettes up from Virginia. I can't even smuggle cigarettes anymore." He hung his head. "I'm a loser. A fuckin' loser. I should shoot *myself*."

"Maybe you just had some bad luck," Lula said. "I bet next time you try to smuggle something it works out fine."

"I got a bum prostate," DeChooch said. "I had to stop to take a leak. That's where they caught me . . . at the rest stop."

"Don't seem fair," Lula said.

"Life isn't fair. There isn't nothing fair

about life. All my life I've worked hard and I've had all these . . . achievements. And now I'm old and what happens? I get arrested taking a leak. It's goddamn embarrassing."

His house was decorated with no special style in mind. Probably it had been furnished over the years with whatever fell off the truck. There was no Mrs. DeChooch. She'd passed away years ago. So far as I knew there'd never been any little DeChooches.

"Maybe you should get dressed," I said. "We really need to go downtown."

"Why not," DeChooch said. "Don't make no difference where I sit. Could just as well be downtown as here." He stood, gave a dejected sigh, and shuffled stoop-shouldered to the stairs. He turned and looked at us. "Give me a minute."

The house was a lot like my parents' house. Living room in front, dining room in the middle, and kitchen overlooking a narrow backyard. Upstairs there'd be three small bedrooms and a bathroom.

Lula and I sat in the stillness and darkness, listening to DeChooch walking around above us in his bedroom.

"He should have smuggled Prozac instead of cigarettes," Lula said. "He could have popped a few."

"What he should do is get his eyes fixed," I said. "My Aunt Rose was operated on for cataracts and now she can see again."

"Yeah, if he got his eyes fixed he could probably shoot a lot more people. I bet that'd cheer him up."

Okay, maybe he shouldn't get his eyes fixed.

Lula looked toward the stairs. "What's he doing up there? How long does it take to put a pair of pants on?"

"Maybe he can't find them."

"You think he's that blind?"

I shrugged.

"Come to think of it, I don't hear him moving around," Lula said. "Maybe he fell asleep. Old people do that a lot."

I went to the stairs and yelled up at DeChooch. "Mr. DeChooch? Are you okay?"

No answer.

I yelled again.

"Oh boy," Lula said.

I took the stairs two at a time. DeChooch's bedroom door was closed, so I rapped on it hard. "Mr. DeChooch?"

Still no answer.

I opened the door and looked inside. Empty. The bathroom was empty and the other two bedrooms were empty. No De-Chooch.

Shit.

"What's going on?" Lula called up.

"DeChooch isn't here."

"Say what?"

Lula and I searched the house. We looked under beds and in closets. We looked in the cellar and the garage. DeChooch's closets were filled with clothes. His toothbrush was still in the bathroom. His car was asleep in the garage.

"This is too weird," Lula said. "How could he have gotten past us? We were sitting right in his front room. We would have seen him sneak by."

We were standing in the backyard, and I cut my eyes to the second story. The bathroom window was directly above the flat roof that sheltered the back door leading from the kitchen to the yard. Just like my parents' house. When I was in high school I used to sneak out that window late at night so I could hang with my friends. My sister, Valerie, the perfect daughter, never did such a thing.

"He could have gone out the window," I said. "He wouldn't have had a far drop either because he's got those two garbage cans pushed against the house."

"Well, he's got some nerve acting all old and feeble and goddamned depressed, and then soon as we turn our backs he goes and jumps out a window. I'm telling you, you can't trust nobody anymore."

"He snookered us."

"Damn skippy."

I went into the house, searched the kitchen, and with minimum effort found a set of keys. I tried one of the keys on the front door. Perfect. I locked the house and pocketed the keys. It's been my experience that sooner or later, everyone comes home. And when DeChooch *does* come home he might decide to shut the house up tight.

I knocked on Angela's door and asked if she wasn't by any chance harboring Eddie DeChooch. She claimed she hadn't seen him all day, so I left her with my card and gave instructions to call me if DeChooch turned up.

Lula and I got into the CR-V, I cranked the engine over, and an image of DeChooch's keys floated to the forefront of my brain.

House key, car key . . . and a third key. I took the key ring out of my purse and looked at it.

"What do you suppose this third key is for?" I asked Lula.

"It's one of them Yale locks that you put on gym lockers and sheds and stuff."

"Do you remember seeing a shed?"

"I don't know. I guess I wasn't paying attention to that. You think he could be hiding in a shed along with the lawn mower and weed whacker?"

I shut the engine off and we got out of the car and returned to the backyard.

"I don't see a shed," Lula said. "I see a couple garbage cans and a garage."

We peered into the dim garage for the second time.

"Nothing in there but the car," Lula said.

We walked around the garage to the rear and found the shed.

"Yeah, but it's locked," Lula said. "He'd have to be Houdini to get himself in there and then lock it from the outside. And on top of that this shed smells *real bad*."

I shoved the key in the lock and the lock popped open.

"Hold on," Lula said. "I vote we leave this

shed locked. I don't want to know what's smelling up this shed."

I yanked at the handle, the door to the shed swung wide, and Loretta Ricci stared out at us, mouth open, eyes unseeing, five bullet holes in the middle of her chest. She was sitting on the dirt floor, her back propped against the corrugated metal wall, her hair white from a dose of lime that wasn't doing much to stop the destruction that follows death.

"Shit, that ain't no ironing board," Lula said.

I slammed the door shut, snapped the lock in place, and put some distance between me and the shed. I told myself I wasn't going to throw up, and took a bunch of deep breaths. "You were right," I said. "I shouldn't have opened the shed."

"You never listen to me. Now look what we got. All on account of you had to be nosy. Not only that, but I know what's gonna happen next. You're gonna call the police, and we're gonna be tied up all day. If you had any sense you'd pretend you didn't see nothing, and we'd go get some fries and a Coke. I could really use some fries and a Coke."

I handed her the keys to my car. "Get yourself some food, but make sure you're back in a half hour. I swear, if you abandon me I'll send the police out after you."

"Boy, that really hurts. When did I ever abandon you?"

"You abandon me all the time!"

"Hunh," Lula said.

I flipped my cell phone open and called the police. Within minutes I could hear the blue-and-white pull up in front of the house. It was Carl Costanza and his partner, Big Dog.

"When the call came in, I knew it had to be you," Carl said to me. "It's been almost a month since you found a body. I knew you were due."

"I don't find that many bodies!"

"Hey," Big Dog said, "is that a Kevlar vest you're wearing?"

"Brand new, too," Costanza said. "Not even got any bullet holes in it."

Trenton cops are top of the line, but their budget isn't exactly Beverly Hills. If you're a Trenton cop you hope Santa will bring you a bulletproof vest because vests are funded primarily with miscellaneous grants and donations and don't automatically come with the badge.

I'd removed the house key from De-Chooch's key ring and had it safely tucked away in my pocket. I gave the two remaining keys to Costanza. "Loretta Ricci is in the shed. And she's not looking too good."

I knew Loretta Ricci by sight, but that was about it. She lived in the Burg and was widowed. I'd put her age around sixty-five. I saw her sometimes at Giovichinni's Meat Market ordering lunch meat.

VINNIE LEANED FORWARD in his chair and narrowed his eyes at Lula and me. "What do you mean you lost DeChooch?"

"It wasn't our fault," Lula said. "He was sneaky."

"Well hell," Vinnie said, "I wouldn't expect you to be able to catch someone who was sneaky."

"Hunh," Lula said. "Your ass."

"Dollars to doughnuts he's at his social club," Vinnie said.

It used to be there were a lot of powerful social clubs in the Burg. They were powerful because numbers were run out of them. Then Jersey legalized gambling and pretty soon the local numbers industry was in the toilet. There are only a few social clubs left in the Burg now, and the members all sit around reading *Modern Maturity* and comparing pacemakers.

"I don't think DeChooch is at his social club," I told Vinnie. "We found Loretta Ricci dead in DeChooch's toolshed, and I think DeChooch is on his way to Rio."

FOR LACK OF something better to do I went home to my apartment. The sky was overcast and a light rain had started to fall. It was midafternoon, and I was more than a little creeped out by Loretta Ricci. I parked in the lot, pushed through the double glass doors that led to the small lobby, and took the elevator to the second floor.

I let myself into my apartment and went straight to the flashing red light on the phone machine.

The first message was from Joe Morelli. "Call me." Didn't sound friendly.

The second message was from my friend MoonMan. "Hey dude," he said. "It's the MoonMan." That was it. No more message.

The third message was from my mother. "Why me?" she asked. "Why do I have to have a daughter who finds dead bodies? Where did I go wrong? Emily Beeber's daughter never finds dead bodies. Joanne Malinoski's daughter never finds dead bodies. Why me!"

News travels fast in the Burg.

The fourth and last message was from my mother again. "I'm making a nice chicken for supper with a pineapple upside-down cake for dessert. I'll set an extra plate in case you don't have plans."

My mother was playing hardball with the cake.

My hamster, Rex, was asleep in his soup can in his cage on the kitchen counter. I tapped on the side of the cage and called hello, but Rex didn't budge. Catching up on his sleep after a hard night of running on his wheel.

I thought about calling Morelli back and decided against it. Last time I talked to Morelli we'd ended up yelling at each other. After spending the afternoon with Mrs. Ricci I didn't have the energy to yell at Morelli.

I shuffled into the bedroom and flopped down on the bed to think. Thinking very often resembles napping, but the intent is different. I was in the middle of some very deep thinking when the phone rang. By the time I dragged myself out of my thinking mode there was no one left on the line, only another message from Mooner.

"Bummer," Mooner said. That was it. Nothing more.

MoonMan has been known to experiment with pharmaceuticals and for the better part of his life has made no sense at all. Usually it's best to ignore MoonMan.

I stuck my head in my refrigerator and found a jar of olives, some slimy brown lettuce, a lone bottle of beer, and an orange with blue fuzz growing on it. No pineapple upside-down cake.

There was a pineapple upside-down cake a couple miles away at my parents' house. I checked out the waistband on my Levi's. No room to spare. Probably I didn't need the cake.

I drank the beer and ate some olives. Not bad, but not cake. I blew out a sigh of resignation. I was going to cave. I wanted the cake.

MY MOTHER AND my grandmother were at the door when I pulled to the curb in front of their house. My Grandmother Mazur moved

in with my parents shortly after my Grandfather Mazur took his bucket of quarters to
the big poker slot machine in the sky. Last
month Grandma finally passed her driver's
test and bought herself a red Corvette. It
took her exactly five days to acquire enough
speeding tickets to lose her license.

"The chicken's on the table," my mother
said. "We were just about to sit."

"Lucky for you the dinner got late,"
Grandma said, "on account of the phone
wouldn't stop ringing. Loretta Ricci is big
news." She took her seat and shook out her
napkin. "Not that I was surprised. I said to
myself a while ago that Loretta was looking
for trouble. She was real hot to trot, that one.
Went wild after Dominic died. Man-crazy."

My father was at the head of the table and
he looked like he wanted to shoot himself.

"She'd just jump from one man to the next
at the seniors' meeting," Grandma said.
"And I heard she was real loosey-goosey."

The meat was always placed in front of
my father so he got first pick. I guess my
mother figured if my father got right down to
the task of eating he wouldn't be so inclined
to jump up and strangle my grandmother.

"How's the chicken?" my mother wanted to know. "Do you think it's too dry?"

No, everyone said, the chicken wasn't dry. The chicken was just right.

"I saw a television show the other week about a woman like that," Grandma said. "This woman was real sexy, and it turned out one of the men she was flirting with was an alien from outer space. And the alien took the woman up to his spaceship and did all kinds of things to her."

My father hunkered lower over his plateful of food and mumbled something indiscernible except for the words . . . *crazy old bat.*

"What about Loretta and Eddie De-Chooch?" I asked. "Do you suppose they were seeing each other?"

"Not that I know of," Grandma said. "From what I know, Loretta liked her men hot, and Eddie DeChooch couldn't get it up. I went out with him a couple times, and that thing of his was dead as a doorknob. No matter what I did I couldn't get nothing to happen."

My father looked up at Grandma, and a piece of meat fell out of his mouth.

My mother was red-faced at the other end of the table. She sucked in some air and made the sign of the cross. "Mother of God," she said.

I fiddled with my fork. "If I left now I probably wouldn't get any pineapple upside-down cake, right?"

"Not for the rest of your life," my mother said.

"So how did she look?" Grandma wanted to know. "What was Loretta wearing? And how was her hair done? Doris Szuch said she saw Loretta at the food store yesterday afternoon, so I'm guessing Loretta wasn't all rotted and wormy yet."

My father reached for the carving knife, and my mother cut him down with a steel-eyed look that said *don't even think about it.*

My father's retired from the post office. He drives a cab part-time, only buys American cars, and smokes cigars out behind the garage when my mother isn't home. I don't think my dad would actually stab Grandma Mazur with the carving knife. Still, if she choked on a chicken bone I'm not sure he'd be all that unhappy.

"I'm looking for Eddie DeChooch," I said to Grandma. "He's FTA. Do you have any ideas about where he might be hiding?"

"He's friends with Ziggy Garvey and

Benny Colucci. And there's his nephew Ronald."

"Do you think he'd leave the country?"

"You mean because he might have put those holes in Loretta? I don't think so. He's been accused of killing people before and he never left the country. At least not that I know of."

"I hate this," my mother said. "I hate having a daughter who goes out after killers. What's the matter with Vinnie for giving this case to you?" She glared at my father. "Frank, he's *your* side of the family. You need to talk to him. And why can't you be more like your sister, Valerie?" my mother asked me. "She's happily married with two beautiful children. She doesn't go around chasing after killers, finding dead bodies."

"Stephanie's *almost* happily married," Grandma said. "She got engaged last month."

"Do you see a ring on her finger?" my mother asked.

Everyone looked at my naked finger.

"I don't want to talk about it," I said.

"I think Stephanie's got the hots for someone else," Grandma said. "I think she's sweet on that Ranger fella."

My father paused with his fork plunged into a mound of potatoes. "The bounty hunter? The black guy?"

My father was an equal opportunity bigot. He didn't go around painting swastikas on churches, and he didn't discriminate against minorities. It was just that with the possible exception of my mother, if you weren't Italian you weren't quite up to standards.

"He's Cuban-American," I said.

My mother did another sign of the cross.

TWO

IT WAS DARK when I left my parents. I didn't expect Eddie DeChooch to be home, but I drove past his house anyway. Lights were blazing in the Marguchi half. The DeChooch half was lifeless. I caught a glimpse of yellow crime-scene tape still stretched across the backyard.

There were questions I wanted to ask Mrs. Marguchi, but they'd keep. I didn't want to disturb her tonight. Her day had been bad enough. I'd catch her tomorrow, and on the way I'd stop at the office and get an address for Garvey and Colucci.

I cruised around the block and headed for

Hamilton Avenue. My apartment building is located a couple miles from the Burg. It's a sturdy, three-story chunk of brick and mortar built in the seventies with economy in mind. It doesn't come with a lot of amenities, but it has a decent super who'll do anything for a six-pack of beer, the elevator almost always works, and the rent is reasonable.

I parked in the lot and looked up at my apartment. The lights were on. Someone was home and it wasn't me. It was probably Morelli. He had a key. I felt a rush of excitement at the thought of seeing him, quickly followed by a sinking sensation in the pit of my stomach. Morelli and I have known each other since we were kids, and life has never been simple between us.

I took the stairs, trying out emotions, settling on conditionally happy. Truth is, Morelli and I are pretty sure we love each other. We're just not sure we can stand to live together for the rest of our lives. I don't especially want to marry a cop. Morelli doesn't want to marry a bounty hunter. And then there's Ranger.

I opened the door to my apartment and found two old guys sitting on my couch, watching a ball game on television. No Morelli in sight. They both stood and smiled when I came into the room.

"You must be Stephanie Plum," one of the men said. "Allow me to make the introductions. I'm Benny Colucci and this is my friend and colleague, Ziggy Garvey."

"How did you get into my apartment?"

"Your door was open."

"No, it wasn't."

The smile widened. "It was Ziggy. He's got the touch with a lock."

Ziggy beamed and wiggled his fingers. "I'm an old coot, but my fingers still work."

"I'm not crazy about people breaking into my apartment," I said.

Benny solemnly nodded. "I understand, but we thought in this instance it would be okay, being that we have something of a very serious nature to discuss."

"And urgent," Ziggy added. "Also of an urgent nature."

They looked at each other and agreed. It was urgent.

"And besides," Ziggy said. "You got some nosy neighbors. We were waiting for you in the hall, but there was a lady who kept opening her door and looking at us. It made us uncomfortable."

"I think she was interested in us, if you know what I mean. And we don't do anything funny like that. We're married men."

"Maybe when we were younger," Ziggy said, smiling.

"So what's this urgent business?"

"Ziggy and me happen to be very good friends of Eddie DeChooch," Benny said. "Ziggy and Eddie and me go way back. So Ziggy and me are concerned about Eddie's sudden disappearance. We're worried Eddie might be in trouble."

"You mean because he killed Loretta Ricci?"

"No, we don't think that's a big issue. People are always accusing Eddie of killing people."

Ziggy leaned forward in a conspiratorial whisper. "Bum raps, all of them."

Of course.

"We're concerned because we think Eddie might not be thinking right," Benny said. "He's been in this depression. We go to see him and he don't want to talk to us. He's never been like that."

"It's not normal," Ziggy said.

"Anyway, we know you're looking for him,

and we don't want him to get hurt, you understand?"

"You don't want me to shoot him."

"Yeah."

"I almost never shoot people."

"Sometimes it happens, but God forbid it would be Choochy," Benny said. "We're trying to prevent it from being Choochy."

"Hey," I said, "if he gets shot it won't be my bullet."

"And then there's something else," Benny said. "We're trying to find Choochy so we can help him."

Ziggy nodded. "We think maybe he should be seeing a doctor. Maybe he needs a psychiatrist. So we figured we could work together being that you're looking for him, too."

"Sure," I said, "if I find him I'll let you know." After I delivered him up to the court and had him safely behind bars.

"And we were wondering if you have any leads?"

"Nope. None."

"Gee, we were counting on you to have some leads. We heard you were pretty good."

"Actually, I'm not all that good . . . it's more that I'm lucky."

Another exchange of glances.

"So, are you, you know, feeling lucky about this?" Benny asked.

Hard to feel lucky when I've just let a depressed senior citizen slip through my fingers, found a dead woman in his shed, and sat through dinner with my parents. "Well, it's sort of too early to tell."

There was some fumbling at the door, the door swung open, and Mooner ambled in. Mooner was wearing a head-to-toe purple spandex bodysuit with a big silver *M* sewn onto the chest.

"Hey dude," Mooner said. "I tried calling you, but you were never home. I wanted to show you my new Super Mooner Suit."

"Cripes," Benny said, "he looks like a flaming fruit."

"I'm a superhero, dude," the Mooner said.

"Super *fruit*cake is more like it. You walk around in this suit all day?"

"No way, dude. This is my secret suit. Ordinarily I only wear this when I'm doing super deeds, but I wanted the dudette here to get the full impact, so I changed in the hall."

"Can you fly like Superman?" Benny asked Mooner.

"No, but I can fly in my mind, dude. Like, I can soar."

"Oh boy," Benny said.

Ziggy looked at his watch. "We gotta go. If you get a line on Choochy you'll let us know, right?"

"Sure." Maybe.

I watched them leave. They were like Jack Sprat and his wife. Benny was about fifty pounds overweight with chins spilling over his collar. And Ziggy looked like a turkey carcass. I assumed they both lived in the Burg and belonged to Chooch's club, but I didn't know that for certain. Another assumption was that they were on file as former Vincent Plum bondees since they hadn't felt it necessary to give me their phone numbers.

"So what do you think of the suit?" Mooner asked me when Benny and Ziggy left. "Dougie and me found a whole box of them. I think they're like for swimmers or runners or something. Dougie and me don't know any swimmers who could use them, but we thought we could turn them into Super Suits. See, you can wear them like underwear and then when you need to be a superhero you just take your clothes off. Only problem is we haven't got any capes. That's probably why the old dude didn't know I was a superhero. No cape."

"You don't really think you're a superhero, do you?"

"You mean like in real life?"

"Yeah."

Mooner looked astonished. "Superheroes are like, fiction. Didn't anyone ever tell you that?"

"Just checking."

I'd gone to high school with Walter "MoonMan" Dunphy and Dougie "The Dealer" Kruper.

Mooner lives with two other guys in a narrow row house on Grant Street. Together they form the Legion of Losers. They're all potheads and misfits, floating from one menial job to the next, living hand-to-mouth. They're also gentle and harmless and utterly adoptable. I don't exactly hang with Mooner. It's more that we keep in touch, and when our paths cross he tends to generate maternal feelings in me. Mooner is like a goofy stray kitten that shows up for a bowl of kibble once in a while.

Dougie lives several units down in the same row of attached houses. In high school Dougie was the kid who wore the dorky button-down shirt when all the other kids wore T-shirts. Dougie didn't get great grades, didn't do sports, didn't play a musical instrument, and didn't have a cool car. Dougie's solitary accomplishment was his ability to suck Jell-O into his nose through a straw.

After graduation it was rumored that Dougie had moved to Arkansas and died. And then several months ago Dougie surfaced in the Burg, alive and well. And last month Dougie got nailed for fencing stolen goods out of his house. At the time of his arrest his dealing had seemed more community service than crime since he'd become the definitive source for cut-rate Metamucil, and for the first time in years Burg seniors were regular.

"I thought Dougie shut down his dealership," I said to Mooner.

"No, man, I mean we really *found* these suits. They were like in a box in the attic. We were cleaning the house out and we came across them."

I was pretty sure I believed him.

"So what do you think?" he asked. "Cool, huh?"

The suit was lightweight Lycra, fitting his gangly frame perfectly without a wrinkle . . . and that included his doodle area. Not much left to the imagination. If the suit was on Ranger I wouldn't complain, but this was more than I wanted to see of the Mooner.

"The suit is terrific."

"Since Dougie and me have these cool suits, we decided we'd be crime-fighters . . . like Batman."

Batman seemed like a nice change. Usually Mooner and Dougie were Captain Kirk and Mr. Spock.

Mooner pushed the Lycra cap back off his head, and his long brown hair spilled out. "We were going to start fighting crime tonight. Only problem is, Dougie's gone."

"Gone? What do you mean gone?"

"Like he just disappeared, dude. He called me on Tuesday and told me he had some stuff to do, but I should come over to watch wrestling last night. We were gonna watch it on Dougie's big screen. It was like an awesome event, dude. Anyway, Dougie never showed up. He wouldn't have missed wrestling unless something awful happened. He wears like four pagers on him and he's not answering any of them. I don't know what to think."

"Did you go out looking for him? Could he be at a friend's house?"

"I'm telling you, it's not like him to miss wrestling," Mooner said. "Like *nobody* misses wrestling, dude. He was all excited about it. I think something bad's happened."

"Like what?"

"I don't know. I just have this bad feeling."

We both sucked in a breath when the phone rang, as if our suspecting disaster would make it happen.

"He's here," Grandma said at the other end of the line.

"Who? Who's where?"

"Eddie DeChooch! Mabel picked me up after you left so we could pay our respects to Anthony Varga. He's laid out at Stiva's and Stiva did a real good job. I don't know how Stiva does it. Anthony Varga hasn't looked this good for twenty-five years. He should have come to Stiva when he was alive. Anyway, we're still here, and Eddie DeChooch just walked into the funeral parlor."

"I'll be right there."

No matter if you're suffering depression or wanted for murder, you still pay your respects in the Burg.

I grabbed my shoulder bag off the kitchen counter and shoved Mooner out the door. "I have to run. I'll make some phone calls and I'll get back to you. In the meantime, you should go home and maybe Dougie will show up."

"Which home should I go to, dude? Should I go to Dougie's home or my home?"

"Your home. And check on Dougie's home once in a while."

Having Mooner worry about Dougie made me uneasy, but it didn't feel critical. Then again, Dougie'd missed wrestling. And Mooner was right . . . *nobody* misses wrestling. At least nobody in Jersey.

I ran down the hall and down the stairs. I bolted through the lobby, out the door, and into my car. Stiva's was a couple miles down Hamilton Avenue. I did a mental equipment inventory. Pepper spray and cuffs in my purse. The stun gun was probably in there, too, but it might not be charged. My .38 was home in the cookie jar. And I had a nail file in case things got physical.

Stiva's Funeral Parlor is housed in a white frame structure that was once a private residence. Garages for the various funeral-type vehicles and viewing rooms for the various dead have been added to accommodate business. There's a small parking lot. Black shutters frame the windows, and the wide front porch is covered in green indoor-outdoor carpet.

I parked in the lot and power-walked to the front entrance. Men stood in a knot on the porch, smoking and swapping stories. They were working-class men, dressed in unmemorable suits, their waists and hairlines showing the years. I moved past them to the foyer. Anthony Varga was in Slumber Room number one. And Caroline Borchek was in Slumber Room number two. Grandma Mazur was hiding behind a fake ficus tree in the lobby.

"He's in with Anthony," Grandma said. "He's talking to the widow. Probably sizing her up, looking for a new woman to shoot and stash in his shed."

There were about twenty people in the Varga viewing room. Most of them were seated. A few stood at the casket. Eddie DeChooch was among those at the casket.

I could go in and quietly maneuver myself to his side and clap on the cuffs. Probably the easiest way to get the job done. Unfortunately, it would also create a scene and upset people who were grieving. More to the point, Mrs. Varga would call my mother and relay the whole gruesome incident. My other choices were that I could approach him at the casket and ask him to come outside with me. Or I could wait until he left and nab him in the parking lot or on the front porch.

"What do we do now?" Grandma wanted to know. "Are we just gonna go in and grab him, or what?"

I heard someone suck in some air behind me. It was Loretta Ricci's sister, Madeline. She'd just come in and spotted DeChooch.

"Murderer!" she shouted at him. "You murdered my sister."

DeChooch went white-faced and stumbled backward, losing his footing, knocking into Mrs. Varga. Both DeChooch and Mrs. Varga grabbed the casket for support, the casket tipped precariously on its skirted trolley, and there was a collective gasp as Anthony Varga lurched to one side, bashing his head against the satin padding.

Madeline shoved her hand into her purse,

someone yelled that Madeline was going for a gun, and everyone scrambled. Some went flat to the floor, and some surged up the aisle to the lobby.

Stiva's assistant, Harold Barrone, lunged at Madeline, catching her at the knees, throwing Madeline into Grandma and me, taking us all down in a heap.

"Don't shoot," Harold yelled to Madeline. "Control yourself!"

"I was just getting a tissue, you moron," Madeline said. "Get off me."

"Yeah, and get off *me*," Grandma said. "I'm old. My bones could snap like a twig."

I pulled myself to my feet and looked around. No Eddie DeChooch. I ran out to the porch where the men were standing. "Have any of you seen Eddie DeChooch?"

"Yep," one of the men said. "Eddie just left."

"Which way did he go?"

"He went to the parking lot."

I flew down the stairs and got to the lot just as DeChooch was pulling away in a white Cadillac. I said a few comforting cuss words and took off after DeChooch. He was about a block ahead of me, driving on the white line and running stoplights. He turned into the Burg, and I wondered if he was going home. I followed him down Roebling Avenue, past the street that would have taken him to his house. We were the only traffic on Roebling, and I knew I'd been made. DeChooch wasn't so blind that he couldn't see lights in his rearview mirror.

He continued to wind his way through the Burg, taking Washington and Liberty streets and then going back up Division. I had visions of myself following DeChooch until one of us ran out of gas. And what then? I didn't have a gun or a vest. And I didn't have backup. I'd have to rely on my powers of persuasion.

DeChooch stopped at the corner of Division and Emory, and I stopped about twenty feet behind him. It was a dark corner without a streetlight, but DeChooch's car was clear in my lights. DeChooch opened his door and got out all creaky-kneed and stooped. He looked at me for a moment, shielding his eyes against my brights. Then he matter-of-factly raised his arm and fired off three shots. *Pow. Pow. Pow.* Two hit the pavement beside my car and one zinged off my front bumper.

Yikes. So much for persuasion. I threw

the CR-V into reverse and floored it. I wheeled around Morris Street, screeched to a stop, rammed the car into drive, and rocketed out of the Burg.

I'd pretty much stopped shaking by the time I parked in my lot and I'd ascertained that I hadn't wet my pants, so all in all, I was sort of proud of myself. There was a nasty gash in my bumper. Could have been worse, I told myself. Could have been a gash in my head. I was trying to cut Eddie DeChooch some slack because he was old and depressed, but truth is, I was starting to dislike him.

Mooner's clothes were still in the hall when I got out of the elevator, so I gathered them up on my way to my apartment. I paused at my door and listened. The television was on. Sounded like boxing. I was almost certain I'd shut the television off. I rested my forehead on the door. Now what?

I was still standing there with my forehead pressed to the door when the door opened and Morelli grinned out at me.

"One of those days, huh?"

I looked around. "Are you alone?"

"Who'd you expect to be here?"

"Batman, the Ghost of Christmas past,

Jack the Ripper." I dumped Mooner's clothes on the foyer floor. "I'm a little freaked. I just had a shoot-out with De-Chooch. Except he was the only one with a gun."

I gave Morelli the lurid details, and when I got to the part about not wetting my pants, the phone rang.

"Are you all right?" my mother wanted to know. "Your grandmother just got home and said you took off after Eddie DeChooch."

"I'm fine, but I lost DeChooch."

"Myra Szilagy told me they're hiring at the button factory. And they give benefits. You could probably get a good job on the line. Or maybe even in the office."

Morelli was slouched on the couch, back to watching boxing, when I got off the phone. He was wearing a black T-shirt and a cream cable-knit sweater over jeans. He was lean and hard-muscled and darkly Med-iterranean. He was a good cop. He could make my nipples tingle with a single look. And he was a New York Rangers fan. This made him just about perfect . . . except for the cop part.

Bob the Dog was on the couch beside Morelli. Bob is a cross between a golden retriever and Chewbacca. He'd originally come to live with me but then decided he liked Morelli's house better. One of those guy things, I guess. So now Bob mostly lives with Morelli. It's okay with me since Bob eats *everything*. Left to his own devices Bob could reduce a house to nothing more than a few nails and some pieces of tile. And because Bob frequently takes in large quantities of roughage such as furniture, shoes, and houseplants, Bob frequently expels mountains of dog doody.

Bob smiled and wagged his tail at me, and then Bob went back to watching television.

"I'm assuming you know the guy who took his clothes off in your hall," Morelli said.

"Mooner. He wanted to show me his underwear."

"Makes perfect sense to me."

"He said Dougie's gone missing. He said Dougie went out yesterday morning and never came back."

Morelli dragged himself away from the boxing. "Isn't Dougie coming up to trial?"

"Yes, but Mooner doesn't think Dougie skipped. Mooner thinks something's wrong."

"Mooner's brain probably looks like a fried

egg. I wouldn't put a lot of stock in what Mooner thinks."

I handed Morelli the phone. "Maybe you could make a few phone calls. You know, check the hospitals." And the morgue. As a cop, Morelli had better access than I did.

Fifteen minutes later Morelli had run through the list. No one meeting Dougie's description had checked into St. Francis, Helen Fuld, or the morgue. I called Mooner and told him our findings.

"Hey man," Mooner said, "it's getting scary. It's not just Dougie. Now my clothes are gone."

"Don't worry about your clothes. I've got your clothes."

"Boy, you're good," Mooner said. "You're really good."

I did some mental eye rolling and hung up.

Morelli patted the seat next to him. "Sit down and let's talk about Eddie DeChooch."

"What about DeChooch?"

"He's not a nice guy."

A sigh inadvertently escaped from my lips.

Morelli ignored the sigh. "Costanza said you got to talk to DeChooch before he took off."

"DeChooch is depressed."

"I don't suppose he mentioned Loretta Ricci?"

"Nope, not a word about Loretta. I found Loretta all by myself."

"Tom Bell's primary on the case. I ran into him after work, and he said Ricci was already dead when she was shot."

"What?"

"He won't know the cause of death until after the autopsy."

"Why would someone shoot a dead person?"

Morelli did a palms-up.

Great. "Do you have anything else to give me?"

Morelli looked at me and grinned.

"Besides that," I said.

I WAS ASLEEP, and in my sleep I was suffocating. There was a terrible weight on my chest and I couldn't breathe. Usually I don't have dreams about suffocating. I have dreams about elevators shooting out the tops of buildings with me trapped inside. I have dreams of bulls stampeding down the street after me. And I have dreams of forgetting to get dressed and going to a shopping center naked. But I never have dreams of suffocating. Until now. I dragged myself awake and opened my eyes. Bob was sleeping next to me with his big dog head and front paws on my chest. The rest of the bed was empty. Morelli was gone. He'd tippy-toed out at the crack of dawn, and he'd left Bob with me.

"Okay, big guy," I said, "if you get off me I'll feed you."

Bob might not understand all the words, but Bob almost never missed the intent when it came to food. His ears perked up and his eyes got bright and he was off the bed in an instant, dancing around all happy-faced.

I poured out a caldron of dog crunchies and looked in vain for people food. No Pop-Tarts, no pretzels, no Cap'n Crunch with Crunchberries. My mother always sends me home with a bag of food, but my mind had been on Loretta Ricci when I left my parents' house, and the food bag had been forgotten, left on the kitchen table.

"Look at this," I said to Bob. "I'm a domestic failure."

Bob gave me a look that said, *Hey lady, you fed me, so how bad could you be*?

I stepped into Levi's and boots, threw a denim jacket on over my nightshirt, and hooked Bob up to his leash. Then I hustled Bob down the stairs and into my car so I could drive him to my archenemy Joyce Barnhardt's house to poop. This way I didn't have to do the pooper-scooper thing, and I felt like I was accomplishing something. Years ago I'd caught Joyce boinking my husband (now my *ex*-husband) on my dining room table, and once in a while I like to re-pay her kindness.

Joyce lives just a quarter mile away, but that's enough distance for the world to change. Joyce has gotten nice settlements from her ex-husbands. In fact, husband number three was so eager to get Joyce out of his life he deeded her their house, free and clear. It's a big house set on a small lot in a neighborhood of upwardly mobile pro-fessionals. The house is red brick with fancy white columns supporting a roof over the front door. Sort of like the Parthenon meets Practical Pig. The neighborhood has a strict pooper-scooper law, so Bob and I only visit Joyce under cover of darkness. Or in this case, early in the morning before the street awakens.

I parked half a block from Joyce. Bob and I quietly skulked to her front yard, Bob did his business, we skulked back to the car, and zipped off for McDonald's. No good deed goes unrewarded. I had an Egg McMuffin and coffee, and Bob had an Egg McMuffin and a vanilla milkshake.

We were exhausted after all this activity, so we went back to my apartment and Bob took a nap and I took a shower. I put some gel in my hair and scrunched it up so there were lots of curls. I did the mascara and eyeliner thing and finished with lip gloss. I might not solve any problems today, but I looked pretty damn good.

A half hour later Bob and I sailed into Vinnie's office, ready to go to work.

"Uh-oh," Lula said, "Bob's on the job." She bent down to scratch Bob's head. "Hey Bob, what's up."

"We're still looking for Eddie DeChooch," I said. "Anyone know where his nephew Ronald lives?"

Connie wrote a couple addresses on a sheet of paper and handed it over to me. "Ronald has a house on Cherry Street, but you'll have more luck finding him at work at this time of the day. He runs a paving company, Ace Pavers, on Front Street, down by the river."

I pocketed the addresses, leaned close to Connie, and lowered my voice. "Is there anything on the street about Dougie Kruper?"

"Like what?" Connie asked.

"Like he's missing."

The door to Vinnie's office burst open and Vinnie stuck his head out. "What do you mean he's missing?"

I looked up at Vinnie. "How did you hear that? I was whispering, and you had your door closed."

"I got ears in my ass," Vinnie said. "I hear everything."

Connie ran her fingers along the desk edges. "Goddamn you," Connie said, "you planted a bug again." She emptied her cup filled with pencils, rifled through her drawers, emptied the contents of her purse onto the desktop. "Where is it, you little worm?"

"There's no bug," Vinnie said. "I'm telling you I got good ears. I got radar."

Connie found the bug stuck to the bottom of her telephone. She ripped it off and smashed it with her gun butt. Then she dropped the gun back into her purse and threw the bug in the trash.

"Hey," Vinnie said, "that was company property!"

"What's with Dougie?" Lula asked. "Isn't he coming up to trial?"

"Mooner said he and Dougie were supposed to watch wrestling together on Dougie's big screen, and Dougie never showed up. He thinks something bad's happened to Dougie."

"Wouldn't catch me missing a chance to see those wrestling guys wearing little spandex panties on a big screen," Lula said.

Connie and I agreed. A girl would have to be crazy to miss all that beefcake on a big screen.

"I haven't heard anything," Connie said, "but I'll ask around."

The front door to the office crashed open and Joyce Barnhardt stormed in. Her red hair was teased out to its full potential. She was wearing SWAT-type pants and shirt, the pants tight across her butt and the shirt unbuttoned halfway down her sternum, showing a black bra and a lot of cleavage. BOND ENFORCEMENT was written in white letters across the back of the shirt. Her eyes were black-rimmed, and her lashes were heavily mascaraed.

Bob hid under Connie's desk, and Vinnie ducked into his office and locked the door. A while back, after a short consultation with his johnson, Vinnie had agreed to hire Joyce on as an apprehension agent. Mr. Nasty was still happy with the decision, but the rest of Vinnie didn't know what to do with Joyce.

"Vinnie, you limp dick, I saw you sneak back into your office. Get the hell out here," Joyce yelled.

"Nice to see you in such a good mood," Lula said to Joyce.

"Some dog did his business on my lawn again. This is the second time this week."

"Guess you have to expect that when you get your dates from the animal shelter," Lula said.

"Don't push me, fatso."

Lula narrowed her eyes. "Who you calling fatso? You call me fatso again and I'll rearrange your face."

"Fatso, fat ass, lard butt, blimpo . . ."

Lula launched herself at Joyce, and the two of them went down to the floor, scratching and clawing. Bob stayed firmly under the desk. Vinnie hid in his office. And Connie moseyed over, waited for her opportunity, and buzzed Joyce on the ass with the stun gun. Joyce let out a squeak and went inert.

"This is the first time I've used one of these things," Connie said. "They're kind of fun."

Bob crept out from under the desk to take a look at Joyce.

"So, how long you been taking care of Bob?" Lula asked, heaving herself to her feet.

"He spent the night."

"You suppose it was Bob-size poop on Joyce's lawn?"

"Anything's possible."

"How possible? Ten percent possible? Fifty percent possible?"

We looked down at Joyce. She was starting to twitch, so Connie gave her another buzz with the stun gun.

"It's just that I hate to use the pooper-scooper. . . ." I said.

"Hah!" Lula said on a bark of laughter. "I knew it!"

Connie gave Bob a doughnut from the box on her desk. "What a good boy!"

THREE

"SINCE BOB WAS such a good boy, and I'm in such a good mood, I'm gonna help you find Eddie DeChooch," Lula said.

Her hair was sticking straight up from where Joyce had pulled it, and she'd popped a button off her shirt. Taking her along would probably ensure my safety because she looked genuinely deranged and dangerous.

Joyce was still on the floor, but she had one eye open and her fingers were moving. Best that Lula and Bob and I left before Joyce got her other eye open.

"So what do you think?" Lula wanted to

know when we were all in the car and on our way to Front Street. "Do you think I'm fat?"

Lula didn't look like she had a lot of fat on her. She looked solid. Bratwurst solid. But it was *a lot* of bratwurst.

"Not exactly fat," I said. "More like *big.*"

"I haven't got none of that cellulite, either."

This was true. A bratwurst does not have cellulite.

I drove west on Hamilton, toward the river, to Front Street. Lula was in front riding shotgun, and Bob was in back with his head out the window, his eyes slitty and his ears flapping in the breeze. The sun was shining and the air was just a couple degrees short of spring. If it hadn't been for Loretta Ricci I'd have bagged the search for Eddie De-Chooch and taken off for the shore. The fact that I needed to make a car payment gave me added incentive to point the CR-V in the direction of Ace Pavers.

Ace Pavers rolled asphalt and they were easy to find. The office was small. The garage was large. A behemoth paver sat in the chain-link holding pen attached to the garage, along with other assorted tar-blackened machinery.

I parked on the street, locked Bob in the car, and Lula and I marched up to the office. I'd expected an office manager. What I found was Ronald DeChooch playing cards with three other guys. They were all in their forties, dressed in casual dress slacks and three-button knit shirts. Not looking like executives and not looking like laborers. Sort of looking like wise guys on HBO. Good thing for television because now New Jersey knew how to dress.

They were playing cards on a rickety card table and sitting on metal folding chairs. There was a pile of money on the table, and no one appeared happy to see Lula or me.

DeChooch looked like a younger, taller version of his uncle with an extra sixty pounds evenly distributed. He put his cards facedown on the table and stood. "Can I help you ladies?"

I introduced myself and told them I was looking for Eddie.

Everyone at the table smiled.

"That DeChooch," one of the men said, "he's something. I heard he left you two sitting in the parlor while he jumped out the bedroom window."

This got a lot of laughs.

"If you'd known Choochy you'd have known to watch the windows," Ronald said. "He's gone out a lot of windows in his time. Once he got caught in Florence Selzer's bedroom. Flo's husband, Joey the Rug, came home and caught Choochy going out the window and shot him in the . . . what do you call it, glutamus maximus?"

A big guy with a big belly tipped back on his chair. "Joey disappeared after that."

"Oh yeah?" Lula said. "What happened to him?"

The guy did a palms-up. "No one knows. Just one of those things."

Right. He was probably an SUV bumper like Jimmy Hoffa. "So, have any of you seen Choochy? Anyone know where he might be?"

"You could try his social club," Ronald said.

We all knew he wouldn't go to his social club.

I put my business card on the table. "In case you think of something."

Ronald smiled. "I'm thinking of something already."

Ugh.

"That Ronald is slime," Lula said when we

got into the car. "And he looked at you like you were lunch."

I gave an involuntary shiver and drove away. Maybe my mother and Morelli were right. Maybe I should get a different job. Or maybe I should get *no* job. Maybe I should marry Morelli and be a housewife like my perfect sister, Valerie. I could have a couple kids and spend my days coloring in coloring books and reading stories about steam shovels and little bears.

"It could be fun," I said to Lula. "I like steam shovels."

"Sure you do," Lula said. "What the hell are you talking about?"

"Kids' books. Remember the book about the steam shovel?"

"I didn't have books when I was a kid. And if I *did* have a book it wouldn't have been about a steam shovel . . . it would have been about a crack spoon."

I crossed Broad Street and headed back into the Burg. I wanted to talk to Angela Marguchi and possibly take a look in Eddie's house. Usually I could count on friends or relatives of the fugitive to help me with the chase. In Eddie's case, I didn't think this was going to work. Eddie's friends and relatives weren't of the snitch mentality.

I parked in front of Angela's house and told Bob I'd only be a minute. Lula and I got halfway to Angela's front door and Bob started barking in the car. Bob didn't like being left alone. And he knew I was fibbing about the minute.

"Boy, that Bob sure can bark loud," Lula said. "He's giving me a headache already."

Angela stuck her head out the door. "What's making all that noise?"

"It's Bob," Lula said. "He don't like being left in the car."

Angela's face lit. "A dog! Isn't he cute. I love dogs."

Lula opened the car door and Bob bounded out. He rushed up to Angela, put his paws on her chest, and knocked her on her ass.

"You didn't break nothing, did you?" Lula asked, picking Angela up.

"I don't think so," Angela said. "I got a pacemaker to keep me going, and I got stainless steel and Teflon hips and knees. Only thing I have to watch out for is getting hit by lightning or getting shoved in a micro-wave."

Thinking about Angela going into a microwave got me to thinking about Hansel and Gretel, who faced a similar horror. This got me to thinking about the unreliability of bread crumbs as trail markers. And that led to the depressing admission that I was in worse shape than Hansel and Gretel because Eddie DeChooch hadn't even left bread crumbs.

"I don't suppose you've seen Eddie," I asked Angela. "He hasn't returned home, has he? Or called and asked you to take care of his houseplants?"

"Nope. I haven't heard from Eddie. He's probably the only one in the whole Burg I haven't heard from. My phone's been ringing off the hook. Everybody wanting to know about poor Loretta."

"Did Eddie have many visitors?"

"He had some men friends. Ziggy Garvey and Benny Colucci. And a couple others."

"Anyone who drove a white Cadillac?"

"Eddie's been driving a white Cadillac. His car's been on the fritz and he borrowed a Cadillac from someone. I don't know who. He kept it parked in the alley behind the garage."

"Did Loretta Ricci visit often?"

"So far as I know that was the first time she visited Eddie. Loretta was a volunteer with that Meals-on-Wheels program for seniors. I saw her go in with a box about suppertime. I figure someone told her Eddie was depressed and not eating right. Or maybe Eddie signed up. Although I can't see Eddie doing something like that."

"Did you see Loretta leave?"

"I didn't exactly see her leave, but I noticed the car was gone. She must have been in there for about an hour."

"How about gunshots?" Lula asked. "Did you hear her get whacked? Did you hear screaming?"

"I didn't hear any screaming," Angela said. "Mom's deaf as a post. Once Mom puts the television on you can't hear *anything* in here. And the television is on from six to eleven. Would you like some coffee cake? I got a nice almond ring from the bakery."

I thanked Angela for the coffee cake offer but told her Lula and Bob and I had to keep on the job.

We exited the Marguchi house and stepped next door to the DeChooch half. The DeChooch half was off limits, of course, ringed with crime-scene tape, still part of an ongoing investigation. There were no cops guarding the integrity of the house or shed, so I assumed they'd worked hard yesterday to finish the collection of evidence.

"We probably shouldn't go in here, being that the tape's still up," Lula said.

I agreed. "The police wouldn't like it."

"Of course, we were in there yesterday. We probably got prints all over the place."

"So you're thinking it wouldn't matter if we went in today?"

"Well, it wouldn't matter if nobody found out about it," Lula said.

"And I have a key so it isn't actually breaking and entering." Problem is, I sort of stole the key.

As a bond enforcement officer I also have the right to enter the fugitive's house if I have good reason to suspect he's there. And if push came to shove, I'm sure I could come up with a good reason. I might be lacking a bunch of bounty hunter skills, but I can fib with the best of them.

"Maybe you should see if that's really Eddie's house key," Lula said. "You know, test it out."

I inserted the key into the lock and the door swung open.

"Damn," Lula said. "Look at what happened now. The door's open."

We scooted into the dark foyer and I closed and locked the door behind us.

"You take lookout," I said to Lula. "I don't want to be surprised by the police or by Eddie."

"You can count on me," Lula said. "Lookout's my middle name."

I started in the kitchen, going through the cabinets and drawers, thumbing through the papers on the counter. I was doing the Hansel and Gretel thing, looking for a bread crumb that would start me on a trail. I was hoping for a phone number scribbled on a napkin, or maybe a map with a big orange arrow pointing to a local motel. What I found was the usual flotsam that collects in all kitchens. Eddie had knives and forks and dishes and soup bowls that had been bought by Mrs. DeChooch and used for the life of her marriage. There were no dirty dishes left on the counter. Everything was neatly stacked in the cupboards. Not a lot of food in the refrigerator, but it was better stocked than mine. A small carton of milk, some sliced turkey breast from Giovichinni's

Meat Market, eggs, a stick of butter, condi-
ments.

I prowled through a small downstairs powder room, the dining room, and living room.
I peered into the coat closet and searched
coat pockets while Lula watched the street
through a break in the living room drape.

I climbed the stairs and searched the bedrooms, still hoping to find a bread crumb.
The beds were all neatly made. There was
a crossword book on the nightstand in the
master bedroom. No bread crumbs. I moved
on to the bathroom. Clean sink. Clean tub.
Medicine chest filled to bursting with Dar-
von, aspirin, seventeen different kinds of
antacids, sleeping pills, a jar of Vicks, den-
ture cleaner, hemorrhoid cream.

The window over the tub was unlocked. I
climbed into the tub and looked out. De-
Chooch's escape seemed possible. I got out
of the tub and out of the bathroom. I stood
in the hall and thought about Loretta Ricci.
There was no sign of her in this house. No
bloodstains. No indication of struggle. The
house was unusually clean and tidy. I'd noticed this yesterday, too, when I'd gone
through looking for DeChooch.

No notes scribbled on the pad by the

phone. No matchbooks from restaurants tossed on the kitchen counter. No socks on the floor. No laundry in the bathroom hamper. Hey, what do I know? Maybe depressed old men get obsessively neat. Or maybe DeChooch spent the entire night scrubbing the blood from his floors and then did the laundry. Bottom line is *no bread crumbs.*

I returned to the living room and made an effort not to grimace. There was one place left to look. The cellar. Yuck. Cellars in houses like this were always dark and creepy, with rumbly oil burners and cobwebby rafters.

"Well, I suppose I should look in the cellar now," I said to Lula.

"Okay," Lula said. "The coast is still clear."

I opened the cellar door and flipped the light switch. Scarred wood stairs, gray cement floor, cobwebby rafters, and creepy rumbly cellar sounds. No disappointment here.

"Something wrong?" Lula asked.

"It's creepy."

"Uh-huh."

"I don't want to go down there."

"It's just a cellar," Lula said.

"How about if you go down."

"Not me. I hate cellars. They're creepy."

"Do you have a gun?"

"Do bears shit in the woods?"

I borrowed Lula's gun and crept down the cellar stairs. I don't know what I was going to do with the gun. Shoot a spider, maybe.

There was a washer and dryer in the cellar. A pegboard with tools . . . screwdrivers, wrenches, hammers. A workbench with a vise attached. None of the tools looked recently used. Some cardboard cartons were stacked in a corner. The boxes were closed but not sealed. The tape that had sealed them was left on the floor. I snooped in a couple of the boxes. Christmas decorations, some books, a box of pie plates and casserole dishes. No bread crumbs.

I climbed the stairs and closed the cellar door. Lula was still looking out the window.

"Uh-oh," Lula said.

"What uh-oh?" I *hate* uh-oh!

"Cop car just pulled up."

"Shit!"

I grabbed Bob's leash, and Lula and I ran for the back door. We exited the house and scooted over to the stoop that served as back porch to Angela's house. Lula wrenched Angela's door open and we all jumped inside.

Angela and her mother were sitting at the small kitchen table, having coffee and cake.

"Help! Police!" Angela's mother yelled when we burst through the door.

"This is Stephanie," Angela shouted to her mother. "You remember Stephanie?"

"Who?"

"*Stephanie!*"

"What's she want?"

"We changed our mind about the cake," I said, pulling a chair out, sitting down.

"What?" Angela's mother yelled. *"What?"*

"Cake," Angela yelled back at her mother. "They want some cake."

"Well for God's sake give it to them before they shoot us."

Lula and I looked at the gun in my hand.

"Maybe you should put that away," Lula said. "Wouldn't want the old lady to mess her pants."

I gave the gun to Lula and took a piece of cake.

"Don't worry," I yelled. "It's a fake gun."

"Looks real to me," Angela's mother yelled back. "Looks like a forty-caliber, fourteen-round Glock. You could put a good hole in a man's head with that. I used to carry one myself, but I switched to a shotgun when my eyesight went."

Carl Costanza rapped on the back door and we all jumped.

"We're making a security patrol and I saw your car outside," Costanza said, helping himself to the piece of cake in my hand. "Wanted to make sure you weren't thinking of doing anything illegal . . . like violating the crime scene."

"Who, me?"

Costanza smiled at me and left with my cake.

We turned our attention back to the table, where there was now an empty cake plate.

"For goodness sakes," Angela said, "there was a whole cake here. What on earth could have happened to it?"

Lula and I exchanged glances. Bob had a piece of white confectioners' sugar icing clinging to his lip.

"We should probably be going anyway," I said, dragging Bob to the front door. "Let me know if you hear from Eddie."

"That didn't do us much good," Lula said when we were on the road. "We didn't find out nothing about Eddie DeChooch."

"He buys sliced turkey breast from Giovi-chinni," I said.

"So what are you saying? We should bait our hook with turkey breast?"

"No. I'm saying this is a guy who's spent his whole life in the Burg and isn't going any-where else. He's right here, driving around in a white Cadillac. I should be able to find him." It would be easier if I'd been able to get the number off the Cadillac's license plate. I had my friend Norma do a search at the DMV for white Cadillacs, but there were too many to check out.

I dropped Lula off at the office and went in search of the Mooner. Mooner and Dougie mostly spend their days watching television and eating Cheez Doodles, living off a shared semi-illegal windfall. Sometime soon I suspect the windfall will all have gone up in wacky tabacky smoke, and Mooner and Dougie will be living a lot less luxu-riously.

I parked in front of Mooner's house and Bob and I marched up to the front stoop and I knocked on the door. Huey Kosa opened the door and grinned out at me. Huey Kosa and Zero Bartha are Mooner's two roommates. Nice guys but, like Mooner, they were living in another dimension.

"Dude," Huey said.

"I'm looking for Mooner."

"He's at Dougie's house. He like had to do laundry, and the Dougster has a machine. The Dougster has everything."

I drove the short distance to Dougie's house and parked. I could have walked, but that wouldn't have been the Jersey way.

"Hey dude," Mooner said when I rapped on Dougie's door. "Nice to see you and the Bob. Mi casa su casa. Well, actually it's the Dougster's casa, but I don't know how to say that."

He was wearing another one of the Super Suits. Green this time and without the *M* sewn onto the chest, looking more like PickleMan than MoonMan.

"Saving the world?" I asked.

"No. Doing the laundry."

"Have you heard from Dougie?"

"Nothing, dude. Nada."

The front door opened to a living room sparsely furnished with a couch, a chair, a single floor lamp, and a big-screen TV. Bob Newhart got offered a bag of roadkill from Larry, Daryl, and Daryl on the big-screen TV.

"It's a Bob Newhart retrospective," Mooner said. "They're playing all the classics. Solid gold."

"So," I said, looking around the room, "Dougie's never disappeared like this before?"

"Not as long as I've known him."

"Does Dougie have a girlfriend?"

Mooner went blank-faced. Like this was too big a question to comprehend.

"Girlfriend," he said finally. "Wow, I never thought of the Dougster with a girlfriend. Like, I've never seen him with a girl."

"How about a boyfriend?"

"Don't think he's got one of them, either. Think the Dougster's more . . . um, self-sufficient."

"Okay, let's try something else. Where was Dougie going when he disappeared?"

"He didn't say."

"He drove?"

"Yep. Took the Batmobile."

"Just exactly what does the Batmobile look like?"

"It looks like a black Corvette. I rode around looking for it, but it's nowhere."

"Probably you should report this to the police."

"No way! The Dougster will be up the creek on his bond."

I was getting a bad vibe here. Mooner was looking nervous, and this was a seldom-seen side of his personality. Mooner is usually Mr. Mellow.

"There's something else going on," I said. "What aren't you telling me?"

"Hey, nothing, dude. I swear."

Call me crazy, but I like Dougie. He might be a schnook and a schemer, but he was kind of an *okay* schnook and schemer. And now he was missing, and I was having a bad feeling in my stomach.

"How about Dougie's family? Have you spoken to any of them?" I asked.

"No, dude, they're all in Arkansas someplace. The Dougster didn't talk about them a lot."

"Does Dougie have a phone book?"

"I've never seen one. I guess he could have one in his room."

"Stay here with Bob and make sure he doesn't eat anything. I'll check out Dougie's room."

There were three small upstairs bedrooms. I'd been in the house before, so I knew which room was Dougie's. And I knew what to expect of the interior design. Dougie didn't waste time with the petty details of housekeeping. The floor in Dougie's room was littered with clothes, the bed was un-made, the dresser was cluttered with scraps of paper, a model of the starship *Enterprise*, girlie magazines, food-encrusted dishes and mugs.

There was a phone at bedside but no ad-dress book beside the phone. There was a piece of yellow notepaper on the floor by the bed. There were a lot of names and num-bers scribbled in no special order on the pa-per, some obliterated by a coffee cup stain. I did a fast scan of the page and discovered several Krupers were listed in Arkansas. None in Jersey. I scrounged through the mess on his dresser and just for the hell of it snooped in his closet.

No clues there.

I didn't have any good reason to look in the other bedrooms, but I'm nosey by na-ture. The second bedroom was a sparsely furnished guest room. The bed was rum-pled, and my guess was Mooner slept there from time to time. And the third bedroom was stacked floor-to-ceiling with hijacked merchandise. Boxes of toasters, telephones, alarm clocks, stacks of T-shirts, and God-knows-what-else. Dougie was at it again.

"Mooner!" I yelled. "Get up here! *Now!*"

"Whoa," Mooner said when he saw me standing at the doorway to the third bed-room. "Where'd all that stuff come from?"

"I thought Dougie gave up dealing?"

"He couldn't help himself, dude. I swear he tried, but it's in his blood, you know? Like, he was born to deal."

Now I had a better idea of the origin of Mooner's nervousness. Dougie was still in-volved with bad people. Bad people are just fine when everything's going good. They be-come a concern when your friend shows up missing.

"Do you know where these boxes came from? Do you know who Dougie was work-ing with?"

"I'm like, clueless. He took a phone call and then next thing there's a truck in the driveway and we've got this inventory. I wasn't paying too much attention. Rocky and Bullwinkle were on, and you know how hard it is to tear yourself away from ol' Rocky."

"Did Dougie owe money? Was there something wrong with the deal?"

"Didn't seem like it. Seemed like he was real happy. He said the stuff he got was a quick sale. Except for the toasters. Hey, you want a toaster?"

"How much?"

"Ten bucks."

"Sold."

I MADE A quick stop at Giovichinni's for a few food-type essentials, and then Bob and I hustled home for lunch. I had my toaster under one arm and my grocery bag in another when I got out of the car.

Benny and Ziggy suddenly materialized from nowhere.

"Let me help you with that bag," Ziggy said. "A lady like you shouldn't be carrying her own bag."

"And what's this? A toaster," Benny said, relieving me of the toaster, looking at the box. "This is a good one, too. It's got those extra-wide slots so you can do English muffins."

"I'm fine," I said, but they already had the

bag and the toaster and were ahead of me, going through the door to my building.

"We just thought we'd stop by and see how things were going," Benny said, punching the elevator button. "You have any luck with Eddie yet?"

"I saw him at Stiva's, but he got away."

"Yeah, we heard about that. That's a shame."

I opened my door and they handed me my bag and toaster and peeked inside my apartment.

"You don't got Eddie in here, do you?" Ziggy asked.

"No!"

Ziggy shrugged. "It was a long shot."

"Nothing ventured, nothing gained," Benny said.

And they left.

"You don't have to pass an intelligence test to get into the mob," I said to Bob.

I plugged my new toaster in and fed it two slices of bread. I made Bob a peanut butter sandwich with untoasted bread, I took the toasted peanut butter sandwich, and we ate, standing in the kitchen, enjoying the moment.

"I guess it's not so hard to be a housewife," I said to Bob, "as long as you have peanut butter and bread."

I called Norma at the DMV and got the license number for Dougie's 'Vette. Then I called Morelli to see if he'd heard anything about anything.

"The autopsy report on Loretta Ricci hasn't come back yet," Morelli said. "No one's nabbed DeChooch, and Kruper hasn't floated in with the tide. The ball's in your court, Cupcake."

Oh great.

"So I guess I'll see you tonight," Morelli said. "I'll pick you and Bob up at five-thirty."

"Sure. Anything special?"

Phone silence. "I thought we were invited to your parents' house for dinner."

"Oh rats! Damn. Shit."

"Forgot, huh?"

"I was just there yesterday."

"Does this mean we don't have to go?"

"If only it was that easy."

"Pick you up at five-thirty," Morelli said, and he hung up.

I like my parents. I really do. It's just that they drive me nuts. First of all, there's my perfect sister, Valerie, with her two perfect children. Fortunately, they live in L.A., so their perfection is lessened by distance. And then there's my alarming marital status, which my mother feels compelled to fix. Not to mention my job, my clothes, my eating habits, my church attendance (or lack of).

"Okay, Bob," I said, "time to get back to work. Let's go cruising."

I thought I'd spend the afternoon looking for cars. I needed to find a white Cadillac and the Batmobile. Start with the Burg, I decided, and then enlarge the search area. And I had a mental list of restaurants and diners with early-bird specials that catered to seniors. I'd save the diners for last and see if the white Cadillac turned up.

I dropped a chunk of bread into Rex's cage and told him I'd be home by five. I had Bob's leash in my hand and was about to take off when there was a knock on my door. It was StateLine Florist.

"Happy Birthday," the kid said. He handed me a vase of flowers and left.

This was a little strange since my birthday's in October and it was now April. I set the flowers on the kitchen counter and read the card.

Roses are red. Violets are blue. I've got a hard-on and it's because of you.

It was signed Ronald DeChooch. Bad enough he creeped me out at the social club, now he was sending me flowers.

FOUR

"YUCK. ICK. GROSS!" I grabbed the flowers and tried to throw them away, but I couldn't bring myself to do it. I had a hard enough time throwing *dead* flowers away, much less flowers that were all fresh and hopeful and pretty. I dropped the card on the floor and jumped up and down on it. Then I tore it into tiny pieces and pitched it into the garbage. The flowers were still on my counter, looking happy and colorful but giving me the creeps. I picked them up and carefully set them out in the hall. I jumped back into my apartment and closed the door. I stood there for a couple beats to see how it felt.

"Okay, I can live with this," I said to Bob.

Bob didn't look like he had much of an opinion.

I snagged a jacket off the hook in the foyer. Bob and I exited my apartment, hustled past the flowers in the hall, then calmly walked down the stairs and out to the car.

After half an hour of riding around the Burg I decided looking for the Cadillac was a dumb idea. I parked on Roebling and dialed Connie on my cell phone.

"What's new?" I asked. Connie was related to half the mob in Jersey.

"Dodie Carmine got a boob job."

This was good stuff but not what I wanted. "Anything else?"

"You're not the only one looking for DeChooch. I got a call from my Uncle Bingo, wondering if we had a line out. After that I talked to my Aunt Flo and she said something went wrong in Richmond when DeChooch went down there for the cigarettes. She didn't know anything more."

"It says on the arrest sheet that DeChooch was alone when he was picked up. Hard to believe he didn't have a partner."

"From what I know he was on his own. He

set the deal up, rented a truck, and drove to Richmond."

"Blind old dude drives to Richmond to heist some cigs."

"You got it."

I had Metallica wailing away. Bob was riding shotgun next to me, digging Lars on the drums. The Burg was conducting business behind closed doors. And I suddenly had a disturbing thought.

"DeChooch was arrested between here and New York?"

"Yeah, the rest stop in Edison."

"Do you think he could have dropped some cigarettes off in the Burg?"

There was a moment of silence. "You're thinking of Dougie Kruper," Connie said.

I snapped the phone closed, put the car in gear, and headed for Dougie's house. I didn't bother knocking when I got there. Bob and I barged right in.

"Hey," Mooner said, ambling out of the kitchen, spoon in one hand, opened can in the other, "I'm having lunch here. You want some orange and brown stuff in a can? I got extra. Shop & Bag was having a two-for-one sale on cans without labels."

I was halfway up the stairs. "No thanks. I

want to take another look at Dougie's inventory. He get anything other than that one shipment?"

"Yeah, some old guy dropped a couple boxes off a couple days ago. Wasn't much to it, though. Just a couple boxes."

"Do you know what's in those boxes?"

"First-quality ciggies. You want some?"

I pushed my way through the merchandise in the third bedroom and found the cartons of cigarettes. Damn.

"This isn't good," I said to Mooner.

"I know. They'll kill you, dude. Better off with weed."

"Superheroes don't do weed," I said.

"No way!"

"It's true. You can't be a superhero if you do drugs."

"Next thing you'll be telling me they don't drink beer."

Hard call. "I don't actually know about beer."

"Bummer."

I tried to imagine Mooner when he wasn't high, but I couldn't get a picture. Would he suddenly start wearing three-piece suits? Would he become a Republican?

"You need to get rid of this stuff," I said.

"You mean like sell it?"

"No. Get rid of it. If the police come in here you'll be charged with possession of stolen property."

"The police are here all the time, dude. They're some of Dougie's best customers."

"I mean officially. Like if they're investigating Dougie's disappearance."

"Ahhhh," Mooner said.

Bob eyed the can in Mooner's hand. The stuff in the can looked a lot like dog food. Of course when you have a Bob dog everything is dog food. I shoved Bob out the door, and we all went back downstairs.

"I have some phone calls to make," I told Dougie. "I'll let you know if anything turns up."

"Yeah, but what about me?" Mooner asked. "What should I do? I should be like . . . helping."

"Get rid of the stuff in the third bedroom!"

THE FLOWERS WERE still in the hall when Bob and I stepped out of the elevator. Bob sniffed at them and ate a rose. I dragged Bob into the apartment and, first thing, checked my phone messages. Both were from Ronald. Hope you like the flowers, the first said, they set me back a couple bucks. The second suggested we should get together because he thought we had something going between us.

Blech.

I made myself another peanut butter sandwich to get my mind off Ronald. Then I made one for Bob. I took the phone to the dining room table and called all of the Krupers on the piece of yellow paper. I told them I was a friend and I was looking for Dougie. When I was given Dougie's Burg address I faked surprise that he was back in Jersey. No need to alarm Dougie's relatives.

"We scored a big zero with the phone thing," I said to Bob. "Now what?"

I could take Dougie's photo and shop it around, but chances of anyone remembering Dougie were slim to nonexistent. I had a hard time remembering Dougie when I was standing in front of him. I called for a credit check and found Dougie had a MasterCard. That was the extent of Dougie's credit history.

Okay, now I was getting into very bleak territory. I'd eliminated friends, relatives, business accounts. This was pretty much my arsenal. And what's worse, my stomach felt hollow and icky. It was the something-is-wrong feeling. I really didn't want Dougie to be dead, but I wasn't finding any proof that he was alive.

Well, that's stupid, I said to myself. Dougie's a goof. God only knows what he could be doing. He could be on a pilgrimage to Graceland. He could be playing blackjack in Atlantic City. He could be losing his virginity to the late-night cashier of the local 7-Eleven.

And maybe the hollow, icky feeling in my stomach is hunger. Sure, that's it! Good thing I went shopping at Giovichinni's. I dug out the Tastykakes, and gave Bob a coconut layer cake. I ate the package of butterscotch krimpets.

"What do you think?" I asked Bob. "Do you feel better now?"

I felt better. Cake always makes me feel better. In fact I felt so good I decided to go out and look for Eddie DeChooch again. Different neighborhood this time. This time I was going to try Ronald's neighborhood. There was the added incentive of knowing Ronald wasn't at home.

Bob and I drove across town to Cherry Street. Cherry Street is part of a residential pocket at the northeast corner of Trenton. It's a neighborhood of mostly two-family houses on small building lots and it feels a little like the Burg. It was late afternoon. School was out. Televisions ran in living rooms and kitchens. Crockpots simmered.

I crept past Ronald's house, looking for the white Cadillac, looking for Eddie De-Chooch. Ronald's house was a single family with red-brick facing. Not as pretentious as Joyce's with her columns but not all that tasteful, either. The garage door was closed. A minivan sat in the driveway. The small front yard was neatly landscaped around a three-foot-tall, blue-and-white statue of the Virgin Mary. She looked composed and at peace in her plaster shrine. More than I could say for myself in my fiberglass Honda.

Bob and I cruised the street, peeking down driveways, straining to see the shadowy figures who moved behind sheer curtains. We drove Cherry Street twice and then began investigating the rest of the neighborhood, dividing it into grids. We saw a lot of big old cars, but we didn't see any big old white Cadillacs. And we didn't see Eddie DeChooch.

"No stone unturned," I said to Bob, trying to justify time wasted.

Bob gave me a look that said *whatever*. He had his head out the window, looking for cute miniature poodles.

I turned onto Olden Avenue and headed for home. I was about to cross Greenwood when Eddie DeChooch sailed past me in the white Caddy, going in the opposite direction.

I hung a **U**-turn in the middle of the intersection. It was coming up to rush hour and there were a lot of cars on the road. A dozen people leaned on their horns and flipped me hand signals. I forced myself into the stream of traffic and tried to keep Eddie in my line of vision. I was about ten cars behind him. I saw him wheel off onto State Street, heading for center city. By the time I was able to make the turn I'd lost him.

I GOT HOME ten minutes before Joe arrived.

"What's with the flowers in the hall?" he wanted to know.

"Ronald DeChooch sent them. And I don't want to talk about it."

Morelli watched me for a beat. "Am I going to have to shoot him?"

"He's laboring under the delusion that we're attracted to each other."

"A lot of us labor under that delusion."

Bob galloped over to Morelli and pushed against him to get Morelli's attention. Morelli gave Bob a hug and a full body rub. Lucky dog.

"I saw Eddie DeChooch today," I said.

"And?"

"And I lost him again."

Morelli grinned. "Famous bounty hunter loses old guy . . . twice." Actually it was three times!

Morelli closed the space between us and slid his arms around me. "Do you need consoling?"

"What did you have in mind?"

"How much time do we have?"

I did a sigh. "Not enough." God forbid I should be five minutes late for dinner. The spaghetti would be overcooked. The pot roast would be dry. And it would all be my fault. I would have ruined dinner. Again. And worse, my perfect sister, Valerie, has never ruined dinner. My sister had the sense to move thousands of miles away. That's how perfect she is.

*   *   *

MY MOTHER OPENED the door to Joe and me. Bob bounded in, ears flopping, eyes bright.

"Isn't he cute," Grandma said. "Isn't he something."

"Get the cake up on the refrigerator," my mother said. "And where's the pot roast? Don't let him near the pot roast."

My father was already at the table, keeping his eye on the pot roast, staking out the end slab of beef.

"So what's happening with the wedding?" Grandma asked when we were all at the table, digging into the food. "I was just at the beauty parlor, and the girls wanted to know about the date. And they wanted to know did we have a hall rented? Marilyn Biaggi tried to get the firehouse for her daughter Carolyn's shower, and it was taken clear through the rest of the year."

My mother slipped a look at my ring finger. No ring on the ring finger. Just like yesterday. My mother pressed her lips together and cut her meat into tiny pieces.

"We're thinking about a date," I said, "but we haven't settled on anything yet." Liar, liar, pants on fire. We have *never* discussed a date. We've avoided a discussion of the date like the plague.

Morelli hung an arm across my shoulders. "Steph suggested we skip the wedding and start living together, but I don't know if that's such a good idea." Morelli was no slouch when it came to lying, either, and sometimes he had a nasty sense of humor.

My mother sucked in some air and stabbed a piece of meat so hard her fork clanked against her plate.

"I hear that's the modern way of doing things," Grandma said. "I don't see nothing wrong with it myself. If I wanted to shack up with a man I'd just go ahead and do it. What's a silly piece of paper mean anyways? In fact I would have shacked up with Eddie DeChooch, but his penis don't work."

"Jesus Christ," my father said.

"Not that I'm only interested in a man for his penis," Grandma added. "It's just that Eddie and me only had a physical attraction. When it came to talking we didn't have too much to say."

My mother was making motions like she was stabbing herself in her chest. "Just kill me," she said. "It would be easier."

"It's the change," Grandma whispered to Joe and me.

"It's not the change," my mother shrieked.

"It's you! You make me crazy!" She pointed her finger at my father. "And you make me crazy! And you, too," she said, glaring at me. "You all make me crazy. Just once I'd like to have a dinner without talk about private parts, and aliens, and shooting. And I want grandchildren at this table. I want them here next year, and I want them here legally. You think I'm going to last forever? Pretty soon I'll be dead and then you'll be sorry."

Everyone sat slack-jawed and paralyzed. No one said anything for a full sixty seconds.

"We're getting married in August," I blurted out. "The third week in August. We were keeping it a surprise."

My mother's face brightened. "Really? The third week in August?"

No. It was an absolute flat-out fabrication. I don't know where it came from. Just popped out of my mouth. Truth is, my engagement was kind of casual, being that the proposal was made at a time when it was difficult to distinguish between the desire to spend the rest of our lives together and the desire to get sex on a regular basis. Since Morelli's sex drive makes mine look insignificant he usually is more frequently in favor of marriage than I am. I suppose it would be most accurate to say we were engaged to be engaged. And that's a comfortable place for us to live because it's vague enough to absolve Morelli and me of serious marital discussion. Serious marital discussion always leads to a lot of shouting and door slamming.

"Have you been looking at dresses?" Grandma asked. "August don't give us much time. You need a gown. And then there's the flowers and the reception. And you need to reserve the church. Have you asked about the church yet?" Grandma jumped out of her chair. "I've got to go call Betty Szajack and Marjorie Swit and tell them the news."

"No, wait!" I said. "It's not official."

"What do you mean . . . not official?" my mother asked.

"Not many people know." Like Joe.

"How about Joe's granny?" Grandma asked. "Does she know? I wouldn't want to cross Joe's granny. She could put the jinx on things."

"Nobody can put the jinx on things," my mother said. "There's no such thing as a jinx." Even as she said it I could see she was fighting back the urge to cross herself.

"And besides," I said, "I don't want a big

wedding with a gown and everything. I want a . . . barbecue." I couldn't believe I was saying this. Bad enough I'd announced my wedding date, now I had it all planned out. A barbecue! Jeez! It was like I had no control over my mouth.

I looked at Joe and mouthed *help!*

Joe draped an arm around my shoulders and grinned. The silent message was, *Sweetheart, you're on your own with this one.*

"Well, it'll be a relief just to see you happily married," my mother said. "Both my girls . . . happily married."

"That reminds me," Grandma said to my mother. "Valerie called last night when you were out at the store. Something about taking a trip, but I couldn't figure out what she was saying on account of there was all this yelling going on behind her."

"Who was yelling?"

"I think it must have been the television. Valerie and Steven never yell. Those two are just the perfect couple. And the girls are such perfect little ladies."

Gag me with a spoon.

"Did she want me to call her back?" my mother asked.

"She didn't say. Something happened and we got cut off."

Grandma sat up straighter in her seat. She had a clear view through the living room to the street, and something caught her attention.

"There's a taxi stopping in front of our house," Grandma said.

Everyone craned their neck to see the taxi. In the Burg a taxi stopping in front of a house is big entertainment.

"For goodness sakes!" Grandma said. "I could swear that's Valerie getting out of the taxi."

We all jumped up and went to the door. Next thing, my sister and her kids swooped into the house.

Valerie is two years older than me and an inch shorter. We both have curly brown hair, but Valerie's dyed her hair blond and has it cut short, like Meg Ryan. I guess that's what they do with hair in California.

When we were kids Valerie was vanilla pudding, good grades, and clean white sneakers. And I was chocolate cake, the dog ate my homework, and skinned knees.

Valerie was married right out of college and immediately got pregnant. Truth is, I'm jealous. I got married and immediately got divorced. Of course I married a womanizing idiot, and Valerie married a really nice guy. Leave it to Valerie to find Mr. Perfect.

My nieces look a lot like Valerie before Valerie did the Meg Ryan thing. Curly brown hair, big brown eyes, skin a shade more Italian than mine. Not much Hungarian made it to Valerie's gene pool. And even less trickled down to her daughters, Angie and Mary Alice. Angie is nine, going on forty. And Mary Alice thinks she's a horse.

My mother was flushed and teary, hormones revved, hugging the kids, kissing Valerie. "I don't believe it," she kept saying. "I don't believe it! This is such a surprise. I had no idea you were coming to visit."

"I called," Valerie said. "Didn't Grandma tell you?"

"I couldn't hear what you were saying," Grandma said. "There was so much noise, and then we got cut off."

"Well, here I am," Valerie said.

"Just in time for dinner," my mother said. "I have a nice pot roast and there's cake for dessert."

We scrambled to add chairs and plates and extra glasses. We all sat down and passed the pot roast and potatoes and green beans. The dinner immediately elevated to a party, the house feeling filled with holiday.

"How long will you be staying with us?" my mother asked.

"Until I can save up enough money to buy a house," Valerie said.

My father's face went pale.

My mother was elated. "You're moving back to New Jersey?"

Valerie selected a single, lean piece of beef. "It seemed like the best thing to do."

"Did Steve get a transfer?" my mother asked.

"Steve isn't coming." Valerie surgically removed the one smidgen of fat that clung to her meat. "Steve left me."

So much for the holiday.

Morelli was the only one who didn't drop his fork. I glanced over at Morelli and decided he was working hard at not smiling.

"Well, isn't this a pisser," Grandma said.

"Left you," my mother repeated. "What do you mean, he left you? You and Steve are perfect together."

"I thought so, too. I don't know what went

wrong. I thought everything was just fine between us and then *poof,* he's gone."

"Poof?" Grandma said.

"Just like that," Valerie answered. "Poof."
She bit into her lower lip to keep it from
trembling.

My mother and father and grandmother
and I panicked at the trembling lip. We didn't
do this sort of emotional display. We did temper and sarcasm. Anything beyond temper
and sarcasm was virgin territory. And we
certainly didn't know what to make of this
from Valerie. Valerie is the ice queen. Not
to mention that Valerie's life has always
been perfect. This sort of thing just *doesn't*
happen to Valerie.

Valerie's eyes got red and teary. "Could
you pass the gravy?" she asked Grandma
Mazur.

My mother jumped out of her chair. "I'll get
you some hot from the kitchen."

The kitchen door swung closed behind my
mother. There was a shriek and the sound
of a dish smashing against the wall. I automatically looked for Bob, but Bob was sleeping under the table. The kitchen door swung
open and my mother calmly walked out with
the gravy dish.

"I'm sure this is just temporary," my mother said. "I'm sure Steve will come to his senses."

"I thought we had a good marriage. I made nice meals. And I kept the house nice. I went to the gym so I'd be attractive. I even got my hair cut like Meg Ryan. I don't understand what went wrong."

Valerie has always been the articulate member of the family. Always in control. Her friends used to call her Saint Valerie because she always looked serene . . . like Ronald DeChooch's statue of the Virgin. So here she was with her world crumbling around her and she wasn't exactly serene, but she wasn't berserk, either. Mostly she seemed sad and confused.

From my point of view it was a little weird since, when my marriage dissolved, people three miles away heard me yelling. And when Dickie and I went into court I was told there was a point when my head spun around like the kid in *The Exorcist*. Dickie and I didn't have such a great marriage, but we got our money's worth out of the divorce.

I got caught up in the moment and sent Morelli a men-are-bastards look.

Morelli's eyes darkened and the hint of a

grin tugged at his mouth. He brushed a fingertip along the back of my neck, and heat rushed through my stomach clear to my doodah. "Jesus," I said.

The smile widened.

"At least you should be okay financially," I said. "Under California law don't you get half of everything?"

"Half of nothing is nothing," Valerie said. "The house is mortgaged beyond its value. And there's nothing in the bank account because Steve's been shipping our money out to the Caymans. He is *such* a good businessman. Everyone always says that. It's one of the things I found most attractive in him." She took a deep breath and cut Angie's meat. And then she cut Mary Alice's meat.

"Child support," I said. "What about child support?"

"In theory, I suppose he should be helping with the girls, but, well, Steve's disappeared. I think he might be in the Caymans with our money."

"That's awful!"

"The truth is, Steve ran away with our baby-sitter."

We all gasped.

"She turned eighteen last month," Valerie said. "I gave her a Beanie Baby for her birthday."

Mary Alice whinnied. "I want some hay. Horses don't eat meat. Horses have to eat hay."

"Isn't that cute," Grandma said. "Mary Alice still thinks she's a horse."

"I'm a man horse," Mary Alice said.

"Don't be a man horse, sweetheart," Valerie said. "Men are scum."

"Some men are okay," Grandma said.

"All men are scum," Valerie said. "Except for Daddy, of course."

No mention of Joe in the exclusion of scumminess.

"Man horses can gallop faster than lady horses," Mary Alice said, and she flicked a spoonful of mashed potatoes at her sister. The potatoes flew past Angie and landed on the floor. Bob lunged out from under the table and ate the potatoes.

Valerie frowned at Mary Alice. "It's not polite to flick potatoes."

"Yeah," Grandma said. "Little ladies don't flick potatoes at their sisters."

"I'm not a little lady," Mary Alice said. "How many times do I have to tell you. I'm a horse!" And she lobbed a handful of potatoes at Grandma.

Grandma narrowed her eyes and bounced a green bean off Mary Alice's head.

"Grammy hit me with a bean!" Mary Alice yelled. "She hit me with a bean! Make her stop throwing beans at me."

So much for the perfect little ladies.

Bob immediately ate the bean.

"Stop feeding the dog," my father said.

"I hope you don't mind me coming home like this," Valerie said. "It's just until I get a job."

"We only have one bathroom," my father said. "I gotta have the bathroom first thing in the morning. Seven o'clock is my time in the bathroom."

"It will be wonderful having you and the girls in the house," my mother said. "And you can help with Stephanie's wedding. Stephanie and Joe have just set a date."

Valerie choked up again with the red, watery eyes. "Congratulations," she said.

"The wedding ceremony of the Tuzi tribe lasts seven days and ends with the ritualistic piercing of the hymen," Angie said. "The bride then goes to live with her husband's family."

"I saw a special on television about aliens," Grandma said. "And they didn't have hymens. They didn't have any parts down there at all."

"Do horses have hymens?" Mary Alice wanted to know.

"Not man horses," Grandma said.

"It's really nice that you're going to get married," Valerie said. And then Valerie burst into tears. Not sniffling, dainty tears, either. Valerie was doing big, loud, wet sobbing, gulping in air and bellowing out misery. The two little ladies started crying, too, doing openmouthed wailing like only a kid can pull off. And then my mother was crying, sniffling into her napkin. And Bob was howling. *Aaa-rooooh. Aaaroooooooh!*

"I'm never going to get married again," Valerie said between sobs. "Never, never, never. Marriage is the work of the devil. Men are the Antichrist. I'm going to become a lesbian."

"How do you do that?" Grandma asked. "I always wanted to know. Do you have to wear a fake penis? I saw a TV show once and the women were wearing these things that were made out of black leather and were shaped like a great big—"

"Kill me," my mother shouted. "Just kill me. I want to die."

My sister and Bob went back to the bawling and howling. Mary Alice whinnied at the top of her lungs. And Angie covered her ears so she couldn't hear. "La, la, la, la," Angie sang.

My father cleaned his plate and looked around. Where was his coffee? Where was his cake?

"You're going to owe me big time for this one," Morelli whispered in my ear. "This is a doggy-sex night."

"I'm getting a headache," Grandma said. "I can't take this racket. Somebody do something. Put the television on. Get the liquor out. Do something!"

I heaved myself out of my chair and went into the kitchen and got the cake. As soon as it hit the table the crying stopped. If we pay attention to anything in this family . . . it's dessert.

MORELLI AND BOB and I rode home in silence, no one knowing what to say. Morelli pulled into my lot, cut the engine, and turned to me.

"August?" he asked, his voice higher than usual, not able to keep out the incredulous. "You want to get married in August?"

"It just popped out of my mouth! It was all that dying stuff from my mother."

"Your family makes my family look like the Brady Bunch."

"Are you kidding me? Your grandmother is crazy. She gives people the eye."

"It's an Italian thing."

"It's a crazy thing."

A car swerved into the lot, jerked to a stop, the door opened, and Mooner rolled out onto the pavement. Joe and I hit the pavement at the same time. When we got to Mooner he'd dragged himself up to a sitting position. He was holding his head, and blood trickled from between his fingers.

"Hey dude," Mooner said, "I think I've been shot. I was watching television and I heard a sound on the front porch, so I turned around and looked and there was this scary face looking in the window at me. It was this scary old lady with real scary eyes. It was, like, dark, but I could see her through the black glass. And next thing she had a gun in her hand and she shot me. And she broke Dougie's window and everything. There should be a law against that sort of thing, dude."

The Mooner lived two blocks from St. Frances Hospital, but he drove past the hospital and came to me for help. Why me? I asked. And then I realized I sounded like my mother and gave myself a mental smack in the head.

We loaded Mooner back into his car. Joe drove the Mooner to the hospital, and I followed in Joe's truck. Two hours later all the medical and police formalities were behind us, and Mooner had a big Band-Aid on his forehead. The bullet had grazed him just above his eyebrow and ricocheted off into Dougie's living room wall.

We stood in Dougie's living room and studied the hole in his front window.

"I should have been wearing the Super Suit," Mooner said. "That would have confounded them, dude."

Joe and I looked at each other. Confounded. Yes, indeed.

"Do you think it's safe for him to stay in his house?" I asked Joe.

"Hard to say what's safe for the Mooner," Joe said.

"Amen," Mooner said. "Safety floats on butterfly wings."

"I don't know what the hell that means," Joe said.

"It means safety is elusive, dude."

Joe pulled me aside. "Maybe we should check him into rehab."

"I heard that, dude. That's a bummer idea. Those people in rehab are weird. They're like, real downers. They're all like, druggies."

"Well jeez, we wouldn't want to put you in with a bunch of druggies," Joe said.

Mooner nodded. "Fuckin' A, man."

"I guess he could stay with me for a couple days," I said. Even as I said it . . . I was regretting it. What was the deal with me today? It was as if my mouth wasn't connected to my brain.

"Wow, you'd do that for the Mooner? That is so awesome." Mooner gave me a hug. "You won't be sorry. I'll be an excellent roommate."

Joe didn't look nearly as happy as the Mooner. Joe had plans for the evening. There'd been that remark at the table about me owing him doggy sex. Probably he'd been teasing. But then, maybe not. Hard to tell with men. Maybe it was best to go with the Mooner.

I sent Joe a shrug that said, *Hey, what's a girl to do*?

"Okay," Joe said, "let's lock up and get out of here. You take the Mooner and I'll take Bob."

MOONER AND I stood in the hall in front of my apartment. Mooner had a small duffel bag with him that I assumed contained a change of clothes and a full range of drugs.

"Okay," I said, "here's the thing. You're welcome to stay here, but you can't do drugs."

"Dude," Mooner said.

"Are there any drugs in the bag?"

"Hey, what do I look like?"

"You look like a stoner."

"Well, yeah, but that's because you know me."

"Empty the bag on the floor."

Mooner dumped the contents of the bag on the floor. I put Mooner's clothes back in the bag, and I confiscated everything else. Pipes and papers and an assortment of controlled substances. I let us into my apartment, flushed the contents of the plasticene bags, and tossed the hardware in the trash.

"No drugs as long as you live here," I said.

"Hey, that's cool," Mooner said. "The Mooner doesn't actually need drugs. The Mooner is a recreational user."

Uh-huh.

I gave Mooner a pillow and a quilt, and I went to bed. At 4:00 A.M. I woke up to the television blaring in the living room. I shuffled out in my T-shirt and flannel boxers and squinted at Mooner.

"What's going on? Don't you sleep?"

"I usually sleep like a rock. I don't know the deal here. I think it's all like, too much. I'm feeling bummed, man. You know what I'm saying? Edgy."

"Yeah. Sounds to me like you need a joint."

"It's medicinal, dude. In California you can get pot by prescription."

"Forget it." I went back to my bedroom, closed and locked the door, and put the pillow over my head.

THE NEXT TIME I straggled out it was seven, Mooner was asleep on the floor, and Saturday morning cartoons were on. I got the coffee machine started, gave Rex some fresh water and food, and dropped a slice of bread into my brand-new toaster. The smell of coffee brewing got Mooner to his feet.

"Yo," he said, "what's for breakfast?"

"Toast and coffee."

"Your grandmother would have made me pancakes."

"My grandmother isn't here."

"You're just trying to make it hard on me, man. Probably you've been scarfing down doughnuts and all I'm allowed to eat is toast. I'm talking about my rights, here." He wasn't exactly yelling, but he wasn't talking softly, either. "I'm a human being and I've got rights."

"What rights are you talking about? The right to have pancakes? The right to have doughnuts?"

"I don't remember."

Oh boy.

He flopped down on the couch. "This apartment is depressing. It makes me, like, nervous. How can you stand to live here?"

"Do you want coffee, or what?"

"Yes! I want coffee and I want it now." His voice ratcheted up a notch. Definitely yelling now. "You can't expect me to wait forever for coffee!"

I slammed a mug down on the kitchen counter, slopped some coffee in it, and shoved it at Mooner. Then I dialed Morelli.

"I need drugs," I said to Morelli. "You have to get me some drugs."

"You mean like antibiotic?"

"No. Like marijuana. I flushed all Mooner's drugs down the toilet last night, and now I hate him. He's completely PMS."

"I thought the plan was to dry him out."

"It isn't worth it. I like him better when he's high."

"Hang in there," Morelli said. And he hung up.

"This is like bogus coffee, dude," Mooner said. "I need a latte."

"Fine! Let's go get a damn latte." I grabbed my bag and keys and shoved Mooner out the door.

"Hey, I need shoes, man," Mooner said.

I performed an exaggerated eye roll and sighed really loudly while Mooner grumped back into the apartment to get his shoes. Great. I wasn't even strung out and now I was PMSing, too.

FIVE

SITTING IN A coffeehouse leisurely sipping a latte wasn't on my morning schedule, so I opted for the McDonald's drive-through, where the breakfast menu listed french vanilla lattes *and* pancakes. They weren't Grandma-caliber pancakes, but they weren't bad, either, and they were easier to come by.

The sky was overcast, threatening rain. No surprise there. Rain is de rigueur for Jersey in April. Steady, gray drizzle that encourages statewide bad hair and couch potato mentality. In school they used to teach us April showers bring May flowers.

April showers also bring twelve-car pileups on the Jersey Turnpike and swollen, snot-clogged sinuses. The upside to this is that we frequently have reason to shop for new cars in Jersey, and we're recognized world-wide for our distinctive nasal version of the English language.

"So how's your head?" I asked Mooner on the way home.

"Filled with latte. My head is mellow, dude."

"No, I mean how are the twelve stitches you have in your head?"

Mooner felt along the Band-Aid. "Feels okay." He sat for a moment with his lips slightly parted and his eyes searching the back recesses of his mind, and then a light flicked on. "Oh yeah," he said. "I was shot by the scary old lady."

That's the good part about smoking pot all your life . . . no short-term memory. Something horrible happens to you and ten minutes later you can't remember a thing.

Of course, that's also the bad part about smoking pot, because when disaster strikes, like your friend goes missing, there's the possibility that important messages and events are lost in the haze. And there's the possibility that you could hallucinate a face in the window when the shot was actually fired by a passing car.

In the case of the Mooner, the possibility was a good probability.

I drove past Dougie's house to make sure it hadn't burned down while we slept.

"Everything looks okay," I said.

"Looks lonely," Mooner said.

WHEN WE GOT back to my apartment Ziggy Garvey and Benny Colucci were in the kitchen. They each had a mug of coffee and a piece of toast.

"Hope you don't mind," Ziggy said. "We were curious about your new toaster."

Benny gestured with his toast. "This is excellent toast. See how evenly brown it is. Not burned on the edges at all. And it's crisp throughout."

"You should get some jelly," Ziggy said. "Some strawberry jelly would be good on this toast."

"You broke into my apartment again! I *hate* when you do that."

"You weren't home," Ziggy said. "We didn't want it to look like you had men loitering in your hall."

"Yeah, we didn't want to sully your good name," Benny said. "We didn't think you were that kind of girl. Although there's been a lot of rumors throughout the years about you and Joe Morelli. You should be careful of him. He has a very bad reputation."

"Hey, look," Ziggy said. "It's the little fruit. Where's your uniform, kid?"

"Yeah, and what's with the Band-Aid? You fall off your high heels?" Benny asked.

Ziggy and Benny elbowed each other and laughed as if this were some great inside joke.

An idea skittered through my head. "You guys wouldn't happen to know anything about the need for the Band-Aid, would you?"

"Not me," Benny said. "Ziggy, you know anything about that?"

"I don't know nothing about it," Ziggy said.

I leaned back against the kitchen counter and crossed my arms. "So what are you doing here?"

"We thought we should check in," Ziggy said. "It's been a while since we talked, and we wanted to see if anything new turned up."

"It's been less than twenty-four hours," I said.

"Yeah, that's what we said. It's been a while."

"Nothing's turned up."

"Gee, that's too bad," Benny said. "You come so recommended. We had high hopes you could help us."

Ziggy finished his coffee, rinsed the mug in the sink, and set it on the dish drain. "We should be going now."

"Pig," Mooner said.

Ziggy and Benny paused at the door.

"That's a rude thing to say," Ziggy said. "We're gonna overlook it because you're Miss Plum's friend." He looked to Benny for backup.

"That's right," Benny said. "We're gonna overlook it, but you should learn some manners. It's not right to talk to old gentlemen like that."

"You called me a fruit!" Mooner yelled.

Ziggy and Benny looked at each other, perplexed.

"Yeah?" Ziggy said. "So?"

"Next time feel free to loiter in the hall," I said. I closed and locked the door behind Ziggy and Benny. "I want you to think," I said to the Mooner. "Do you have any idea why someone shot at you? Are you sure about the woman's face in your window?"

"I don't know, man. I'm having a hard time thinking. My mind is like, busy."

"How about strange phone calls?"

"There was just one, but it wasn't all that strange. A woman called up while I was at Dougie's and said she thought I had something that wasn't mine. And I was like, well, yeah."

"Did she say anything else?"

"No. I asked her if she wanted a toaster or a Super Dude Suit, and she hung up."

"Is that all the inventory you've got left? What happened to the cigarettes?"

"Got rid of the cigarettes. I know this real heavy smoker . . ."

It was as if Mooner had been caught in a time warp. I had memories of him in high school, looking exactly like this. Long, thin brown hair, parted in the middle and tied back into a ponytail. Pale skin, slim build, average height. He was wearing a Hawaiian shirt and jeans that probably had been delivered to Dougie's house under cover of darkness. He'd floated through high school in a grass-induced fog of mellow well-being, talking and giggling through lunch, nodding off in English class. And here he was . . . still floating through life. No job. No responsibility. Now that I thought about it, it sounded pretty good.

Connie usually worked mornings on Saturday. I phoned the office and waited while she got off a call.

"That was my Aunt Flo on the line," she said. "Remember I told you there was trouble in Richmond when DeChooch was down there? She thinks it's related to Louie D buying the farm."

"Louie D. He's a *businessman,* right?"

"He's a real big businessman. Or at least he was. He died of a heart attack while DeChooch was making his pickup."

"Maybe it was a bullet that caused the heart attack."

"I don't think so. If Louie D was whacked we would have heard. That kind of news travels. Especially since his sister lives here."

"Who's his sister? Do I know her?"

"Estelle Colucci. Benny Colucci's wife."

Holy shit. "Small world."

I hung up and my mother called.

"We need to pick out a gown for the wedding," she said.

"I'm not wearing a gown."

"You should at least look."

"Okay, I'll look." Not.

"When?"

"I don't know. I'm busy right now. I'm working."

"It's Saturday," my mother said. "What kind of a person works on Saturday? You need to relax more. Your grandmother and I will be right over."

"No!" Too late. She was gone.

"We have to get out of here," I said to Mooner. "It's an emergency. We have to leave."

"What kind of an emergency? I'm not going to get shot again, am I?"

I took the dirty dishes off the counter and threw them into the dishwasher. Then I grabbed Mooner's quilt and pillow and ran into the bedroom with them. My grandmother lived with me for a short while and I was pretty sure she still had a key to my apartment. God forbid my mother would let herself into my apartment and find it a wreck. The bed was unmade, but I didn't want to take time to make it. I gathered up stray clothes and towels and threw it all in the hamper. I barreled through the living room, back to the kitchen, grabbed my bag and my jacket, and yelled at Mooner to get moving.

We met my mother and grandmother in the lobby.

Damn!

"You didn't have to wait for us in the lobby," my mother said. "We would have come up."

"I'm not waiting for you," I said. "I'm on my way out. I'm sorry, but I have to work this morning."

"What are you doing?" Grandma wanted to know. "Are you tracking down some insane killer?"

"I'm looking for Eddie DeChooch."

"I was half right," Grandma said.

"You can find Eddie DeChooch some other time," my mother said. "I have an appointment for you at Tina's Bridal Shoppe."

"Yeah, you better take it," Grandma said. "We only got this one on account of there was a last-minute cancellation. And besides, we needed an excuse to get out of the house because we couldn't stand any more galloping and whinnying."

"I don't want a wedding gown," I said. "I want a small wedding." Or none at all.

"Yes, but it doesn't do any harm to look," my mother said.

"Tina's Bridal Shoppe rocks," Mooner said.

My mother turned to Mooner. "Is this Walter Dunphy? My goodness, I haven't seen you in ages."

"Dude!" Mooner said to my mother.

Then he and Grandma Mazur did one of those complicated handshakes I could never remember.

"We better get a move on," Grandma said. "We don't want to be late."

"I don't want a gown!"

"We're just looking," my mother said. "We'll only spend a half hour looking, and then you can be on your way."

"Fine! A half hour. That's it. No more. And we're just *looking*."

TINA'S BRIDAL SHOPPE is in the heart of the Burg. It occupies half of a red-brick duplex. Tina lives in a small apartment upstairs and conducts business in the bottom half of the house. The other half of the duplex is rental property owned by Tina. Tina is known far and wide as being a bitch of a landlady, and the tenants of the rental almost always leave when their year's lease expires. Because rental properties are scarce as hen's teeth in the Burg, Tina never has a problem finding hapless victims.

"It's *you,*" Tina said, standing back, eyeballing me. "It's perfect. It's stunning."

I was all decked out in a floor-length satin gown. The bodice had been pinned to fit, the scoop neckline showed just a hint of cleavage, and the full bell skirt had a four-foot train.

"It *is* lovely," my mother said.

"Next time I get married I might get myself a dress just like that," Grandma said. "Or I might go to Vegas and get married in one of them Elvis churches."

"Dude," Mooner said, "go for it."

I twisted slightly to better see myself in the three-way mirror. "You don't think it's too . . . white?"

"Definitely not," Tina said. "This is cream. Cream is very different from white."

I *did* look good in the gown. I looked like Scarlett O'Hara getting ready for a big wedding at Tara. I moved around a little to simulate dancing.

"Jump up and down so we can see how it'll look when you do the bunny hop," Grandma said.

"It's pretty, but I don't want a gown," I said.

"I can order one in her size at no obligation," Tina said.

"No obligation," Grandma said. "You can't beat that."

"As long as there's no obligation," my mother said.

I needed chocolate. A *lot* of chocolate. "Oh gee," I said, "look at the time. I have to go."

"Cool," Mooner said. "Are we going to fight crime now? I've been thinking I need a utility belt for my Super Suit. I could put all my crime-fighting gear in it."

"What crime-fighting gear are you talking about?"

"I haven't totally thought it through, but I guess things like anti-gravitation socks that would let me walk up the sides of buildings. And a spray that would make me invisible."

"You sure your head feels okay where you were shot? You don't have a headache or feel dizzy?"

"No. I feel fine. Hungry, maybe."

*   *   *

A LIGHT RAIN was falling when Mooner and I left Tina's shop.

"That was a total experience," Mooner said. "I felt like a bridesmaid."

I wasn't sure what I felt like. I tried *bride* on for size and found it didn't fit as well as *big fat dope*. I couldn't believe I let my mother talk me into trying on wedding gowns. What was I thinking? I smacked myself on the forehead with the heel of my hand and grunted.

"Dude," Mooner said.

No shit. I turned the key in the ignition and shoved Godsmack into the CD player. I didn't want to think about the wedding fiasco, and there's nothing like metal to wipe your mind clean of anything resembling thought. I pointed the car in the direction of Mooner's house and by the time we got to Roebling, Mooner and I were doing serious head banging.

We were strumming and flipping hair and I almost missed the white Cadillac. It was parked in front of Father Carolli's house, next to the church. Father Carolli is as old as dirt and has been in the Burg for as long as I can remember. It would make sense that he and Eddie DeChooch were friends, and that DeChooch would come to him for counsel.

I said a short prayer that DeChooch was inside the house. I could apprehend him there. Inside the church was another matter. There was all that sanctuary stuff to worry about inside the church. And if my mother found out I violated the church there'd be hell to pay.

I walked to Carolli's front door and knocked. No answer.

Mooner waded through the shrubs and peered into a window. "Don't see anybody in here, dude."

We both looked to the church.

Drat. Probably DeChooch was giving confession. *Forgive me, Father, because I snuffed Loretta Ricci.*

"Okay," I said, "let's try the church."

"Maybe I should go home and put my Super Dude Suit on."

"Not sure that would be right for church."

"Not dressy enough?"

I opened the door to the church and squinted into the dim interior. On sunny days the church glowed with light streaming through the stained-glass windows. On rainy days the church felt bleak and without passion. Today the only warmth came from a few votive candles flickering in front of the Virgin Mary.

The church seemed empty. No mumbling coming from the confessionals. No one at prayer. Just the candles burning and the smell of incense.

I was about to leave when I heard someone giggle. The sound was coming from the altar area.

"Hello," I called. "Anyone here?"

"Just us chickens."

It sounded like DeChooch.

Mooner and I cautiously walked down the aisle and peeked around the altar. DeChooch and Carolli were sitting on the floor, their backs to the altar, sharing a bottle of red wine. An empty bottle lay on the floor a couple feet away.

Mooner gave them a peace sign. "Dude," he said.

Father Carolli peaced him back and repeated the mantra. "Dude."

"What do you want?" DeChooch asked. "Can't you see I'm in church?"

"You're drinking!"

"It's medicinal. I'm depressed."

"You need to accompany me back to the

courthouse so you can get bonded out again," I said to DeChooch.

DeChooch took a long drag on the bottle and wiped his mouth with the back of his hand. "I'm in church. You can't arrest me in church. God'll be pissed. You'll rot in hell."

"It's a commanderment," Carolli said.

Mooner smiled. "These guys are shit-faced."

I searched through my bag and came up with cuffs.

"Eek, cuffs," DeChooch said. "I'm so scared."

I slapped the cuffs on his left wrist and grabbed for his other hand. DeChooch took a 9-mil out of his coat pocket, told Carolli to hold the free bracelet, and fired a round off at the chain. Both men yelped when the bullet severed the chain and sent shock waves up their boney arms.

"Hey," I said, "those cuffs cost sixty dollars."

DeChooch narrowed his eyes and stared at Mooner. "Do I know you?"

"I'm the Mooner, dude. You've seen me at Dougie's house." Mooner held up two fingers pressed tight together. "Dougie and me are like this. We're a team."

"I knew I recognized you!" DeChooch said. "I hate you and your rotten, thieving partner. I should have guessed Kruper wouldn't be in this alone."

"Dude," Mooner said.

DeChooch leveled the gun at Mooner. "Think you're smart, don't you? Think you can take advantage of an old man. Holding out for more money . . . is that your angle?"

Mooner rapped on his head with his knuckles. "No grass growing here."

"I want it, now," DeChooch said.

"Happy to do business with you," Mooner said. "What are we talking about here? Toasters or Super Suits?"

"Asshole," DeChooch said. And he squeezed off a shot that was aimed at Mooner's knee but missed by about six inches and zinged into the floor.

"Cripes," Carolli said, hands over his ears, "you're gonna make me go deaf. Put the piece away."

"I'll put it away after I make him talk," DeChooch said. "He's got something that belongs to me." DeChooch leveled the gun again, and Mooner took off up the aisle, at a dead run.

In my mind I was heroic, knocking the gun

out of DeChooch's hand. In real time I was paralyzed. Wave a gun under my nose and everything in my body turns to liquid.

DeChooch got off another one that sailed by Mooner and took out a chunk of the baptismal font.

Carolli smacked DeChooch in the back of the head with the flat of his hand. "Knock it off!"

DeChooch stumbled forward and the gun discharged and shot a hole in a four-foot crucifixion painting hanging on the far wall.

Our mouths dropped open. And we all made the sign of the cross.

"Holy crap," Carolli said. "You shot Jesus. That's gonna take a lot of Hail Marys."

"It was an accident," DeChooch said. He squinted at the painting. "Where did I get him?"

"In the knee."

"That's a relief," DeChooch said. "At least it wasn't no place fatal."

"So about your court appearance," I said. "I'd take it as a personal favor if you'd go down to the station with me and reschedule."

"Boy, you're a real pain in the ass," DeChooch said. "How many times do I have to tell you . . . forget about it. I'm depressed. I'm not gonna go sit in jail when I'm feeling depressed. You ever been in jail?"

"Not exactly."

"Well, take my word for it, it's no place to be when you're depressed. And anyway, there's something I've got to do."

I was sorting through my bag. I had pepper spray in there somewhere. And probably my stun gun.

"Besides, there's people looking for me, and they're a lot tougher than you," De-Chooch said. "And locking me up in jail would make it real easy for them to find me."

"I'm tough!"

"Lady, you're amateur hour," DeChooch said.

I pulled out a can of hair spray, but I couldn't find the pepper spray. I needed better organization. Probably I should put the pepper spray and stun gun in the zipper compartment, but then I'd have to find another place for my gum and mints.

"I'm going now," DeChooch said. "And I don't want you to follow me or I'll have to shoot you."

"Just one question. What did you want from Mooner?"

"That's private between him and me."

DeChooch left through a side door, and Carolli and I stared after him.

"You just let a murderer get away," I said to Carolli. "You were sitting here drinking with a murderer!"

"Nah. Choochy's no murderer. We go way back. He's got a real good heart."

"He tried to shoot Mooner."

"He got excited. Ever since that stroke he's been excitable like that."

"He had a stroke?"

"Just a small one. Hardly counted at all. *I've* had worse strokes."

Oh boy.

I caught up with Mooner half a block from his house. He was scooting along, running and walking, looking over his shoulder, doing the Mooner version of a rabbit fleeing the hounds. By the time I parked, Mooner was already through the door, had located a roach, and was lighting up.

"People are shooting at you," I said. "You shouldn't be smoking dope. Dope makes you stupid, and you need to be smart."

"Dude," Mooner said on an exhale.

Yeesh.

I dragged Mooner out of his house and

down to Dougie's house. We had a new development here. DeChooch was after something and he thought Dougie had it. And now he thinks Mooner's got it.

"What was DeChooch talking about?" I asked Mooner. "What's he after?"

"I don't know, man, but it's not a toaster."

We were standing in Dougie's living room. Dougie isn't the world's best housekeeper, but the room seemed unusually disrupted. Cushions were askew on the couch, and the coat closet door was open. I stuck my head into the kitchen and found a similar scene. The cabinet doors and counter drawers were open. The door to the cellar was open, and the door to the small pantry was open. I didn't remember things as looking like this last night.

I dumped my bag onto the small kitchen table and pawed through the contents, picking out the pepper spray and stun gun.

"Someone's been in here," I said to Mooner.

"Yeah, it happens a lot."

I turned and stared at him. "A lot?"

"This is the third time this week. I figure someone's looking for our stash. And that old guy, what's with him? He was real friendly with Dougie, coming over to the house a second time and all. And now he's yelling at me. It's like, confusing, dude."

I stood there with my mouth open and my eyes slightly bulging for several beats. "Wait a minute, are you telling me DeChooch came back after he delivered the cigarettes?"

"Yeah. Except I didn't know it was De-Chooch. I didn't know his name. Dougie and me just called him the old dude. I was here when he dropped the cigs. Dougie called me to help unload the truck. And then he came back to see Dougie a couple days later. I didn't see him the second time. I just know from Dougie telling me." Mooner took one last drag on the roach. "Boy, talk about a coincidence. Who would have thought you were looking for the old dude."

Mental head-slap.

"I'm going to check the rest of the house. You stay here. If you hear me scream, call the police."

Am I brave, or what? Actually I was pretty sure no one was in the house. It had been raining for at least an hour, maybe more, and there were no signs that someone had come in with wet feet. Most likely, the house was searched last night after we left.

I flipped the light switch for the cellar and started down the stairs. It was a small house and a small cellar, and I didn't have to go far to see that the cellar had been thoroughly searched and abandoned. I did the second story next and had the same experience. Boxes in the cellar and in the extra bedroom had been ripped open and emptied onto the floor.

Clearly, Mooner had no idea what De-Chooch was after. Mooner wasn't smart enough to be devious.

"Is anything missing?" I asked Mooner. "Has Dougie ever noticed anything missing after the house is searched?"

"A rump roast."

"Excuse me?"

"I swear to God. There was a rump roast in the freezer and someone took it. It was a small one. Two and a half pounds. It was left over from a side of beef Dougie happened to come across. You know . . . fell off a truck. It was all that was left of it. We saved it for ourselves in case we felt like cooking something someday."

I returned to the kitchen and checked out

the freezer and refrigerator. Ice cream and a frozen pizza in the freezer. Coke and left-over pizza in the refrigerator.

"This is a real downer," Moon said. "The house doesn't feel right without the Doug-ster here."

I hated to admit it, but I needed help with DeChooch. I suspected he held the key to Dougie, and he kept walking away from me.

CONNIE WAS GETTING ready to close up the office when Mooner and I walked in. "I'm glad you're here," she said. "I have an FTA for you. Roseanne Kreiner. Businesswoman of the ho variety. Has her office on the corner of Stark and Twelfth. Accused of beating the crap out of one of her clients. Guess he didn't want to pay for services rendered. She shouldn't be hard to find. Probably didn't want to give up work time to go to court."

I took the file from Connie and stuffed it into my bag. "Hear anything from Ranger?"

"He delivered his man this morning."

Hooray. Ranger was back. I could get Ranger to help me.

I called his number, but there was no an-swer. I left a message and tried his pager.

A moment later my cell phone rang and a rush skittered through my stomach. Ranger.

"Yo," Ranger said.

"I could use some help with an FTA."

"What's your problem?"

"He's old, and I'll look like a loser if I shoot him."

I could hear Ranger laughing at the other end. "What's he done?"

"Everything. It's Eddie DeChooch."

"Do you want me to talk to him?"

"No. I want you to give me some ideas on how to bring him in without killing him. I'm afraid if I zap him with the stun gun he'll go toes-up."

"Tag team him with Lula. Bookend him and cuff him."

"Already tried that."

"He got away from you and Lula? Babe, he must be eighty. He can't see. He can't hear. He takes an hour and a half to empty his bladder."

"It was complicated."

"You could try shooting him in the foot next time," Ranger said. "That usually works." And he severed the connection.

Great.

I called Morelli next.

"I've got news for you," Morelli said. "I ran into Costanza when I went out for the paper. He said the autopsy report came in on Loretta Ricci, and she died of a heart attack."

"And then she was shot?"

"You got it, Cupcake."

Too weird.

"I know this is your day off, but I was wondering if you'd do me a favor," I said to Morelli.

"Oh boy."

"I was hoping you'd baby-sit Mooner. He's tied up in this DeChooch mess, and I don't know if it's safe to leave him alone in my apartment."

"Bob and I are all set to watch the game. We've been planning this all week."

"Mooner can watch it with you. I'll drop him off."

I hung up before Morelli could say no.

ROSEANNE KREINER WAS standing on her corner, in the rain, looking totally wet and pissed off. If I was a guy I wouldn't let her within twenty feet of my wanger. She was dressed in high-heeled boots and a black garbage bag. It was hard to tell what she was wearing under the bag. Maybe nothing.

She was pacing and waving at passing cars, and when the cars didn't stop she'd give them the finger. Her arrest sheet said she was fifty-two.

I pulled to the curb and rolled my window down. "Do you do women?"

"Honey, I do pigs, cows, ducks, and women. You got the dime I put in my time. Twenty for a hand thing. You go into over-time if you take all day."

I showed her a twenty, and she got into the car. I hit the auto door locks and took off for the police station.

"Any side street will do," she said.

"I have a confession."

"Oh shit. Are you a cop? Tell me you're not a cop."

"I'm not a cop. I'm bond enforcement. You missed your court date and you have to re-schedule."

"Do I get to keep the twenty?"

"Yeah, you can keep the twenty."

"Do you want a diddle for it?"

"No!"

"Jeez. No need to yell. I just didn't want you to feel cheated. I give people their money's worth."

"How about the guy you clocked?"

"He tried to stiff me. You think I'm out there on that corner for my health? I got a mother in assisted living. I don't make the monthly payment and she's living with me."

"Would that be so bad?"

"I'd rather fuck a rhino."

I parked in the police lot, reached over to cuff her, and she started waving her hands around.

"You're not gonna cuff me," she was saying. "No way."

And then somehow with all the hand waving and struggling the automatic door lock got popped and Roseanne jumped out of the car and ran for the street. She had a head start, but she was in heels and I was in cross-trainers, and I caught her after a two-block chase. Neither of us was in good shape. She was wheezing and I felt like I was breathing in fire. I clapped the bracelets on her and she sat down.

"No sitting," I said.

"Tough. I'm not going anywhere."

I'd left my bag in the car and the car looked a long way off. If I ran back to the car to get my cell phone Roseanne wouldn't be here when I returned. She was sitting, sulking, and I was standing, fuming.

Some days it didn't pay to get out of bed.

I had a really strong urge to give her a good kick in the kidney, but that'd probably leave a bruise and then she might sue Vinnie for bounty hunter brutality. Vinnie hated when that happened.

It was raining harder and we were both soaked. My hair was stuck to my face, and my Levi's were drenched. The two of us settled in for a standoff. The standoff ended when Eddie Gazarra drove by on his way to lunch. Eddie's a Trenton cop, and he's married to my cousin Shirley-the-Whiner.

Eddie rolled his window down, shook his head, and made *tsch-tsch-tsch* sounds.

"I've got a situation with an FTA," I said to Eddie.

Eddie grinned. "No shit."

"How about helping me get her into your car."

"It's raining! I'll get soaked."

I narrowed my eyes at him.

"It'll cost you," Gazarra said.

"I'm *not* baby-sitting." His kids were cute, but last time I stayed with them I fell asleep and they cut two inches off my hair.

He did another *tsch*. "Hey, Roseanne," he yelled. "You want a ride?"

Roseanne got up and looked at him. Deciding.

"If you get into the car, Stephanie'll give you ten bucks," Gazarra said.

"No I won't," I yelled. "I already gave her twenty."

"Did you get a diddle for it?" Gazarra asked.

"No!"

He made another *tsch*.

"Well," Roseanne said, "what's it gonna be?"

I pushed the hair out of my face. "It's going to be a kick in the kidney if you don't get your butt in that cop car."

When up against it . . . try an empty threat.

SIX

I PARKED IN my lot and slogged up to my apartment, leaving puddles in my wake. Benny and Ziggy were waiting in the hall.

"We brought you some strawberry preserves," Benny said. "It's the good kind, too. It's Smucker's."

I took the jam and opened my door. "What's up?"

"We heard you caught Chooch having a snort with Father Carolli."

They were smiling, enjoying the moment.

"That Choochy, he's a pip," Ziggy said. "Did he really shoot Jesus?"

I smiled with them. Choochy was indeed a pip. "News travels fast," I said.

"We're what you call plugged in," Ziggy said. "Anyhow, we just want to get it straight from you. How did Choochy look? Was he okay? Was he, you know, crazy?"

"He took a couple shots at Mooner, but he missed. Carolli said Chooch has been excitable ever since his stroke."

"He don't hear so good, either," Benny said.

They exchanged glances on that one. No smiles.

Water was dripping from my Levi's, forming a pool on the kitchen floor. Ziggy and Benny were standing clear of it.

"Where's the little geeky guy?" Benny asked. "Isn't he hanging out with you anymore?"

"He had things to do."

I PEELED MY clothes off the minute Benny and Ziggy left. Rex was running on his wheel, occasionally pausing to watch me, not understanding the concept of rain. Sometimes he sat under his water bottle and it dripped on his head, but mostly his experience with weather was limited.

I slipped into a new T-shirt and clean Levi's and blasted my hair with the hair dryer. When I was done I had a lot of volume but not much shape, so I created a distraction by applying bright blue eyeliner.

I was pulling my boots on when the phone rang.

"Your sister's on her way over," my mother said. "She needs someone to talk to."

Valerie must really be desperate to choose me to talk to. We like each other okay, but we've never been close. Too many basic personality differences. And when she moved to California we drifted even further apart.

Funny how things turn out. We all thought Valerie had the perfect marriage.

The phone rang again and it was Morelli.

"He's humming," Morelli said. "When are you going to come get him?"

"Humming?"

"Bob and I are trying to watch the game and this yodel won't stop humming."

"Maybe he's nervous."

"Fuckin' A. He *should* be nervous. If he doesn't stop humming I'm going to strangle him."

"Try feeding him."

And I hung up.

"I wish I knew what everyone is looking for," I said to Rex. "I know it's tied to Dougie's disappearance."

There was a rap on the door and my sister bounced in, looking Doris Day–Meg Ryan perky. Probably perfect for California, but we don't do *perky* in Jersey.

"You're awfully perky," I said. "I don't remember you as being this perky."

"I'm not perky . . . I'm cheerful. I am absolutely not crying anymore, ever again. No one likes a Gloomy Gus. I'm going to get on with my life and I'm going to be happy. I'm going to be so goddamn happy Mary Sunshine's going to look like a loser."

Yikes.

"And do you know why I can be happy? I can be happy because I'm well adjusted."

Good thing Valerie moved back to Jersey. We'd fix that.

"So this is your apartment," she said, looking around. "I've never been here."

I looked, too, and I wasn't impressed by what I saw. I have lots of good ideas for my apartment, but somehow I never get around to buying the glass candle holders at Illuminations or the brass fruit bowl at Pottery Barn. My windows have utilitarian shades and drapes. My furniture is relatively new but uninspired. I live in a cookie-cutter, inexpensive seventies apartment that looks exactly like a cookie-cutter, inexpensive seventies apartment. Martha Stewart would have a cow over my apartment.

"Jeez," I said, "I'm really sorry about Steve. I didn't know you two were having problems."

Valerie flopped onto the couch. "I didn't know, either. He broadsided me. I came home from the gym one day and realized Steve's clothes were gone. Then I found a note on the kitchen counter about how he felt trapped and had to get away. And the next day I got a foreclosure notice on the house."

"Wow."

"I'm thinking this could be a good thing. I mean, this could open up all sorts of new experiences for me. For instance, I have to get a job."

"Any ideas?"

"I want to be a bounty hunter."

I was speechless. Valerie. A bounty hunter.

"Did you tell Mom?"

"No. Do you think I should?"

"No!"

"The thing about being a bounty hunter is that you make your own hours, right? So I could be home when the girls get out of school. And bounty hunters are kind of tough, and that's what I want the new Valerie to be . . . cheerful but tough."

Valerie was wearing a red cardigan sweater from Talbots, designer jeans that had been ironed, and snakeskin loafers.

Tough seemed like a stretch.

"I'm not sure you're the bounty hunter type," I told Valerie.

"Of course I'm the bounty hunter type," she said enthusiastically. "I just have to get into the right mind-set." She sat up straighter on my couch and started singing the rubber tree ant song.

"He's got hiiiigh hopes . . . hiiiigh hopes!"

Good thing my gun was in the kitchen, because I had an urge to shoot Valerie. This was taking the cheerful thing way beyond where I wanted to go.

"Grandma said you were working on a big case and I thought maybe I could help," Valerie said.

"I don't know . . . this guy is a killer."

"But he's old, right?"

"Yeah. He's an old killer."

"That sounds like a good place to start," Valerie said, bouncing up off the couch. "Let's go get him."

"I don't exactly know where to find him," I said.

"He's probably feeding ducks at the lake. That's what old men do. At night they watch television and during the day they feed the ducks."

"It's raining. I don't think he'd feed the ducks in the rain."

Valerie glanced over at the window. "Good point."

There was a sharp rap at the door and then the sound of someone testing the door to see if it was locked. Then there was another rap.

Morelli, I thought. Returning Mooner.

I opened the door and Eddie DeChooch stepped into my foyer. He had his gun in his hand, and he looked serious.

"Where is he?" DeChooch asked. "I know he's living with you. Where is the rat bastard?"

"Are you talking about Mooner?"

"I'm talking about the worthless little piece of shit who's screwing around with me. He's got something that belongs to me and I want it back."

"How do you know Mooner has it?"

DeChooch pushed past me and went into my bedroom and bathroom. "His friend don't have it. And I don't have it. The only one left is this Mooner moron." DeChooch opened closet doors and slammed them shut. "Where is he? I know you've got him locked away some place."

I shrugged. "He said he had errands to run and that's the last I've seen of him."

He put his gun to Valerie's head. "Who's Miss Cutesy here?"

"That's my sister Valerie."

"Maybe I should shoot her."

Valerie looked sideways at the gun. "Is that a real gun?"

DeChooch moved the gun six inches to the right and squeezed off a shot. The bullet missed my television by a millimeter and lodged in my wall.

Valerie went white and made a squeaky sound.

"Cripes, she sounds like a mouse," De-Chooch said.

"What am I supposed to do about that wall?" I asked him. "You made a big bullet hole in it."

"You can show the bullet hole to your friend. You can tell him his head's gonna look like that wall if he doesn't shape up."

"Maybe I could help you get this thing back if you'd tell me what it is."

DeChooch eased out my front door with the gun pointed at Valerie and me. "Don't follow me," he said, "or I'll shoot you."

Valerie's knees wobbled and she sat down hard on the floor.

I waited a couple beats before going to the door and looking out, down the hall. I believed DeChooch about the shooting part. When I finally checked the hall DeChooch was nowhere to be seen. I closed and locked my door and ran to the window. My apartment is at the back of the building, and my windows overlook the parking lot. Not especially scenic, but handy for checking out fleeing crazy old men.

I watched DeChooch leave the building and take off in the white Cadillac. The police were looking for him and I was looking for him and he was riding around in the white Cadillac. Not exactly the stealth felon. So why weren't we able to catch him? I knew the answer on my side. I was inept.

Valerie was still on the floor, still looking pale.

"You might want to rethink the bounty hunter thing," I suggested to Valerie. Maybe I should rethink it, too.

VALERIE RETURNED TO my parents' house to locate her Valium, and I called Ranger back.

"I'm going to bail on this case," I said to Ranger. "I'm going to hand it off to you."

"You don't usually bail," Ranger said. "What's the deal here?"

"DeChooch is making me look like an idiot."

"And?"

"Dougie Kruper is missing and I think his disappearance is somehow tied to De-Chooch. I'm worried that I'm endangering Dougie because I keep screwing up with DeChooch."

"Dougie Kruper was probably abducted by aliens."

"Do you want to take the case, or what?"

"I don't want it."

"Fine. The hell with you." I hung up and stuck my tongue out at the phone. I grabbed my bag and my rain jacket and stomped out of my apartment and down the stairs.

Mrs. DeGuzman was in the lobby. Mrs. DeGuzman is from the Philippines and doesn't speak a word of English.

"Humiliating," I said to Mrs. DeGuzman.

Mrs. DeGuzman smiled and bobbed her head like one of those dogs people put in their car rear window.

I got into the CR-V and sat there for a moment thinking things like, *Prepare to die, DeChooch.* And, *No more Ms. Nice Guy, this is war.* But then I couldn't figure out how to find DeChooch, so I did a quick run to the bakery.

It was close to five when I got back to my apartment. I opened my door and stifled a shriek. There was a man in my living room. I took another look and realized it was Ranger. He was sitting in a chair, looking relaxed, thoughtfully watching me.

"You hung up on me," he said. "Don't ever hang up on me."

His voice was quiet, but as always the authority was unmistakable. He was wearing black dress slacks, a long-sleeved light-weight black sweater pushed up on his fore-arms, and expensive black loafers. His hair was cut very short. I was used to seeing him in SWAT dress with long hair, and I hadn't immediately recognized him. I guess that was the point.

"Are you in disguise?" I asked.

He watched me without answering. "What's in the bag?"

"An emergency cinnamon bun. What are you doing here?"

"I thought we might make a deal. How bad do you want DeChooch?"

Oh boy. "What did you have in mind?"

"You find DeChooch. If you need help bringing him in you call me. If I succeed in the capture, you spend a night with me."

My heart stopped beating. Ranger and I had been playing this game for a while now, but it had never been articulated in quite this way.

"I'm sort of engaged to Morelli," I said.

Ranger smiled.

Shit.

There was the sound of a key being inserted in my front door lock and the door swung open. Morelli strode in and he and Ranger nodded to each other.

"Game over?" I asked Morelli.

Morelli gave me a death look. "The

game's over and the baby-sitting is over. And I don't ever want to see this guy again."

"Where is he?"

Morelli turned and looked. No Mooner. "Christ," Morelli said. He went back to the hall and yanked Mooner into the room by Mooner's jacket collar, the Trenton PD equivalent to a mother cat dragging a demented offspring by the scruff of his neck.

"Dude," Mooner said.

Ranger stood and passed me a card with a name and address written on it. "The owner of the white Cadillac," he said. He slipped into a black leather jacket and left. Mr. Sociable.

Morelli deposited Mooner in a chair in front of the television, pointed his finger at him, and told him to stay.

I raised my eyebrows at Morelli.

"It works with Bob," Morelli said. He put the television on and motioned me into the bedroom. "We need to talk."

There was a time when the idea of being in a bedroom with Morelli scared the hell out of me. Now mostly it makes my nipples get hard.

"What's up?" I said, closing the door.

"Mooner tells me you picked out a wedding gown today."

I closed my eyes and flopped back onto the bed. "I did! I let myself get sucked into it." I groaned. "My mother and grandmother showed up and next thing I was trying on gowns at Tina's."

"You'd tell me if we were getting married, wouldn't you? I mean, you wouldn't just appear on my doorstep in the gown one day and say we were due at the church in an hour."

I sat up and narrowed my eyes at him. "No need to get snippy about it."

"Men don't get snippy," Morelli said. "Men get pissed. Women get snippy."

I jumped up from the bed. "That's so typical of you to make a sexist remark!"

"Lighten up," Morelli said. "I'm Italian. I'm supposed to make sexist remarks."

"This is *not* going to work."

"Cupcake, you'd better figure this out before your mother gets her Visa bill for that dress."

"Well, what do you want to do? Do you want to get married?"

"Sure. Let's get married now." He reached

behind him and locked the bedroom door. "Take your clothes off."

"What?"

Morelli pushed me down and leaned over me. "Marriage is a state of mind."

"Not in my family."

He picked up my shirt and looked under it.

"Hold it! Wait a minute!" I said. "I can't do this with Mooner in the next room!"

"Mooner's watching television."

His hand cupped my pubic bone, he did something magical with his index finger, my eyes glazed over, and some drool trickled out of the corner of my mouth. "The door's locked, right?"

"Right," Morelli said. He had my pants down to my knees.

"Maybe you should check."

"Check on what?"

"On Mooner. Make sure he's not listening at the door."

"I don't care if he's listening at the door."

"I care."

Morelli sighed and rolled off me. "I should have fallen in love with Joyce Barnhardt. She would have invited Mooner in to watch."

He opened the door a crack and looked out. He opened it wider. "Oh shit," he said.

I was on my feet with my pants up. "What? *What?*"

Morelli was out of the room, moving through the house, opening and closing doors. "Mooner's gone."

"How could he be gone?"

Morelli stopped and faced me. "Do we care?"

"Yes!"

Another sigh. "We were only in the bedroom for a couple minutes. He can't have gone far. I'll go look for him."

I crossed the room to the window and looked down into the parking lot. A car was leaving. It was hard to see the car in the rain, but it looked like Ziggy and Benny. Dark, American-made midsize. I grabbed my bag, locked my door, and ran the length of the hall. I caught up with Morelli in the lobby. We pushed through the doors to the lot and stopped. No Mooner in sight. The dark sedan no longer in view.

"I think it's possible he's with Ziggy and Benny," I said. "I think we should try their social club." I couldn't imagine where else they'd take Mooner. I didn't think they'd take him home with them.

"Ziggy and Benny and Chooch belong to Domino on Mulberry Street," Morelli said, both of us climbing into his truck. "Why do you think Mooner's with Benny and Ziggy?"

"I thought I saw their car pull out of the lot. And I have a feeling Dougie and DeChooch and Benny and Ziggy are all mixed up in something that started with the cigarette deal."

We wound our way through the Burg to Mulberry and sure enough, Benny's dark blue sedan was parked in front of the Domino Social Club. I got out and felt the hood. Warm.

"How do you want to play this?" Morelli asked. "Do you want me to wait in the truck? Or do you want me to muscle you in?"

"Just because I'm a liberated woman doesn't mean I'm a moron. Muscle me in."

Morelli knocked on the door, and an old man opened the door with the security chain attached.

"I'd like to talk to Benny," Morelli said.

"Benny's busy."

"Tell him it's Joe Morelli."

"He's still gonna be busy."

"Tell him if he doesn't come to the door right now I'm going to set his car on fire."

The old guy disappeared and returned in less than a minute. "Benny says if you set his car on fire he's gonna hafta kill you. And he'll tell your grandmother on you, too."

"Tell Benny he better not have Walter Dunphy in there because Dunphy is under my grandmother's protection. Anything happens to Dunphy and Benny gets *the eye*."

Two minutes later the door opened for a third time and Mooner got pitched out.

"Dang," I said to Morelli. "I'm impressed."

"Dude," Morelli said.

We put Mooner in the truck and drove him back to my apartment. He got the giggles halfway there, and Morelli and I knew what kind of bait Benny had used on Mooner.

"How lucky was that," Mooner said, smiling and awestruck. "I stepped out for a minute to find some shit, and the two dudes were right there in the lot. And now they like me."

FOR AS LONG as I can remember my mother and grandmother have gone to church on Sunday morning. And on the way home from church, my mother and grandmother stop at the bakery and buy a bag of jelly doughnuts for my father, the sinner. If Mooner and I timed it right we'd arrive a minute or two behind the doughnuts. My mother would be happy because I'd come to visit. Mooner would be happy because he'd get a doughnut. And I'd be happy because my grandmother would have gotten the very latest gossip relating to everybody and everything, including Eddie DeChooch.

"I've got big news," Grandma said when she came to the door. "Stiva got hold of Loretta Ricci yesterday and the first viewing's going to be tonight at seven. It'll be one of those closed-casket ones, but it should be worth something, anyway. Maybe Eddie will even show up. I'm going to wear my new red dress. There'll be a packed house tonight. Everybody'll be there."

Angie and Mary Alice were in the living room in front of the television with the sound turned up so loud the windows were vibrating. My father was in the living room, too, staked out in his favorite chair, reading the paper, his knuckles white with the effort.

"Your sister's in bed with a migraine," Grandma said. "Guess the cheerful thing was too much of a strain. And your mother's making cabbage rolls. We've got doughnuts in the kitchen and if that don't do it for you, I've got a bottle in my bedroom. This place is bedlam."

Mooner took a doughnut and drifted into the living room to watch television with the kids. I helped myself to coffee and sat at the kitchen table with my doughnut.

Grandma sat across from me. "What are you up to today?"

"I have a lead on Eddie DeChooch. He's been driving around in a white Cadillac, and I just got the owner's name. Mary Maggie Mason." I took the card from my pocket and looked at it. "Why does that name sound so familiar?"

"Everybody knows Mary Maggie Mason," Grandma said. "She's a star."

"I never heard of her," my mother said.

"That's because you never go anywhere," Grandma said. "Mary Maggie's one of them mud wrestlers at The Snake Pit. She's the best."

My mother looked up from her pot of beef and rice and tomatoes. "How do you know all this?"

"Elaine Barkolowski and me go to The Snake Pit sometimes after bingo. On Thursdays they got men wrestling and they only wear little Baggies on their privates. They're not as good as The Rock, but they're pretty good all the same."

"That's disgusting," my mother said.

"Yeah," Grandma said. "It costs five dollars to get in but it's worth it."

"I have to go to work," I said to my mother. "Is it okay if I leave Mooner here for a while?"

"He doesn't do drugs anymore, does he?"

"Nope. He's clean." For a whole twelve hours. "You might want to lock up the glue and cough syrup, though . . . just in case."

The address Ranger had given me for Mary Maggie Mason was an upscale high-rise condo building that looked out at the river. I rode through the underground parking, checking out cars. No white Cadillac, but there was a silver Porsche with MMM-YUM on the license plate.

I parked in a slot reserved for guests and rode the elevator to the seventh floor. I was wearing jeans and boots and a black leather jacket over a black knit shirt, and I didn't feel dressed right for the building. The building called for gray silk and heels and skin that had been lasered and buffed to perfection.

Mary Maggie Mason answered on the second knock. She was wearing sweats, and her brown hair was pulled back into a ponytail. "Yes?" she asked, peering at me from behind tortoiseshell glasses, a Nora Roberts book in her hand. Mary Maggie, the mud wrestler, reads romance. In fact, from what I could see beyond her door, Mary Maggie read *everything*. There were books everywhere.

I gave her my card and introduced myself. "I'm looking for Eddie DeChooch," I said. "It's been brought to my attention that he's driving your car around town."

"The white Cadillac? Yeah. Eddie needed a car, and I never drive the Caddy. I inherited it when my Uncle Ted died. I should probably sell it, but it's nostalgic."

"How do you know Eddie?"

"He's one of the owners of The Snake Pit. Eddie and Pinwheel Soba and Dave Vincent. Why are you looking for Eddie? You're not going to arrest him, are you? He's really a sweet old guy."

"He missed his court date and he needs to reschedule. Do you know where I can find him?"

"Sorry. He stopped by one day last week.

I don't remember which day. He wanted to borrow the car. His car is a real lemon. Always something wrong with it. So I loan him the Cadillac a lot. He likes to drive it because it's big and white and he can find it at night in a parking lot. Eddie doesn't see all that well."

It's none of my business, but I wouldn't be loaning my car to a blind guy. "Looks like you do a lot of reading."

"I'm a book junkie. When I retire from wrestling I'm going to open a mystery bookstore."

"Can you make a living selling mysteries?"

"No. Nobody makes a living selling mysteries. The stores are all fronts for numbers operations."

We were standing in the foyer and I was looking around as best I could for evidence that DeChooch might be hiding out with Mary Maggie.

"This is a great building," I said. "I didn't realize there was this much money in mud wrestling."

"Mud wrestling doesn't pay anything. I stay alive with the endorsements. And I've got a couple corporate sponsors." Mary

Maggie glanced at her watch. "Yikes, look at the time. I have to go. I'm supposed to be at the gym in a half hour."

I pulled out of the underground garage and parked on a side street so I could make a few calls. First call was to Ranger's cell phone.

"Yo," Ranger said.

"Do you know DeChooch owns a third of The Snake Pit?"

"Yeah, he won it in a crap game two years ago. I thought you knew."

"I didn't know!"

Silence.

"So what else do you know that I don't know?" I asked.

"How much time do we have?"

I hung up on Ranger and called Grandma.

"I want you to look up a couple names in the phone book," I said to Grandma. "I need to know where Pinwheel Soba and Dave Vincent live."

I listened to Grandma thumbing through pages, and finally she came back on the line. "Neither of them's listed."

Rats. Morelli would be able to get me the addresses, but Morelli wouldn't want me messing around with Snake Pit owners. Morelli would give me a big lecture about being careful, we'd get into a shouting match, and then I'd have to eat a lot of cake to calm down.

I took a deep breath and redialed Ranger.

"I need addresses," I told Ranger.

"Let me guess," Ranger said. "Pinwheel Soba and Dave Vincent. Pinwheel's in Miami. He moved last year. Opened a club in South Beach. Vincent lives in Princeton. There's supposed to be bad feelings between DeChooch and Vincent." He gave me Vincent's address and disconnected.

A flash of silver caught my eye and I looked up to see Mary Maggie zip around the corner in her Porsche. I pulled out after her. Not exactly following her, but keeping her in view. We were both going in the same direction. North. I stayed with her and it seemed to me she was going pretty far afield to get to a gym. I bypassed my turnoff and stayed with her through center city to north Trenton. If she'd been on guard she would have spotted me. It's hard for a single car to do a decent tail. Fortunately, Mary Maggie wasn't looking for a tail.

I dropped back when she turned onto Cherry Street. I parked around the corner from Ronald DeChooch's house and watched Mary Maggie get out of her car, walk to the door, and ring the doorbell. The door opened and Mary Maggie stepped inside. Ten minutes later, the front door opened again and Mary Maggie Mason came out. She stood on the front porch for a minute or two talking to Ronald. Then she got into her car and drove away. This time she went to a gym. I watched her park and go into the building and then I left.

I took Route 1 to Princeton, hauled out a map, and located Vincent's house. Princeton isn't actually part of New Jersey. It's a small island of wealth and intellectual eccentricity floating in the Sea of Central Megalopolis. It's an honest-to-god town awash in the land of the strip mall. Hair is smaller, heels are shorter, asses are tighter in Princeton.

Vincent owned a large yellow-and-white colonial set onto a half-acre lot on the edge of town. There was a detached two-car garage. No cars in the driveway. No flag proclaiming that Eddie DeChooch was in residence. I parked one house down on the opposite side of the street and watched the house. Very boring. Nothing happening. No cars cruising by. No children playing on the sidewalk. No metal blaring out of a second-story boom box. A bastion of respectability and decorum. And a little intimidating. Knowing it was bought with Snake Pit profits did nothing to alter the feeling of old-money snootiness. I didn't think Dave Vincent would appreciate having his peaceful Sunday disturbed by a bounty hunter looking for Eddie DeChooch. And I could be going out on a limb here, but I suspected Mrs. Vincent wouldn't take a chance on tarnishing her social standing by harboring the likes of Choochy.

After I'd done an hour of worthless surveillance a cop car crept down the street and pulled up behind me. Great. I was about to get rousted out of the neighborhood. If someone caught me sitting in front of their house in the Burg, they'd send their dog out to take a leak on my car wheel. Backup action would be a string of profanities yelled at me to get the hell out of there. In Princeton they send a perfectly pressed, perfectly polite officer of the law to make an inquiry. Is this class, or what?

There didn't seem to be anything gained by stressing Officer Perfect so I got out of my car and walked back to him while he was checking my plate. I passed him my card and the bond contract stating my right to apprehend Eddie DeChooch. And I gave him the standard explanation of routine surveillance.

Then he explained to me that the good people in this neighborhood aren't used to being under surveillance, and probably it'd be best if I conducted my surveillance in a more discreet manner.

"Sure," I said. And then I left. If a cop is your friend he's the best friend you'll ever have. On the other hand, if you're not on intimate terms with a cop it's smart not to annoy him.

Watching the Vincent house wasn't going to do me any good, anyway. If I wanted to talk to Dave Vincent better to see him at work. Besides, it wouldn't hurt to take a look at The Snake Pit. Not only would I get to talk to Vincent, I'd also get another shot at Mary Maggie Mason. She'd seemed like a nice enough person, but clearly there was more to the story.

I took Route 1 south and on a whim decided to take another look around at Mary Maggie's garage.

SEVEN

I CRUISED INTO the garage and rode around looking for the Cadillac. I went up and down every aisle, but I didn't have any luck. Good thing, too, because I didn't know what I'd do if I found Choochy. I didn't feel capable of bringing him in on my own. And the thought of agreeing to Ranger's deal gave me an orgasm on the spot, followed by a panic attack.

I mean, what if I spent the night with Ranger? What then? Suppose he was so amazing I got ruined for all other men. Suppose he was better in the sack than Joe. Not that Joe was a slouch in bed. It was just that

Joe was mortal, and I wasn't sure about Ranger.

And what about my future? Was I going to marry Ranger? No. Ranger wasn't marriage material. Hell, Joe was barely marriage material.

And then there was the other side of it. Suppose I didn't measure up. I involuntarily squinched my eyes closed. Argh! It would be awful. Beyond embarrassing.

Suppose *he* didn't measure up! The fantasy would be ruined. What would I think about when it was just me and the shower massage?

I shook my head to clear my brain. I didn't want to contemplate a night with Ranger. It was too complicated.

IT WAS DINNERTIME when I got back to my parents'. Valerie was out of bed and at the table, wearing dark glasses. Angie and Mooner were eating peanut butter sandwiches in front of the television. Mary Alice was galloping around the house, pawing at the carpet and snorting. Grandma was dressed for the viewing. My father had his head down over his meat loaf. And my mother was at the head of the table, having a full-blown hot flash. Her face was flushed, her hair was damp on her forehead, and her eyes darted feverishly around the room, daring anyone to imply she was in the throes of the change.

Grandma ignored my mother and passed me the applesauce. "I was hoping you'd show up for dinner. I could use a ride to the viewing."

"Sure," I said. "I was going, anyway."

My mother gave me a pained expression.

"What?" I asked.

"Nothing."

"What?"

"It's your clothes. You go to the Ricci viewing dressed like that, and I'll be getting phone calls for a week. What will I say to people? They'll think you can't afford decent clothes."

I looked down at my jeans and boots. They looked decent to me, but I wasn't about to argue with a menopausal woman.

"I have clothes you can wear," Valerie said. "In fact, I'll go with you and Grandma. It'll be fun! Does Stiva still serve cookies?"

There must have been a mix-up at the hospital. Surely I don't have a sister who thinks funeral parlors are fun.

Valerie popped up out of her chair and pulled me upstairs by the hand. "I know just the outfit for you!"

There's nothing worse than wearing someone else's clothes. Well, maybe world famine or a typhoid epidemic, but aside from that, borrowed clothes never feel right. Valerie is an inch shorter than me and five pounds lighter. Our shoe sizes are identical, and our taste in clothes couldn't be more different. Wearing Valerie's clothes to the Ricci viewing equates to Halloween in hell.

Valerie whisked a skirt out of her closet. *"Ta-dah!"* she sang. "Isn't this wonderful? It's perfect. And I have the perfect top for it, too. And I have the perfect shoes. They're all coordinated."

Valerie has always been coordinated. Her shoes and her handbags always match. Her skirts and shirts match, too. And Valerie can actually wear a scarf without looking like an idiot.

Five minutes later, Valerie had me completely outfitted. The skirt was mauve and lime green, patterned with pink and yellow lilies. The material was diaphanous and the hemline hit midcalf. Probably looked great on my sister in L.A., but I felt like a seventies shower curtain. The top was a stretchy little white cotton shirt with cap sleeves and lace around the neck. The shoes were pink strappy sandals with three-inch heels.

Never in my life had I ever considered wearing pink shoes.

I looked at myself in the full-length mirror and tried not to grimace.

"LOOK AT THIS," Grandma said when we got to Stiva's. "It's a packed house. We should have gotten here sooner. All the good seats up front by the casket are going to be gone."

We were in the foyer, barely able to push our way through the mourners who were spilling in and out of the viewing rooms. It was precisely seven o'clock, and if we'd gotten to Stiva's any sooner we would have had to line up outside like fans at a rock concert.

"I can't breathe," Valerie said. "I'm going to be squashed like a bug. My girls will be orphans."

"You have to step on people's feet and kick them in the back of the leg," Grandma said, "then they move away from you."

Benny and Ziggy were standing just inside the door to room one. If Eddie came through the door they had him. Tom Bell, the primary on the Ricci case, was also here. Plus half the population of the Burg.

I felt a hand cup my ass and I whirled around to catch Ronald DeChooch leering down at me. "Hey, chicky," he said, "I like the flimsy skirt. I bet you're not wearing any panties."

"Listen, you dickless sack of shit," I said to Ronald DeChooch, "you touch my ass again and I'll get someone to shoot you."

"Spunky," Ronald said. "I like that."

Meanwhile, Valerie had disappeared, swept away with the crowd surging forward. And Grandma was worming her way up to the casket ahead of me. A closed casket is a dangerous situation, since lids have been known to mysteriously spring open in Grandma's presence. Best to stay close to Grandma and keep watch that she doesn't get her nail file out to work at the latch.

Constantine Stiva, the Burg's favorite undertaker, spotted Grandma and rushed to stand guard, beating Grandma to the deceased.

"Edna," he said, nodding and smiling his understanding undertaker smile, "so nice to see you again."

Once a week Grandma caused chaos at

Stiva's, but Stiva wasn't about to alienate a future customer who was no spring chicken and had her eye on a top-of-the-line mahogany, hand-carved eternal resting box.

"I thought it only right that I pay my respects," Grandma said. "Loretta was in my seniors group."

Stiva had himself wedged between Grandma and Loretta. "Of course," he said. "Very kind of you."

"I see it's another one of them closed-coffin things," Grandma said.

"The family's preference," Stiva said, his voice as smooth as custard, his expression benign.

"I guess it's best, being that she was shot and then all carved up in the autopsy."

Stiva showed a flicker of nervousness.

"Shame they had to do the autopsy," Grandma said. "Loretta was shot in the chest and she could have had an open casket except I guess when they do the autopsy they take your brain out and I suppose that makes it hard to get a good hairdo."

Three people who had been standing nearby sucked in air and speed-walked to the door.

"So what did she look like?" Grandma

asked Stiva. "Would you have been able to do anything with her if it wasn't for the brain thing?"

Stiva had Grandma by the elbow. "Why don't we go into the lobby where it's not so crowded and we can have some cookies."

"That's a good idea," Grandma said. "I could use a cookie. Nothing interesting to see here, anyway."

I followed them out and on the way stopped to talk to Ziggy and Benny.

"He's not going to show up here," I said. "He's not that crazy."

Ziggy and Benny shrugged in unison.

"Just in case," Ziggy said.

"What was the deal with Mooner yesterday?"

"He wanted to see the club," Ziggy said. "He came out of your apartment building to get some air and we got to talking and one thing led to another."

"Yeah, we didn't mean to kidnap the little guy," Benny said. "And we don't want old lady Morelli putting the eye on us. We don't believe in any of that Old World stuff, but why take a chance."

"We heard she put the eye on Carmine

Scallari, and he couldn't, uh, *perform* after that," Ziggy said.

"The story goes he even tried that new medicine but nothing helped," Benny said.

Benny and Ziggy both gave an involuntary shiver. They didn't want to be in the same predicament as Carmine Scallari.

I looked past Benny and Ziggy into the lobby and spotted Morelli. He was standing to one side, against the wall, surveying the crowd. He was wearing jeans and black cross-trainers and a black T-shirt under a tweed sportcoat. He looked lean and predatory. Men approached him to talk sports and then move on. Women watched from a distance, wondering if Morelli was as dangerous as he looked, if he was as bad as his reputation.

He caught my eye from across the room and crooked his finger at me, doing the universal *come here* gesture. He draped a proprietary arm around me when I reached him and kissed me on my neck, just below my ear. "Where's Mooner?"

"Watching television with Valerie's kids. Are you here because you're hoping to catch Eddie?"

"No. I'm here hoping to catch you. I think

you should let Mooner overnight with your parents, and you should come home with me."

"Tempting, but I'm with Grandma and Valerie."

"I just got here," Morelli said. "Did Grandma manage to get the lid up?"

"Stiva intercepted her."

Morelli ran his finger along the lace edging on the shirt. "I like the lace."

"What about the skirt?"

"The skirt looks like a shower curtain. Sort of erotic. Makes me wonder if you're wearing underwear."

Omigod! "That's the same thing Ronald DeChooch said to me."

Morelli looked around. "I didn't see him when I came in. I didn't know Ronald and Loretta Ricci moved in the same circles."

"Maybe Ronald is here for the same reason Ziggy and Benny and Tom Bell are here."

Mrs. Dugan came over to us, all smiles. "Congratulations," she said. "I heard about the wedding. I'm so thrilled for you. And you are so lucky to have gotten the PNA Hall for your reception. Your grandmother must have pulled some strings on that one."

PNA Hall? I looked up at Morelli and rolled my eyes and Morelli gave me the silent head-shake.

"Excuse me," I said to Mrs. Dugan, "I have to find Grandma Mazur."

I put my head down and plowed through the crowd to Grandma. "Mrs. Dugan just told me we have the PNA Hall rented for my reception," I stage-whispered to her. "Is that true?"

"Lucille Stiller had it reserved for her parents' fiftieth wedding anniversary and her mother died just last night. As soon as we heard we snapped the hall right up. Things like this don't happen every day!"

"I don't want a reception in the PNA Hall."

"Everyone wants a reception in the PNA," Grandma said. "It's the best place in the Burg."

"I don't want a big reception. I want to have the reception in the backyard." Or not at all. I'm not even sure if I'm having a *wedding*!

"What if it rains? Where will we put all the people?"

"I don't want a lot of people."

"There's gotta be a hundred people in Joe's family alone," Grandma said.

Joe was standing behind me. "I'm having a panic attack," I said to him. "I can't breathe. My tongue is swelling. I'm going to choke."

"Choking might be the best thing," Joe said.

I looked at my watch. The viewing wasn't over for an hour and a half. My luck, I'd leave and Eddie would waltz in. "I need some air," I said. "I'm going outside for a couple minutes."

"There's people I haven't talked to yet," Grandma said. "I'll meet up with you later."

Joe followed me out and we stood on the porch, breathing in street air, happy to get away from the carnations, enjoying the car fumes. Lights were on and there was a steady stream of traffic on the street. The funeral home sounded festive behind us. No rock music, but plenty of talking and laughing. We sat on a step and watched the traffic in companionable silence. We were sitting there relaxing when the white Cadillac rolled by.

"Was that Eddie DeChooch?" I asked Joe.

"Looked like him to me," Joe said.

Neither of us moved. Not much we could

do about DeChooch driving by. Our cars were parked two blocks away.

"We should do something to apprehend him," I said to Joe.

"What do you have in mind?"

"Well, it's too late now, but you should have shot out a tire."

"I'll have to remember that for next time."

Five minutes later we were still sitting there, and DeChooch rolled by again.

"Jesus," Joe said. "What's with this guy?"

"Maybe he's looking for a parking place."

Morelli was on his feet. "I'm getting my truck. You go inside and tell Tom Bell."

Morelli took off and I went to get Bell. I passed Myron Birnbaum on the stairs. Hold on. Myron Birnbaum was leaving. He was giving up his parking place and DeChooch was looking for a parking place. And knowing Myron Birnbaum, I was betting he'd parked close by. All I had to do was keep Birnbaum's space open until DeChooch came along. DeChooch would park and I'd have him trapped. Goddamn, I was *so clever.*

I followed Birnbaum, and just as I'd expected he was parked at the corner, three cars down from Stiva's, nicely sandwiched between a Toyota and a Ford SUV. I waited for him to pull out, and then I jumped into the empty space and started waving people away. Eddie DeChooch could barely see past the front bumper of his car, so I didn't have to worry about him spotting me from a distance. My plan was to save the space for him and then hide behind the SUV when the Cadillac came into view.

I heard heels clacking on the sidewalk and turned to see Valerie clippity-clopping over to me.

"What's going on?" Valerie said. "Are you holding a parking place for someone? Do you want me to help?"

An old lady in a ten-year-old Oldsmobile stopped short of the parking space and put her right turn signal on.

"Sorry," I said, motioning for her to move on. "This spot is taken."

The old lady responded by gesturing for me to get out of the way.

I shook my head no. "Try the parking lot."

Valerie was standing to my side, waving her arms, pointing to the lot, looking like one of those guys who direct planes onto the runway. She was dressed almost exactly like me with the exception of a slightly different color scheme. Valerie's shoes were lavender.

The old lady beeped her horn at me and started creeping forward into the space. Valerie jumped back but I put my hands on my hips and glared at the woman and refused to budge.

There was another old lady in the passenger seat. She rolled her window down and stuck her head out. "This is *our* parking place."

"This is a police operation," I said. "You're going to have to park someplace else."

"Are you a police officer?"

"I'm bail enforcement."

"That's right," Valerie said. "This is my sister and she's a bail bonds enforcement person."

"Bail bonds is different from police," the woman said.

"The police are on their way," I told her.

"I think you're a big fibber. I think you're saving this spot for your boyfriend. Nobody in police work would dress like you."

The Oldsmobile was about a third into the parking space with the rear of the car blocking off half of Hamilton. From the corner of my eye I caught a flash of white and before I had a chance to react, DeChooch smashed into the Oldsmobile. The Oldsmobile bounced forward and smashed into the back of the SUV, missing me by half an inch. The Cadillac careened off the left rear quarter panel of the Oldsmobile, and I could see DeChooch struggling to get control. He turned and looked directly at me, for a moment we all seemed suspended in time, and then he took off.

Damn!

The two old ladies wrenched open the doors to the Oldsmobile and struggled out.

"Look at my car!" the driver said. "It's a wreck!" She whirled around at me. "It's all your fault. You did this. I hate you." And she hit me in the shoulder with her purse.

"Yow," I said, "that hurts."

She was a couple inches shorter than me but had me by a few pounds. Her hair was cut short and was newly permed. She looked to be in her sixties. She was wearing bright red lipstick, had crayoned dark brown eyebrows onto herself, and her cheeks were decorated with spots of rose-toned rouge. Definitely not from the Burg. Probably Hamilton Township.

"I should have run you over when I had the chance," she said.

She hit me with the purse again, and this time I grabbed it by the strap and yanked it out of her hand.

Behind me I could hear Valerie give a little yelp of surprise.

"My purse," the woman shrieked. "Thief! Help. She took my purse!"

A crowd had started to form around us. Motorists and mourners. The old lady grabbed one of the men on the fringe. "She's stealing my purse. She caused the accident and now she's stealing my purse. Get the police."

Grandma jumped out of the crowd. "What's going on? I just got here. What's the ruckus about?"

"She stole my purse," the woman said.

"Did not," I said back.

"Did so."

"Did not!"

"Yes you did," the woman said, and she shoved me back with a hand to my shoulder.

"Keep your hands off my granddaughter," Grandma said.

"Yes. And she's *my* sister," Valerie chimed in.

"Mind your own business," the woman yelled at Grandma and Valerie.

The woman shoved Grandma and Grandma shoved back and next thing they were slapping at each other and Valerie was standing to the side, shrieking.

I stepped forward to stop them and in the confusion of flailing arms and shrill threats someone smacked me in the nose. Little twinkle lights spread across my field of vision and I went down on one knee. Grandma and the old lady stopped slapping at each other and offered me tissues and advice on how to stop the blood that was dripping from my nose.

"Someone get a paramedic," Valerie shouted. "Call nine-one-one. Get a doctor. Get the undertaker."

Morelli arrived and hauled me to my feet. "I think we can cross boxing off the list of possible alternative professions."

"The old lady started it."

"From the way your nose looks I'd say she also finished it."

"Lucky punch."

"DeChooch passed me going about seventy in the opposite direction," Morelli said. "I couldn't turn in time to go after him."

"That is the story of my life."

* * *

WHEN MY NOSE stopped bleeding Morelli loaded Grandma and Valerie and me into my CR-V and followed us to my parents' house. He waved good-bye at that point, not wanting to be around when my mother saw us. I had bloodstains on Valerie's skirt and knit shirt. The skirt had a small tear in it. My knee was skinned and bleeding. And I had the beginning of a black eye. Grandma was in about the same condition but without the black eye and torn skirt. And something had happened to Grandma's hair so that it was standing straight up, making her look like Don King.

Because news travels at the speed of light in the Burg, by the time we got home, my mother had already taken six phone calls on the subject and knew every detail of our brawl. She clamped her mouth shut tight when we walked in and ran to get ice for my eye.

"It wasn't so bad," Valerie said to my mother. "The police got it all straightened out. And the EMT people said they didn't think Stephanie's nose was broken. And they don't do much for a broken nose, anyway, do they, Stephanie? Maybe put a

Band-Aid on it." She took the ice pack from my mother and put it on her own head. "Do we have any liquor in the house?"

Mooner ambled over from the television. "Dude," he said. "What's up?"

"Had a little dispute over a parking place."

He nodded his head. "It's all about standing in line, isn't it?" And he went back to the television.

"You're not leaving him here, are you?" my mother asked. "He's not living with me, too, is he?"

"Do you think that would work?" I asked hopefully.

"No!"

"Then I guess I'm not leaving him."

Angie looked around from the television. "Is it true you got hit by an old lady?"

"It was an accident," I told her.

"When a person gets hit in the head the blow makes their brain swell. It kills brain cells and they don't regenerate."

"Isn't it late for you to be watching television?"

"I don't have to go to bed because I don't have to go to school tomorrow," Angie said. "We haven't registered in this new school system. And besides, we're used to staying up late. My father frequently had business dinners, and we were allowed to stay up until he got home."

"Only now he's gone," Mary Alice said. "He left us so he could sleep with the baby-sitter. I saw them kissing once and Daddy had a fork in his pants and it was sticking straight out."

"Forks do that sometimes," Grandma said.

I collected my clothes and Mooner and headed for home. If I was in better shape I would have driven over to The Snake Pit, but that was going to have to wait for another day.

"So tell me again why everyone is looking for this Eddie DeChooch guy," Mooner said.

"I'm looking for him because he failed to appear for a court date. And the police are looking for him because they think he might be involved in a murder."

"And he thinks I've got something that's his."

"Yeah." I watched Mooner as I drove, wondering if something was shaking loose in his head, wondering if a piece of important information would float to the surface.

"So what do you think?" Mooner said. "Do

you think Samantha can do all that magic stuff if she doesn't twitch her nose?"

"No," I said. "I think she has to twitch her nose."

Mooner gave this serious consideration. "That's what I think, too."

IT WAS MONDAY morning, and I felt like I'd been run over by a truck. A scab had formed on my knee and my nose ached. I dragged myself out of bed and limped into the bathroom. Eek! I had two black eyes. One was considerably blacker than the other. I got into the shower and stood there for what might have been a couple hours. When I staggered out my nose felt better, but my eyes looked worse.

Mental note. Two hours in a hot shower not good in early stages of black eye.

I blasted my hair with the dryer and pulled it back into a ponytail. I dressed in my usual uniform of jeans and stretchy T-shirt and went out to the kitchen in search of breakfast. Ever since Valerie showed up, my mother had been too distracted to send me home with the traditional food bag, so there was no pineapple upside-down cake in my refrigerator. I poured a glass of orange juice and dropped a slice of bread in the toaster. It was quiet in my apartment. Peaceful. Nice. Too nice. Too peaceful. I stepped out of the kitchen and looked around. Everything seemed to be in order. Except for the rumpled quilt and pillow on the couch.

Oh shit! There was no Mooner. Damn, damn, damn.

I ran to the door. It was closed and locked. The security chain was hanging loose, not securing the door. I opened the door and looked out. No one in the hall. I looked out the living room window, down at the parking lot. No Mooner. No suspicious characters or cars. I called Mooner's house. No answer. I scribbled a note to Mooner that I'd be back and he should wait for me. He could wait in the hall or he could break into my apartment. Hell, everybody breaks into my apartment. I taped the note to my front door and took off.

First stop was Mooner's house. Two roommates. No Mooner. Second stop, Dougie's house. No luck there. I cruised by the social club, Eddie's house, and Ziggy's house. I went back to my apartment. No sign of Mooner.

I called Morelli. "He's gone," I said. "He was gone when I got up this morning."

"Is that bad?"

"Yes, it's bad."

"I'll keep my eyes open."

"There haven't been any, uh . . ."

"Bodies washed up on the shore? Bodies found in Dumpsters? Dismembered limbs stuffed into the overnight drop at the video store? No. It's been slow. None of those."

I hung up and called Ranger. "Help," I said.

"Heard you got trashed by some old lady last night," Ranger said. "We've got to get you some self-defense lessons, babe. Not good for the image to get trashed by an old lady."

"I have bigger problems than that. I was baby-sitting Mooner and he disappeared."

"Maybe he just split."

"Maybe he didn't."

"He driving a car?"

"His car's still in my lot."

Ranger let the silence lie there for a beat. "I'll ask around and get back to you."

I called my mother. "You haven't seen Mooner, have you?" I asked.

"What?" she yelled. "What did you say?"

I could hear Angie and Mary Alice running around in the background. They were screaming at each other and it sounded like they were banging on pots.

"What's going on?" I shouted into the phone.

"Your sister's gone off on a job interview, and the girls are having a parade."

"It sounds more like they're having World War Three. Has Mooner been around this morning?"

"No. I haven't seen him since last night. He's a little strange, isn't he? Are you sure he's not on drugs?"

I LEFT THE note to Mooner taped to my front door, and I drove down to the office. Connie and Lula were sitting at Connie's desk, watching the door to Vinnie's private lair.

Connie made a gesture for me to be quiet. "Joyce is in there with Vinnie," she whispered. "They've been at it for ten minutes now."

"You should have been here in the beginning when Vinnie was making sounds like a cow. Think Joyce must have been milking him," Lula said.

Some low-key grunting and moaning was going on beyond the closed door. The grunting stopped and Lula and Connie leaned forward expectantly.

"This is my favorite part," Lula said. "This is where they get to the spanking and Joyce barks like a dog."

I leaned forward with them, listening for the spanking, wanting Joyce to bark like a dog, feeling embarrassed but not able to walk away.

I was firmly pulled back by my ponytail. Ranger had come in behind me and had me by the hair. "Glad to see you're hard at work looking for Mooner."

"Shhh. I want to hear Joyce bark like a dog."

Ranger had me flat against him, and I could feel the heat from his body seeping into mine. "Not sure that's worth waiting for, babe."

There was some slapping and some squealing and then there was silence.

"Well, that was fun," Lula said, "but there's gonna be a price for the entertainment. Joyce only goes in there when she wants something. And there's only one high-bond case pending right now."

I looked at Connie. "Eddie DeChooch?

Vinnie wouldn't give Eddie over to Joyce, would he?"

"Usually he only sinks that low when there are horses involved," Connie said.

"Yeah, equine sex is the dollar ticket," Lula said.

The door opened and Joyce flounced out. "I'll need the paperwork on DeChooch," she said.

I lunged at her, but Ranger still had hold of my hair, so I didn't get very far. "Vinnie," I yelled, "get out here!"

The door to Vinnie's inner office crashed closed and there was the sound of the lock clicking into place.

Lula and Connie glared at Joyce.

"It's going to take a while to get the paperwork together," Connie said. "Maybe days."

"No problem," Joyce said. "I'll be back." She glanced over at me. "Nice eye. Very attractive."

I was going to have to do another Bob on her lawn. Maybe I could sneak into her house somehow and do a Bob on her bed.

Ranger released my ponytail but kept a hand on my neck. I tried to act calm, but his touch was humming through me all the way to my toes and points in between.

"None of my contacts have seen anyone meeting Mooner's description," Ranger said. "I thought we might discuss the subject with Dave Vincent."

Lula and Connie looked my way. "What's happened to Mooner?"

"Disappeared," I said. "Just like Dougie."

EIGHT

RANGER WAS DRIVING a black Mercedes that looked fresh off the showroom floor. Ranger's cars were always black and always new and always of questionable ownership. He had a pager and a cell phone clipped to his visor and a police scanner under the dash. And I knew from past experience that there'd be a sawed-off shotgun and an assault weapon hidden somewhere in the car and a semi-automatic clipped to his belt. Ranger is one of the few civilians in Trenton with a permit to carry concealed. He owns office buildings in Boston, has a daughter in Florida by a failed marriage, has worked worldwide as a mercenary, and has a moral code that isn't entirely in sync with our legal system. I have no idea who the heck he is . . . but I like him.

The Snake Pit wasn't open for business, but there were cars parked in the small lot adjacent to the building and the front door was ajar. Ranger parked next to a black BMW, and we went inside. A cleaning crew worked at polishing the bar and washing the floor. Three muscle-bound guys stood to one side, drinking coffee and talking. I assumed they were wrestlers going over the game plan. And I could see why Grandma left bingo early to come to The Snake Pit. The possibility that one or more of the coffee drinkers could have his underwear ripped off in the mud held some appeal. Truth is, I think naked men are kind of strange looking what with their doodles and ding-dong hanging loose like they do. Nevertheless, there's the curiosity thing. I guess it's another one of those car crash experiences, where you feel compelled to look even if you know you'll be horrified.

Two men were sitting at a table reviewing what looked like a spreadsheet. They were in their fifties with health club bodies, dressed in slacks and lightweight sweaters. They looked up when we entered. One of them acknowledged Ranger.

"Dave Vincent and his accountant," Ranger said to me. "Vincent is the one in the tan sweater. The one who nodded hello."

Perfect for the house in Princeton.

Vincent stood and came over to us. He smiled when he saw my eye up close. "You must be Stephanie Plum."

"I could have taken her out," I said. "She caught me by surprise. It was an accident."

"We're looking for Eddie DeChooch," Ranger said to Vincent.

"Everyone is looking for DeChooch," Vincent said. "The guy's nutty."

"We thought he might be keeping in touch with his business partners."

Dave Vincent shrugged. "I haven't seen him."

"He's driving Mary Maggie's car."

Vincent showed some annoyance. "I don't get involved with my employees' private lives. If Mary Maggie wants to loan Chooch a car that's *her* business."

"If she's hiding him it becomes *my* business," Ranger said.

And we turned and left.

"So," I said when we got to the car. "That seemed to go well."

Ranger grinned at me. "We'll see."

"Now what?"

"Benny and Ziggy. They'll be at the club."

"OH JEEZ," BENNY said when he came to the door. "Now what?"

Ziggy was a step behind him. "We didn't do it."

"Do what?" I asked.

"Anything," Ziggy said. "We didn't do anything."

Ranger and I exchanged glances.

"Where is he?" I asked Ziggy.

"Where's who?"

"Mooner."

"Is this a trick question?"

"No," I said. "It's a real question. Mooner is missing."

"Are you sure?"

Ranger and I gave them the silent staredown.

"Crap," Ziggy finally said.

WE LEFT BENNY and Ziggy with as much information as we had when we arrived.

Which meant we had nothing. Not to mention that I felt as if I'd just participated in an Abbott and Costello routine.

"So that seemed to go almost as well as the interview with Vincent," I said to Ranger.

This got me another smile. "Get in the car. We're visiting Mary Maggie next."

I gave him a salute and got into the car. I wasn't sure we were accomplishing anything but it was a nice day to be riding around with Ranger. Riding with Ranger absolved me of responsibility. I was clearly the underling. And I was protected. No one would dare shoot at me when I was with Ranger. Or if they did shoot at me, I was pretty certain I wouldn't die.

We drove in silence to Mary Maggie's condo building, parked one row over from her Porsche, and took the elevator to the seventh floor.

Mary Maggie answered on the second knock. Her breath caught when she saw us and she took a step backward. Ordinarily this reaction might be construed as a sign of fear or guilt. In this case it was the normal reaction women have when confronted with Ranger. To Mary Maggie's credit it wasn't followed by flushing and stammering. Her attention traveled from Ranger to me. "You again," she said.

I gave her a finger wave.

"What happened to your eye?"

"Parking dispute."

"Looks like you lost."

"Looks can be deceiving," I said. Not necessarily in this case . . . but sometimes.

"DeChooch was riding around town last night," Ranger said. "We thought you might have seen him."

"Nope."

"He was driving your car, and he was involved in an accident. Hit-and-run."

It was clear from the expression on Mary Maggie's face that this was the first she'd heard of the accident.

"It's his eyes. He shouldn't be driving at night," she said.

No shit. Not to mention his mind, which should be keeping him off the road all together. The man was a lunatic.

"Was anyone hurt?" Mary Maggie asked.

Ranger shook his head.

"You'll call us if you see him, right?" I said.

"Sure," Mary Maggie said.

"She's not going to call us," I said to Ranger when we were in the elevator.

Ranger just looked at me.

"What?" I asked.

"Patience."

The elevator doors opened to the under-ground garage and I jumped out. "Patience? Mooner and Dougie are missing, and I've got Joyce Barnhardt breathing down my neck. We ride around and talk to people, but we don't learn anything and nothing hap-pens and no one even seems to be worried."

"We're leaving messages. Applying pres-sure. You apply pressure in the right spot and things start to break down."

"Hmm," I said, still not feeling like we'd ac-complished a lot.

Ranger unlocked his car with the remote. "Don't like the sound of that *hmm*."

"The pressure stuff sounds a little . . . ob-scure."

We were alone in the dimly lit garage. Just Ranger and me and two levels of cars and concrete. It was the perfect setting for a gangland murder or an attack by a deranged rapist.

"Obscure," Ranger repeated.

He grabbed me by my jacket lapels, pulled me to him, and kissed me. His tongue touched mine and I got a rush that was just a millimeter below climax. His hands slid inside my jacket and circled my waist. He was hard against me. And suddenly nothing mattered but a Ranger-induced orgasm. I wanted one. Now. The hell with Eddie DeChooch. One of these days he'd drive himself into a bridge abutment and that'd be the end of that.

"Yes, but what about the wedding?" a small voice murmured from deep in my brain.

Shut up, I told the voice. *I'll worry about it later.*

"And what about your legs?" the voice asked. *"Did you shave your legs this morning?"*

Cripes, I was barely able to breathe with needing this goddamn orgasm and now I was supposed to worry about the hair on my legs! Where's the justice in this world? Why me? Why am *I* the one worrying about the hair on my legs? Why is it always the woman worrying about the freaking hair?

"Earth to Steph," Ranger said.

"If we do it now does it count as a credit toward capturing DeChooch?"

"We aren't doing it now."

"Why not?"

"We're in a parking garage. And by the time I get you out of the garage you'll have changed your mind."

I narrowed my eyes at him. "So what's the point here?"

"The point is that you can break down a person's defense system if you apply the right pressure."

"Are you telling me this was just a demonstration? You got me into this . . . this *state* to prove a point?"

His hands were still at my waist, holding me against him. "How serious is this *state*?" he asked.

If it was any more serious I'd spontaneously combust. "It's not that serious," I told him.

"Liar."

"How serious is *your state*?"

"Frighteningly serious."

"You're complicating my life."

He opened the car door for me. "Get in. Ronald DeChooch is next on the list."

The front room to the paving company offices was empty when Ranger and I walked in. A young guy poked his head around a corner and asked what we wanted. We said we wanted to talk to Ronald. Thirty seconds later Ronald strolled in from somewhere in the back of the building.

"I heard an old lady popped you in the eye, but I didn't realize she did such a good job," Ronald said to me. "That's a first-class shiner."

"Have you seen your uncle lately?" Ranger asked Ronald.

"No, but I heard he was involved in the accident outside the funeral parlor. He shouldn't be driving at night."

"The car he was driving belongs to Mary Maggie Mason," I said. "Do you know her?"

"I've seen her around." He looked at Ranger. "Are you working this case, too?"

Ranger gave a barely perceptible nod.

"Good to know," Ronald said.

"What was that?" I asked Ranger when we got outside. "Was that what I think it was? Was that hemorrhoid saying it made a difference with you on board? Like, now he was going to take the search seriously?"

"Let's take a look at Dougie's house," Ranger said.

Dougie's house hadn't changed since the last time I was there. No evidence of a new search. No evidence that Dougie or Mooner had passed through. Ranger and I went room by room. I filled Ranger in on the previous searches and the missing pot roast.

"Do you think it's significant that they took a pot roast?" I asked Ranger.

"One of life's mysteries," Ranger said.

We walked around back and snooped in Dougie's garage.

The little yappy dog that lives next door to Dougie left his post on the Belskis' back porch and skipped around us, yipping and snapping at our pants legs.

"Think anyone would notice if I shot him?" Ranger asked.

"I think Mrs. Belski would come after you with a meat cleaver."

"Have you talked to Mrs. Belski about the people searching the house?"

I smacked myself in the forehead with the heel of my hand. Why hadn't I thought to talk to Mrs. Belski? "No."

The Belskis have lived in their row house forever. They're in their sixties now. Hard-working, sturdy Polish stock. Mr. Belski is retired from Stucky Tool and Die Company. Mrs. Belski raised seven children. And now they have Dougie for a neighbor. Lesser people would have been at war with Dougie, but the Belskis have accepted their fate as God's will and coexist.

The Belskis' back door opened, and Mrs. Belski stuck her head out. "Is Spotty bothering you?"

"Nope," I said. "Spotty is fine."

"He gets excited when he sees strangers," Mrs. Belski said, coming across the yard to get Spotty.

"I understand there've been some strangers going through Dougie's house."

"There are always strangers in Dougie's house. Were you there when he held his *Star Trek* party?" She shook her head. "Such goings-on."

"How about lately? In the last couple days."

Mrs. Belski scooped Spotty up in her arms and held him close. "Nothing like the *Star Trek* party."

I explained to Mrs. Belski that someone had broken into Dougie's house.

"No!" she said. "How terrible." She gave a worried glance at Dougie's back door. "Dougie and his friend Walter get a little wild sometimes, but they're really nice young people at heart. They're always nice to Spotty."

"Have you seen anyone suspicious hanging around the house?"

"There were two women," Mrs. Belski said. "One was my age. Maybe a little older. In her sixties. The other was a couple years younger. I was coming back from walking Spotty and these women parked their car and let themselves into Dougie's house. They had a key. I assumed they were relatives. Do you suppose they were thieves?"

"Do you remember the car?"

"Not really. All cars look alike to me."

"Was it a white Cadillac? Was it a sports car?"

"No. It wasn't either of those. I would have remembered a white Cadillac or a fancy sports car."

"Anyone else?"

"An older man has been stopping by. Thin. In his seventies. Now that I think about it, he might have been driving a white Cadillac. Dougie gets lots of visitors. I don't always pay attention. I haven't noticed anyone looking suspicious, except for the women who had a key. I remember them because the older one looked at me and there was something about her eyes. Her eyes were scary. Angry and crazy."

I thanked Mrs. Belski and gave her my card.

When I was alone in the car with Ranger I got to thinking about the face Mooner saw in the window the night he got shot. It had seemed so improbable we hadn't given it a lot of attention. He hadn't been able to identify the face or even give it much detail . . . with the exception of the scary eyes. And now here was Mrs. Belski telling me about a sixty-something woman with scary eyes. There was also the woman who'd called Mooner and accused him of having something that belonged to her. Maybe this was the woman with the key. And how did she get a key? From Dougie, maybe.

"Now what?" I said to Ranger.

"Now we wait."

"I've never been very good at waiting. I have another idea. How about if we use me as bait? How about if I call Mary Maggie and tell her I have the *thing* and I'm willing to trade it for Mooner. And then I ask her to pass it on to Eddie DeChooch."

"You think Mary Maggie's the contact?"

"It's a shot in the dark."

*   *   *

MORELLI CALLED A half hour after Ranger dropped me off. "You're what?" Morelli yelled.

"Bait."

"Jesus."

"It's a good idea," I said. "We're going to let people think I have whatever it is that they're after. . . ."

"We?"

"Ranger and me."

"Ranger."

I had a mental picture of Morelli clenching his teeth.

"I don't want you working with Ranger."

"It's my job. We're bounty hunters."

"I don't want you doing that job, either."

"Well, guess what? I'm not crazy about you being a cop."

"At least my job is legitimate," Morelli said.

"My job is just as legitimate as yours."

"Not when you work with Ranger," Morelli said. "He's a nut case. And I don't like the way he looks at you."

"How does he look at me?"

"The same way I do."

I could feel myself hyperventilating. Breathe slow, I told myself. Don't panic.

I got rid of Morelli, made myself a peanut

butter and olive sandwich, and called my sister.

"I'm worried about this marriage thing," I said. "If *you* couldn't stay married, what are *my* chances?"

"Men don't think right," Valerie said. "I did everything I was supposed to do and it was wrong. How can that be?"

"Do you still love him?"

"I don't think so. Mostly I'd like to punch him in the face."

"Okay," I said. "I have to go now." And I hung up.

Next, I paged through the phone book, but there was no Mary Maggie Mason listed. No surprise there. I called Connie and asked her to get me the number. Connie had sources for unlisted phones.

"While you're on the line, I've got a quickie for you," Connie said. "Melvin Baylor. He didn't show up for court this morning."

Melvin Baylor lives two blocks from my parents. He's a perfectly nice forty-year-old guy who got taken to the cleaners in a divorce settlement that stripped him of everything but his underwear. To add insult to injury, two weeks after the settlement his ex-wife Lois announced her engagement to their unemployed next-door neighbor.

Last week the ex and the neighbor got married. The neighbor is still unemployed but now driving a new BMW and watching his game shows on a big-screen TV. Melvin, meanwhile, lives in a one-room apartment over Virgil Selig's garage and drives a ten-year-old brown Nova. On the night of his ex's wedding Melvin gulped down his usual dinner of cold cereal and skim milk and in profound depression drove his sputtering Nova to Casey's Bar. Not being any kind of a drinker, Melvin got properly snockered after two martinis. He then got into his wreck of a car, and for the first time in his life showed some backbone by crashing his ex-wife's wedding reception and relieving himself on the cake in front of two hundred people. He was roundly applauded by every man in the room.

Lois's mother, having paid eighty-five dollars for the three-tiered extravaganza, had Melvin arrested for indecent exposure, lewd conduct, trespass on a private party, and destruction of private property.

"I'll be right there," I said. "Have the paperwork ready for me. And I'll get Mason's number when I come in."

I grabbed my bag and yelled to Rex that I wouldn't be gone long. I ran down the hall, down the stairs, and slammed into Joyce in the lobby.

"I heard from people that you've been going all over this morning asking about DeChooch," Joyce said. "DeChooch is mine now. So back off."

"Sure."

"And I want the file."

"I lost it."

"Bitch," Joyce said.

"Snot."

"Fat ass."

"Douche bag."

Joyce whirled around and stormed out of the building. Next time my mother had chicken I was going to wish on the wishbone that Joyce got herpes.

The office was quiet when I got there. Vinnie's door was closed. Lula was asleep on the couch. Connie had Mary Maggie's phone number and Melvin's permission-to-capture paper ready.

"There's no answer at his house," Connie said. "And he called in sick from work. He's probably at home hiding under the bed, hoping it's all a bad dream."

I tucked the permission-to-capture into my bag and used Connie's phone to call Mary Maggie.

"I've decided I want to make a deal with Eddie," I said to Mason when she answered. "Trouble is, I don't know how to get in touch with him. I thought since he's using your car he might call you or something . . . let you know the car's okay."

"What's the deal?"

"I have something Eddie's looking for and I want to trade Mooner for it."

"Mooner?"

"Eddie will understand."

"Okay," Mason said. "If he calls in I'll pass it on, but there's no guarantee I'll be talking to him."

"Sure," I said. "Just in case."

Lula opened one eye. "Uh-oh, are you telling fibs again?"

"I'm bait," I said.

"No kidding."

"What is this thing Chooch is looking for?" Connie wanted to know.

"I don't know," I said. "That's part of the problem."

* * *

Usually people move out of the Burg when they get divorced. Melvin was one of the exceptions. I think at the time of his divorce he was simply too exhausted and downtrodden to conduct any kind of a search for a place to stay.

I parked in front of Selig's house and walked around back to the garage. It was a ramshackle two-car garage with a second-story, one-man, one-room ramshackle apartment. I climbed the stairs to the apartment and knocked. I listened at the door. Nothing. I banged on the door some more, put my ear to the scarred wood, and listened again. Someone was moving around in there.

"Hey Melvin," I yelled. "Open up."

"Go away," Melvin said through the door. "I'm not feeling well. Go away."

"It's Stephanie Plum," I said. "I need to talk to you."

The door opened and Melvin looked out. His hair was uncombed and his eyes were bloodshot.

"You were supposed to appear in court this morning," I said.

"I couldn't go. I feel sick."

"You should have called Vinnie."

"Oops. I didn't think of that."

I sniffed at his breath. "Have you been drinking?"

He rocked back on his heels and a loopy grin spread across his face. "Nope."

"You smell like cough medicine."

"Cherry schnapps. Someone gave it to me for Christmas."

Oh boy. I couldn't take him in like this. "Melvin, we have to sober you up."

"I'm okay. Except I can't feel my feet." He looked down. "I could feel them a minute ago."

I steered him out of the apartment, locked the door behind us, and went down the rickety stairs in front of him to prevent him from breaking his neck. I poured him into my CR-V and buckled him in. He hung there suspended by the shoulder harness, mouth open, eyes glazed. I drove him to my parents' house and half dragged him inside.

"Company, how nice," Grandma Mazur said, helping me haul Melvin into the kitchen.

My mother was ironing and tunelessly singing.

"I've never heard her sing like that," I said to Grandma.

"She's been doing it all day," Grandma said. "I'm starting to get worried. And she's been ironing that same shirt for an hour."

I sat Melvin at the table and gave him some black coffee and made him a ham sandwich.

"Mom?" I said. "Are you okay?"

"Yes, of course. I'm just ironing, dear."

Melvin rolled his eyes in Grandma's direction. "Do you know what I did? I urrrrrinated on the cake at my ex-wife's wedding. Pissssssed all over the icing. In front of everyone."

"It could have been worse," Grandma said. "You could have pooped on the dance floor."

"Do you know what happens when you pissss on icing? It gets rrrruined. Makes it all drippy."

"How about the little bride and groom at the top of the cake," Grandma said. "Did you piss on them, too?"

Melvin shook his head. "I couldn't reach them. I only got the bottom tier." He put his head down on the table. "I can't believe I embarrassed myself like that."

"Maybe if you practice you could get the top tier next time," Grandma said.

"I'm never going to another wedding," Melvin said. "I wish I was dead. Maybe I should just kill myself."

Valerie came into the kitchen carrying a laundry basket. "What's up?"

"I pissed on the cake," Melvin said. "I was shit-faced." And then he passed out face-down in his sandwich.

"I can't take him in like this," I said.

"He can sleep it off on the couch," my mother said, putting the iron down. "Everybody take a body part and we'll drag him in there."

ZIGGY AND BENNY were in the parking lot when I got home.

"We heard you want to make a deal," Ziggy said.

"Yep. Do you have Mooner?"

"Not exactly."

"Then it's no deal."

"We went all through your apartment and it wasn't there," Ziggy said.

"That's because it's someplace else," I told him.

"Where?"

"I'm not telling until I see Mooner."

"We could hurt you real bad," Ziggy said. "We could make you talk."

"My future grandmother-in-law wouldn't like that."

"You know what I think?" Ziggy said. "I think you're fibbing about having it."

I shrugged and turned to go into the building. "When you find Mooner, let me know and we'll deal."

Ever since I've had this job people have been breaking into my apartment. I buy the best locks available and it doesn't matter. Everyone gets in. The scary part is that I'm starting to get used to it.

Not only did Ziggy and Benny leave everything as they found it . . . they improved on it. They did my dishes and wiped down my counter. The kitchen was nice and tidy.

The phone rang and it was Eddie De-Chooch.

"I understand you've got it."

"Yes."

"Is it in good shape?"

"Yes."

"I'm sending someone over to get it."

"Hold on. Wait a minute. What about

Mooner? The deal is that I'm willing to trade Mooner for it."

DeChooch made a derisive sound. "Mooner. I don't know why you even care about that loser. Mooner isn't part of the deal. I'll give you money."

"I don't want money."

"Everyone wants money. Okay, how about this? How about I kidnap you and torture you until you hand it over?"

"My future grandmother-in-law would put the eye on you."

"The old bat is a crackpot. I don't believe in that bunk."

DeChooch hung up.

I was getting a lot of fast action on the bait scheme, but I wasn't making any progress getting Mooner back. A big sad lump was sitting in the middle of my throat. I was scared. No one seemed to have Mooner to trade. I didn't want Mooner or Dougie to be dead. Even worse, I didn't want to be like Valerie, sitting at the table blubbering with her mouth open.

"Damn!" I yelled. *"Damn, damn, damn!"*

Rex backed out of his soup can and looked up at me, whiskers whirring. I broke off a corner of a strawberry Pop-Tart and handed it to Rex. He shoved the Pop-Tart into his cheek and returned to his can. A hamster of simple pleasures.

I called Morelli and asked him over for dinner. "Except you have to bring the dinner," I said.

"Fried chicken? Meatball sub? Chinese?" Morelli asked.

"Chinese."

I rushed into the bathroom, took a shower, shaved my legs so the stupid voice in my head wouldn't screw things up again, and washed my hair with the shampoo that smells like root beer. I rummaged through my lingerie drawer until I found my black lace thong underpants and matching bra. I covered the undies with my usual T-shirt and jeans and swiped on some mascara and lip gloss. If I was going to get kidnapped and tortured I was going to have some fun first.

Bob and Morelli bounded in just as I was pulling on socks.

"I've got egg rolls, vegetable stuff, shrimp stuff, pork stuff, rice stuff, and some stuff that I think was supposed to go to somebody else but found its way into my bag," Morelli said. "And I got beer."

We put everything on the coffee table and turned the television on. Morelli flipped Bob an egg roll. Bob caught it midair and ate it in one gulp.

"We've talked about it, and Bob has agreed to be my best man," Morelli said.

"So there's going to be a wedding?"

"I thought you bought a dress."

I scooped out some shrimp stuff. "It's on hold."

"What's the problem?"

"I don't want a big wedding. It feels dopey. But my grandmother and my mother keep dragging me into one. All of a sudden I've got this dress on. And then next thing we've got a hall reserved. It's like someone sucked my mind out of my head."

"Maybe we should just go get married."

"When?"

"Can't be tonight. The Rangers are playing. Tomorrow? Wednesday?"

"Are you serious?"

"Yeah. Are you going to eat that last egg roll?"

My heart stopped dead in my chest. When it started back up again it was skipping beats. Married. *Shit!* I was excited, right? That's why I felt like I might throw up. It was the excitement. "Don't we need blood tests and licenses and stuff?"

Morelli turned his attention to my T-shirt. "Pretty."

"The shirt?"

He traced a line with his fingertip along the lace edge of my bra. "That, too." His hands slid under the cotton fabric and the shirt was suddenly over my head and discarded. "Maybe you should show me your stuff," he said. "Convince me you're worth marrying."

I raised a single eyebrow. "Maybe you're the one who should be doing the convincing."

Morelli slid the zipper on my jeans. "Cupcake, before the night's over you're going to be begging me to marry you."

I knew from past experience that this was true. Morelli knew how to make a girl wake up smiling. Tomorrow morning walking might be difficult, but smiling would be easy.

NINE

MORELLI'S PAGER WENT off at 5:30 A.M. Morelli looked at the readout and sighed. "In-
former."

I squinted into the darkness as he moved
around the room. "Do you have to go?"

"No. I just have to make a phone call."

He walked into the living room. There was
a moment of silence. And then he reap-
peared in the bedroom doorway. "Did you
get up in the middle of the night and put the
food away?"

"No."

"There's no food on the coffee table."

Bob.

I dragged myself out of bed, shoved my arms into my robe, and shuffled out to see the carnage.

"I found a couple little wire handles," Morelli said. "Looks like Bob ate the food *and* the cartons."

Bob was pacing at the door. His stomach was distended, and he was drooling.

Perfect. "You make your phone call and I'll walk Bob," I told Morelli.

I ran back to the bedroom, pulled on jeans and a sweatshirt, and rammed my feet into boots. I clipped the leash onto Bob and grabbed my car keys.

"Car keys?" Morelli asked.

"In case I need a doughnut."

Doughnut my foot. Bob was going to do a great big Chinese-food poop. And he was going to do it on Joyce's lawn. Maybe I could even get him to hurl.

We took the elevator because I didn't want Bob moving around any more than was necessary. We rushed to the car and roared out of the lot.

Bob had his nose pressed to the window. He was panting and belching. His stomach was swollen to bursting.

I had the gas pedal almost to the floor.

"Hold on, big fella," I said. "We're almost there. Not long now."

I screeched to a stop in front of Joyce's house. I ran around to the passenger side, opened the door, and Bob flew out. He rocketed to Joyce's lawn, hunched over, and pooped what appeared to be twice his body weight. He paused for a second and horked up a mixture of cardboard box and shrimp chow mein.

"Good boy!" I whispered.

Bob gave himself a shake and bolted back to the car. I slammed the door after him, jumped in on my side, and we took off before the stench could catch up with us. Another job well done.

Morelli was at the coffeemaker when I came in. "No doughnuts?" he asked.

"I forgot."

"I've never known you to forget doughnuts."

"I had other things on my mind."

"Like marriage?"

"That, too."

Morelli poured out two mugs of coffee and handed one to me. "Ever notice how marriage seems a lot more urgent at night than it does in the morning?"

"Does that mean you no longer want to get married?"

Morelli leaned against the counter and sipped his coffee. "You're not getting off the hook that easy."

"There are lots of things we've never talked about."

"Such as?"

"Children. Suppose we have children and it turns out we don't like them?"

"If we can like Bob, we can like anything," Morelli said.

Bob was in the living room licking lint off the carpet.

EDDIE DECHOOCH CALLED ten minutes after Morelli and Bob left for work.

"What's it gonna be?" he asked. "Do you want to make a deal?"

"I want Mooner."

"How many times do I have to tell you, I haven't got him. And I don't know where he is. Nobody I know has him, either. Maybe he got scared and ran away."

I didn't know what to say because it was a possibility.

"You're keeping it cold, right?" DeChooch

said. "I need to get it in good shape. My ass is on the line for this."

"Yep. It's cold, all right. You're not going to believe what good shape it's in. Just find Mooner and you can see for yourself." And I hung up.

What the heck was he talking about?

I called Connie, but she wasn't in the office yet. I left a message for her to get back to me and I took a shower. While I was in the shower I summarized my life. I was after a depressed senior citizen who was making me look like a dunce. Two of my friends were missing without a trace. I looked like I'd just gone a round with George Foreman. I had a wedding gown I didn't want to wear and a hall I didn't want to use. Morelli wanted to marry me. And Ranger wanted to . . . Hell, I didn't want to think about what Ranger wanted to do to me. Oh yeah, and there was Melvin Baylor, who, for all I knew, was still on my parents' couch.

I got out of the shower, got dressed, put in minimum effort on my hair, and Connie called.

"Have you heard any more from Aunt Flo or Uncle Bingo?" I asked Connie. "I need to know what went wrong in Richmond. I need to know what everyone's looking for. It's something that needs to be kept cold. Pharmaceuticals, maybe."

"How do you know it needs to be kept cold?"

"DeChooch."

"You talked to DeChooch?"

"He calls me." Sometimes I can't believe my own life. I have an FTA who calls me. How weird is that?

"I'll see what I can find out," Connie said.

I called Grandma next.

"I need some information about Eddie DeChooch," I said. "I thought you might ask around."

"What do you want to know?"

"He had a problem in Richmond, and now he's looking for something. I want to know what he's looking for."

"Leave it to me!"

"Is Melvin Baylor still there?"

"Nope. He went home."

I said good-bye to Grandma, and there was a knock on my door. I opened the door a crack and looked out. It was Valerie. She was dressed in a tailored black suit jacket and slacks with a white starched shirt and a man's black-and-red striped tie. The Meg

Ryan shag was plastered back behind her ears.

"New look," I said. "What's the occasion?"

"It's my first day as a lesbian."

"Yeah, right."

"I'm serious. I said to myself, why wait? I'm making a fresh start here. I decided I should just jump right in. I'm going to get a job. And I'm going to get a girlfriend. No reason to sit home sulking over a failed relationship."

"I didn't think you were serious the other night. Have you had any . . . um, experience as a lesbian?"

"No, but how hard can it be?"

"I don't know if I like this," I said. "I'm used to being the black sheep of the family. This could change my standing."

"Don't be silly," Valerie said. "No one will care that I'm a lesbian."

Valerie was in California *way* too long.

"Anyhoo," she said, "I've got a job interview. Do I look okay? I want to be honest about my new sexual orientation, but I don't want to be overly butch."

"You don't want the dykes-on-bikes look."

"Exactly. I want the lesbian-chic look."

Having had limited lesbian experience I

wasn't sure what lesbian chic looked like. Mostly I knew television lesbians.

"I'm not certain about the shoes," she said. "Shoes are always so difficult."

She was wearing delicate black patent sandals with a little heel. Her toes were painted bright red.

"I guess it depends if you want men's shoes or women's shoes," I said. "Are you a girl lesbian or a boy lesbian?"

"There are two kinds of lesbians?"

"I don't know. Didn't you research this?"

"No. I just assumed lesbians were uni-sex."

If she was having trouble being a lesbian with her clothes *on*, I couldn't imagine what was going to happen when she took the clothes *off*.

"I'm applying for a job at the mall," Valerie said. "And then I have a second job interview downtown. I was wondering if I could swap cars with you. I want to make a good appearance."

"What car are you driving now?"

"Uncle Sandor's '53 Buick."

"Muscle car," I said. "Very lesbian. Much better than my CR-V."

"I never thought of that."

I felt a little guilty because the truth is I didn't know if a '53 Buick would be favored by lesbians. It was just that I really didn't want to swap. I hate the '53 Buick.

I waved good-bye and wished her luck as she sashayed down the hall. Rex was out of his can and looking at me. Either he was thinking I was very clever, or else he was thinking I was a rotten sister. Hard to tell with hamsters. That's why they make such good pets.

I slung my black leather bag over my shoulder, grabbed my denim jacket, and locked up. Time to check back on Melvin Baylor. I felt a twinge of nervousness. Eddie DeChooch was worrisome. I didn't like the way he felt comfortable shooting at people on a moment's notice. And now that I was among the threatened I liked it even less.

I crept down the stairs and scurried through the lobby. I looked beyond the glass doors, into the lot. No DeChooch anywhere.

Mr. Morganstern stepped out of the elevator.

"Hello, cutie," Mr. Morganstern said. "Whoa. Looks like you ran into a doorknob."

"All part of the job," I said to Mr. Morganstern.

Mr. Morganstern was very old. Possibly two hundred.

"I saw your young friend leaving yesterday. He might be a little funny in the head, but he travels in style. You've got to like a man who travels in style," Mr. Morganstern said.

"What young friend?"

"The Mooner person. The one who wears the Superman suit and has long brown hair."

My heart skipped a beat. It never occurred to me that any of my neighbors would have information about Mooner. "When did you see him? What time?"

"It was early in the morning. The bakery down the street opens at six and I walked there and back, so I guess I saw your friend around seven o'clock. He came out of the door just as I was going in. He was with a lady and they both got into a big black limousine. I never rode in a limousine. It must be something."

"Did he say anything to you?"

"He said . . . *dude.*"

"Did he look okay? Did he look worried?"

"Nope. He looked same as always. You know, like nobody's home."

"What did the woman look like?"

"Nice-looking woman. Short, sort of brown hair. Young."

"How young?"

"About sixty, maybe."

"I don't suppose the limo had anything written on it? Like the name of the limo company?"

"Not that I recall. It was just a big black limo."

I turned on my heel, went back upstairs, and started calling limo companies. It took me a half hour to go through all the listings in the phone book. Only two companies made pickups that early yesterday morning. Both pickups were Town Cars and they were both making airport runs. Neither was booked by or picked up a woman.

Dead end again.

I drove over to Melvin's apartment and knocked on his door.

Melvin answered with a bag of frozen corn on his head. "I'm dying," he said. "My head's exploding. My eyes are on fire."

He looked awful. Worse than yesterday and that was going some. "I'll be back later," I told him. "Don't do any more drinking, okay?"

Five minutes later I was at the office.

"Hey," Lula said. "Look at this. Your eyes are sort of black and green today. That's a good sign."

"Has Joyce been in yet?"

"She came in about fifteen minutes ago," Connie said. "She was nuts, raving about shrimp chow mein."

"She was gonzo," Lula said. "Made no sense at all. Never seen her so mad. I don't suppose you know anything about the shrimp?"

"Nope. Not me."

"How's Bob? He know anything about the chow mein?"

"Bob's fine. He had a stomach problem earlier this morning, but he's okay now."

Connie and Lula did a high five.

"I knew it!" Lula said.

"I'm driving around checking out a few houses," I said. "I was wondering if anyone wanted to go with me."

"Uh-oh," Lula said. "The only time you want company is when you're worried someone's out to get you."

"Eddie DeChooch might sort of be looking for me." Probably other people were after me, too, but Eddie DeChooch seemed the craziest and most likely to shoot me. Although the old lady with the scary eyes was starting to run a close second.

"I guess we can handle Eddie DeChooch," Lula said, getting her handbag out of the bottom file drawer. "He's just a little bitty depressed old man."

With a gun.

Lula and I dropped in on Mooner's roommates first.

"Is Mooner here?" I asked.

"Nope. Haven't seen him. He might be at Dougie's. He's there a lot."

We went to Dougie's house next. I had taken Dougie's keys when Mooner got shot and I'd never given them back. I opened the front door and Lula and I did a walk-through. Nothing seemed out of the ordinary. I went back to the kitchen and looked in the freezer and refrigerator.

"What's that about?" Lula asked.

"Just checking."

After Dougie's house we drove to Eddie DeChooch's house. The crime-scene tape was gone, and the DeChooch half looked dark and unlived in.

I parked the car and Lula and I did a walk-through in DeChooch's house. Again, nothing out of the ordinary. Just for the hell of it

I looked in the freezer and refrigerator. There was a pot roast in the freezer.

"I could see that pot roast turns you on," Lula said.

"Dougie had a pot roast stolen from his freezer."

"Uh-huh."

"This could be it. This could be the stolen pot roast."

"Let me get this straight. You think Eddie DeChooch broke into Dougie's house and stole a pot roast."

Now that I heard it said out loud it sounded kind of dumb. "It could happen," I said.

We drove by the social club and the church, cruised through Mary Maggie's parking garage, cut over to Ace Pavers, and ended with Ronald DeChooch's house in north Trenton. In the course of our travels we covered most of Trenton and all of the Burg.

"That's it for me," Lula said. "I need fried chicken. I want some of that Cluck in a Bucket extra spicy, extra greasy. And I want biscuits and cole slaw and one of them shakes that are so thick you gotta suck your guts out to get it up a straw."

Cluck in a Bucket is just a couple blocks from the office. It has a big revolving chicken impaled on a pole that sprouts out of the macadam parking lot, and it has excellent fast-food fried chicken.

Lula and I got a bucket and took it to a table.

"So let me get this straight," Lula said. "Eddie DeChooch goes to Richmond and picks up some cigarettes. While DeChooch is in Richmond, Louie D buys the farm and something gets screwed up. We don't know what."

I selected a piece of chicken and nodded.

"Choochy comes back to Trenton with the cigarettes, drops some off with Dougie, and then gets himself arrested trying to take the rest of the cigarettes to New York."

I nodded some more.

"Next thing Loretta Ricci is dead and Chooch takes off on us."

"Yep. And then Dougie goes missing. Benny and Ziggy are looking for Chooch. Chooch is looking for *something*. Again, we don't know what. And somebody steals Dougie's pot roast."

"And now Mooner's missing, too," Lula said. "Chooch thought Mooner had the *something.* You told Chooch *you* had the *something.* And Chooch offered you money but no Mooner."

"Yeah."

"That's the dumbest load of shit I ever heard," Lula said, biting into a chicken thigh. She stopped talking and chewing and opened her eyes wide. "Urg," she said. Then she started waving her arms and clutching her throat.

"Are you okay?" I asked.

More throat clutching.

"Whack her on the back," someone offered from another table.

"That doesn't work," someone else said. "You're supposed to do that Heimlich thing."

I ran around to Lula and tried to wrap my arms around her to do the Heimlich, but my arms wouldn't go all the way around.

A big guy walked over from the counter, got Lula in a bear hug from behind, and squeezed.

"Ptoooh," Lula said. And a piece of chicken flew out of her mouth and hit a kid two tables over in the head.

"You've got to lose some weight," I said to Lula.

"It's just I've got big bones," Lula said.

Everything quieted down, and Lula sucked on her milk shake.

"I had an idea while I was dying," Lula said. "It's clear what you've got to do next. Tell Chooch you've decided to make the deal for money. Then we snatch him when he comes to pick up the *thing*. And after we got him we make him talk."

"We haven't had much luck snatching him so far."

"Yeah, but what have you got to lose here? He's gonna be picking up nothing."

True.

"You should call up Mary Maggie the mud wrestler and tell her we'll deal," Lula said.

I found my cell phone and dialed Mary Maggie, but there was no answer. I left my name and number and asked her to return my call.

I was putting my cell phone back in my shoulder bag when Joyce stormed in.

"I saw your car in the lot," Joyce said. "You expect to find DeChooch in here eating chicken?"

"He just left," Lula said. "We could have brought him in, but we thought it was too easy. We like a challenge."

"You two wouldn't know what to do with a

challenge," Joyce said. "You're losers. Fatso and Ditzo. You two are pathetic."

"Yeah, well we're not so pathetic we got a chow mein problem," Lula said.

That caught Joyce short for a moment, not sure if Lula was in on the dastardly deed or merely provoking her.

Joyce's pager chirped. Joyce checked the readout and her lips curled back in a smile. "I have to go. I have a lead on DeChooch. It's a shame you two bimbos don't have anything better to do than sit here filling your faces. But then from the looks of you I guess that's what you do best."

"Yeah, and from the looks of you I guess what you do best is fetch sticks and howl at the moon," Lula said.

"Fuck you," Joyce said and flounced off to her car.

"Hunh," Lula said. "I expected something more original than that. Think Joyce must be off her form today."

"Know what we should do?" I said. "We should follow her."

Lula was already gathering the food together. "You read my mind," Lula said.

The moment Joyce left the lot we were out the door and into the CR-V. Lula had the bucket of chicken and biscuits on her lap, we shoved the shakes into the drink holders, and took off.

"I bet she's a big liar," Lula said. "I bet there's no lead. She's probably going to the mall."

I stayed a couple cars back so she wouldn't make me, and Lula and I kept our eyes glued to the back bumper of Joyce's SUV. There were two heads visible through Joyce's rear window. She had someone riding shotgun with her.

"She's not going to the mall," I said. "She's going in the opposite direction. Looks like she's heading for center city."

Ten minutes later I had a bad feeling about Joyce's destination.

"I know where she's going," I said to Lula. "She's going to talk to Mary Maggie Mason. Someone told her about the white Cadillac."

I followed Joyce into the parking garage, keeping well behind. I parked two lanes over from her and Lula and I sat tight and watched.

"Uh-oh," Lula said, "there she goes. Her and her flunky. They're going up to talk to Mary Maggie."

Damn. I know Joyce too well. I've seen

her work. She would go in like gangbusters, guns drawn, and search room-to-room, claiming just cause. It's the sort of behavior that gives bounty hunting a bad reputation. And even worse, it sometimes gets results. If Eddie DeChooch is hiding under Mary Maggie's bed, Joyce will find him.

I didn't recognize her partner from this distance. They were both dressed in black T-shirts and black cargo pants with BOND ENFORCEMENT printed in bright yellow on the back of their shirts.

"Boy," Lula said, "they got costumes. How come we don't have costumes?"

"Because we don't want to look like a couple goons?"

"Yep. That's the answer I was thinking of."

I jumped out of the car and yelled at Joyce. "Hey Joyce!" I said. "Wait a minute. I want to talk to you."

Joyce whirled around in surprise. Her eyes narrowed when she saw me, and she said something to her partner. The conversation didn't carry to me. Joyce punched the up button. The elevator doors opened and Joyce and her partner disappeared.

Lula and I got to the elevator seconds after the doors closed. We pressed the button and waited a few minutes.

"Know what I think?" Lula said. "I don't think this elevator's going to show up. I think Joyce is holding on to it."

We started up the stairs, fast at first, and then slower.

"Something wrong with my legs," Lula said at the fifth floor. "I got rubber legs. They don't want to work anymore."

"Keep going."

"Easy for you to say. You're dragging that boney-ass body of yours up these stairs. Look what I'm hauling."

It wasn't easy for me to say at all. I was sweating and I could barely breathe. "We've got to get into shape," I said to Lula. "We should go to a gym or something."

"I'd sooner set myself on fire."

That about summed it up for me, too.

We staggered out of the stairwell into the hall at the seventh floor. Mary Maggie's door was open and Mary Maggie and Joyce were shouting at each other.

"If you don't get out of here this second I'm calling the police," Mary Maggie yelled.

"I *am* the police," Joyce yelled back.

"Oh yeah? Where's your badge?"

"It's here on this chain on my neck."

"That's a fake badge. You bought that badge from a catalogue. I'm telling on you. I'm calling the police and telling them you're impersonating a cop."

"I'm not impersonating anybody," Joyce said. "I never said I was the *Trenton* police. I happen to be the *bond* police."

"You happen to be the *dodo* police," Lula said, wheezing.

Now that I was closer I recognized Joyce's partner. It was Janice Molnari. I went to school with Janice. Janice was an okay person. I couldn't help wondering what she was doing working for Joyce.

"Stephanie," Janice said. "Long time no see."

"Not since Loretta Beeber's shower."

"How's it going?" Janice asked.

"Pretty good. How's it with you?"

"Pretty good. My kids are all in school now, so I thought I'd try working part-time."

"How long have you been with Joyce?"

"About two hours," Janice said. "This is my first job."

Joyce had a sidearm strapped to her thigh, and she had her hand on the sidearm. "So what are you doing here, Plum? Following me around so you can see how it's done?"

"That's it," Mary Maggie said. "I want all of you out! *Now!*"

Joyce shoved Lula toward the door. "You heard her. Move it."

"Hey," Lula said, giving Joyce a shot in the shoulder. "Who you telling to move it?"

"I'm telling you to move it, you big tub of lard," Joyce said.

"Better to be a tub of lard than chow mein barf and dog doody," Lula said.

Joyce gave a gasp. "How do you know? I didn't tell you all that." Her eyes opened wide. "It's you! You're the one!" Besides the gun, Joyce was wearing a utility belt complete with cuffs, defense spray, stun gun, and baton. She pulled the stun gun out of the belt and flipped it on. "I'm going to make you pay," Joyce said. "I'm going to fry you. I'm going to stick this to you until my battery is dead and you're nothing but a pool of liquefied fat slime."

Lula looked down at her hands. No purse in either of them. We left our purses in the car. She felt her pockets. No weapons there, either. "Uh-oh," Lula said.

Joyce lunged at her and Lula shrieked

and whipped around and ran down the hall to the stairs. Joyce took off after her. And we all ran after Lula and Joyce. Me first, then Mary Maggie, then Janice. Lula might not be much going *up* the stairs, but once she got momentum going down she was un-catchable. Lula was a freight train in motion.

Lula got to the garage level and crashed through the door. She was halfway to the car when Joyce caught her and straight-armed her with the stun gun. Lula stopped short, swayed in place for a second, and went down like a sack of wet cement. Joyce reached out to give Lula another buzz, and I tackled Joyce from behind. The stun gun flew out of her hand, and we fell to the floor. And just then, Eddie DeChooch pulled into the underground garage in Mary Maggie's white Cadillac.

Janice saw him first. "Hey, is that the old guy in the white Cadillac?" she asked.

Joyce and I picked up our heads and looked. DeChooch was inching along, look-ing for a parking space.

"Get out!" Mary Maggie yelled to De-Chooch. "Get out of the garage!"

Joyce scrambled to her feet and took off

running toward DeChooch. "Get him!" Joyce
yelled to Janice. "Don't let him get away."

"Get him?" Janice asked, standing beside
Lula. "What is she, crazy? How am I supposed to get him?"

"I don't want anything to happen to my
car," Mary Maggie shouted to Joyce and
me. "That was my Uncle Ted's car."

Lula was on all fours and drooling.
"What?" she said. "Who?"

Janice and I got Lula to her feet. Mary
Maggie was still yelling to DeChooch and
DeChooch was still not seeing her.

I left Lula with Janice and ran for my
Honda. I cranked the engine over and
wheeled around behind DeChooch. I don't
know how I expected to catch him, but it
seemed like the thing to do.

Joyce jumped out in front of DeChooch,
gun drawn, and shouted for him to stop.
DeChooch stomped on the gas and plowed
ahead. Joyce stumbled to safety and fired
off a shot, missing DeChooch but hitting a
back window.

DeChooch left-turned down a lane of
parked cars. I followed after him, taking corners on two wheels as he raced in blind

panic. We were doing a loop, DeChooch not able to find the exit.

Mary Maggie was still yelling. And Lula was on her feet waving her arms.

"Wait for me!" Lula yelled, looking like she wanted to run, not sure of the direction.

I did a lap past Lula, and she jumped into the car. The back door was wrenched open, and Janice catapulted herself into the backseat.

Joyce had gone back for her car and had positioned it partially across the exit. She had the driver door open and stood behind the open door with her gun steadied.

DeChooch finally found the right lane and headed for the exit. He drove straight at Joyce. She fired off a shot that missed entirely and then threw herself to the side as DeChooch roared past, ripping Joyce's car door off its hinges, the impact rocketing the door into the air.

I zipped out the exit, behind DeChooch. The Cadillac's right front quarter panel had suffered some damage, but clearly it wasn't anything that bothered Choochy. He turned onto Spring Street with me close on his bumper. He followed Spring to Broad and suddenly we were in stopped traffic.

"We got him," Lula yelled. "Everybody out of the car!"

Lula and Janice and I bolted from the car and ran to apprehend DeChooch. De-Chooch threw the Cadillac into reverse and rammed the CR-V, bouncing it back several feet into the car behind. He pulled the wheel around and angled himself out, grazing the bumper on the car in front of him.

Lula was yelling at him the whole time. "We got the *thing*," she yelled. "And we want the money. We decided we want the money!"

DeChooch didn't look like he was hearing anything. He did a **U**-turn and took off, leaving us in his dust.

Lula and Janice and I watched him hurtle down the street and then we turned our attention to the CR-V. It was crumpled up like an accordion.

"Now this really makes me mad," Lula said. "He made my shake get spilled, and I paid good money for that shake."

"Let me get this straight," Vinnie said. "You're telling me that DeChooch smashed up your car and broke Barnhardt's leg."

"Actually it was the car door that broke

Joyce's leg," I said. "When it flew off her car it kind of did a flip in the air and came down on her leg."

"We wouldn't have known about her except the ambulance had to squeeze past us on the way to the hospital. They were just getting ready to tow our car away when the ambulance came along, and there was Joyce all trussed up inside," Lula said.

"So where is DeChooch now?" Vinnie wanted to know.

"We don't exactly got the answer to that question," Lula said. "And being that we haven't got transportation we have no way of finding out."

"What about *your* car?" Vinnie asked Lula.

"In the shop. I'm having it detailed, and then they're putting some custom paint on it. I won't get it back until next week."

He turned to me. "What about the Buick? You always drive the Buick when you have car problems."

"My sister's driving the Buick."

TEN

"I GOT A motorcycle out back I can let you have," Vinnie said. "I just took it in on a bond. The guy was short money, so he gave me the bike. I already got my garage filled with crap. I can't fit a bike in there."

People cleaned out their houses to buy their bonds. Vinnie took in stereos, televisions, mink coats, computer systems, and gym equipment. He bonded out Madam Zaretsky once and took her whip and her trained dog.

Ordinarily I'd jump at the chance to have a bike. I got my license a couple years ago when I was dating a guy who owned a cycle shop. I've looked at bikes from time to time but never had the money to buy one. The problem now is that a bike isn't the ideal vehicle for a bounty hunter.

"I don't want a bike," I said. "What am I going to do with a bike? I can't bring an FTA in on a bike."

"Yeah, and what about me?" Lula said. "How're you gonna fit a full-figured woman like me on a bike? And what about my hair? I'll have to put one of them helmets on, and it'll ruin my hair."

"Take it or leave it," Vinnie said.

I did a big sigh and rolled my eyes. "This bike come with helmets?"

"They're in the back room."

Lula and I shuffled out to see the bike.

"This is gonna be an embarrassment," Lula said, opening the back door. "This is gonna be . . . hold on, look at this. Holy crap. This isn't just a dumb-ass bike. This is a *hog*."

It was a Harley-Davidson FXDL Dyna Low Rider. It was black with custom green flames and custom pipes. Lula was right. It wasn't just a dumb-ass bike. It was a wet dream.

"You know how to drive one of these?" Lula asked.

I smiled at her. "Oh yeah," I said. "*Oh yeah.*"

Lula and I strapped on the helmets and straddled the bike. I put the key in the ignition, kicked it over, and the Harley rumbled under me. "Houston, we have liftoff," I said. And then I had a small orgasm.

I rode up and down the alley behind Vinnie's office a couple times, getting the feel of the bike, and then I headed for Mary Maggie's condo building. I wanted to take another crack at talking to Mary Maggie.

"Don't look like she's here," Lula said, after the first turn around the parking garage. "I don't see her Porsche."

I wasn't surprised. She was probably off somewhere inspecting the damage on the Cadillac.

"She's wrestling tonight," I said to Lula. "We can talk to her then."

I CHECKED OUT the cars in the lot to my apartment building when I pulled in. No white Cadillac, no black limo, no Ziggy and Benny car, no MMM-YUM Porsche, no mega-bucks-

and-probably-stolen Ranger car. Only Joe's truck.

Joe was slouched in front of the television with a beer in his hand when I walked in.

"I heard you smashed up your car," he said.

"Yeah, but I'm okay."

"I heard that, too."

"DeChooch is whacko. He shoots at people. He deliberately runs people down. What's the deal with him? That's not normal behavior . . . even for an old mob guy. I mean, I know he's depressed, but *yeesh*." I went into the kitchen and gave Rex a piece of biscuit I'd saved from lunch.

Morelli followed me into the kitchen. "How'd you get home?"

"Vinnie loaned me a bike."

"A bike? What kind of bike?"

"A Harley. A Dyna Low Rider."

His eyes and his mouth creased in a smile. "You're riding around on a hog?"

"Yes. And I had a sexual experience on it already."

"All by yourself?"

"Yes."

Morelli gave a bark of laughter and moved toward me, pressing me against the counter, his hands circling my rib cage, his mouth brushing my ear, my neck. "Bet I can improve on it."

THE SUN HAD gone down and it was dark in my bedroom. Morelli was asleep beside me. Even in sleep Morelli radiated contained energy. His body was lean and hard. His mouth was soft and sensual. The planes of his face had become more angular with age. His eyes more wary. He'd seen a lot as a cop. Too much, maybe.

I glanced over at the clock. Eight. *Eight!* Yikes. I must have been asleep, too. One minute we were making love and the next thing it was eight o'clock!

I shook Morelli awake.

"It's eight o'clock!" I said.

"Uh-huh."

"Bob! Where's Bob?"

Morelli bolted out of bed. "Shit! I came here right from work. Bob hasn't had supper!"

The unspoken thought was that Bob would have eaten everything by now . . . the couch, the television, the baseboards.

"Get your clothes on," Morelli said. "We'll

feed Bob and go out for pizza. And then you can spend the night."

"I can't. I have to work tonight. Lula and I didn't get to talk to Mary Maggie today, so I'm going to The Snake Pit. She's wrestling at ten."

"I don't have time to argue," Morelli said. "Bob's probably eaten through a wall by now. Come over when you're done at the Pit." He grabbed me and kissed me and ran down the hall.

"Okay," I said, but Morelli was already gone.

I wasn't sure what one wore to the Pit, but slut hair seemed like a good idea, so I did the hot roller and teasing thing. This increased my height from five foot seven inches to five foot ten. I tarted myself up with a lot of makeup, added a short black spandex skirt and four-inch heels, and I felt very kick-ass. I grabbed my leather jacket and took the car keys from the kitchen counter. Hold on. These weren't car keys. These were motor-cycle keys. Shit! I'd never get my hair in the helmet.

Don't panic, I told myself. Just think about this a minute. Where can you get a car? Valerie. Valerie has the Buick. I'll call her up and tell her I'm going out to a place where there are half-naked women. I mean, that's what lesbians want to see, right?

Ten minutes later, Valerie picked me up in the lot. She still had her hair slicked back behind her ears and was devoid of makeup with the exception of blood-red lipstick. She was wearing men's black wing tips, a charcoal pinstripe suit with slacks, and a white shirt that was open at the neck. I resisted the urge to check to see if there was chest hair sprouting from the open neck.

"How'd it go today?" I asked her.

"I got new shoes! Look at them. Aren't they excellent? I think they're perfect lesbian shoes."

You have to give Valerie credit. She never did anything halfway. "I mean about the job."

"The job didn't work out. I guess that's to be expected. If at first you don't succeed . . ." She put her weight behind the wheel and managed to get the Buick to take a corner. "I got the girls enrolled in school, though. I guess that's something positive."

Lula was waiting on the curb when we got to her house.

"This is my sister, Valerie," I told Lula.

"She's coming along because she has the car."

"Looks like she shops in the men's department."

"She's taking it for a test drive."

"Hey, whatever," Lula said.

The parking lot to The Snake Pit was jammed, so we parked a half mile down on the street. By the time we got to the door my feet were killing me, and I was thinking there were advantages to being a lesbian. Valerie's shoes looked nice and comfy.

We got a table in the back and ordered drinks.

"How are we going to get to talk to Mary Maggie?" Lula wanted to know. "We can't hardly see from here."

"I checked this place out. There are only two doors, so after Mary Maggie does the mud thing we'll each take a door and catch her leaving."

"Sounds like a plan to me," Lula said, belting back her drink and ordering another.

There were a few women with dates, but mostly the room was filled with men, looking serious, hoping a G-string would get ripped off in the mud, which I assume is the equivalent to sacking the quarterback.

Valerie's eyes were wide. Hard to tell if they were reflecting excitement or hysteria.

"Are you sure I'll meet lesbians here?" she shouted above the noise.

Lula and I looked around. We didn't see any lesbians. At least not any who looked like Valerie.

"You never know when lesbians are gonna show up," Lula said. "Probably you should have another drink. You look kind of pale."

I sent the note to Mary Maggie on the next drink order. I told her my table and told her I had a message I wanted passed on to Eddie DeChooch.

A half hour later I still hadn't heard from Mary Maggie. Lula had put away four Cosmopolitans and was looking stone-cold sober, and Valerie had chugged two glasses of Chablis and was looking *very* happy.

Women were whaling away at each other in the pit. Once in a while a hapless drunken male would get pulled into the ooze and flail around until he swallowed a gallon of muck and was expelled by the bouncer. There was a lot of hair pulling and bitch slapping and sliding around. I guess mud is slippery. So far no one got their G-string removed, but there was a bunch of mud-slicked bare breasts that were bloated to the bursting point with implants. All in all, the whole thing didn't look too appealing, and I was happy I had a job where people shot at me. Better than wallowing in the mud half naked.

Mary Maggie's match was announced, and Mary Maggie came out dressed in a silver bikini. I was beginning to see a theme here. Silver Porsche, silver bikini. There was a lot of cheering. Mary Maggie is famous. Then the other woman came out. Her name was Animal, and just between you and me I didn't think it looked good for Mary Maggie. Animal's eyes were glowing red and it was hard to tell from the distance, but I'm pretty sure she had snakes in her hair.

The announcer rang the bell and the two women circled and then lunged. They did this with little success for a while and then Mary Maggie slipped and Animal pounced on her.

This brought the entire room to standing, including Lula and Valerie and me. We were all yelling, wanting Mary Maggie to disembowel Animal. Of course Mary Maggie had too much class to disembowel Animal, so they thrashed in the mud for a few minutes and then started taunting the audience, wanting their own unfortunate drunken male.

"You," Mary Maggie said, pointing in my direction.

I looked around, hoping to find a sex-crazed guy waving a twenty standing just behind me.

Mary Maggie took the microphone. "We have a special guest here tonight. We have The Bounty Hunter. Also known as The Cadillac Wrecker. Also known as The Harasser."

Oh boy.

"You want to talk to me, Bounty Hunter?" Mary Maggie asked. "Step right up."

"Maybe later," I said, thinking Mary Maggie's stage personality wasn't at all like the bookworm I'd met earlier. "We'll talk after the show," I told her. "Don't want to take up your valuable time while you're onstage."

And then suddenly I was being lifted into the air by two very large men. I was being carried, still seated in my chair, six feet off the floor, to the ring.

"Help!" I yelped. *"Help!"*

I was held high above the ring. Mary Maggie smiled. And Animal growled and rotated her head. And then the chair tipped and I did a free fall into the mud.

Animal pulled me to my feet by my hair. "Relax," she said. "This will be painless."

Then she tore my shirt off. Good thing I was wearing my good lace bra from Victoria's Secret.

In the next instant, we all went down in a screaming pack. Mary Maggie Mason, Animal, and me. And then Lula waded in.

"Hey," Lula said. "We just come here to talk and you're ruining my friend's skirt. We're gonna give you a dry-cleaning bill."

"Oh yeah? Well, bill this," Animal said and she yanked Lula's foot out from under her, sending Lula to her ass in the mud.

"Now you made me mad," Lula said. "I was trying to explain things to you, but now you made me mad."

I'd managed to pull myself to my feet while Lula was sparring with Animal. I was wiping the mud from my eyes when Mary Maggie Mason took a flying leap at me and pinned me facedown in the mud again. "Help," I yelled. *"Help!"*

"Stop picking on my friend," Lula said. And she grabbed Mary Maggie by the hair and flung her out of the ring like a rag doll. *Crash!* Direct hit on a table at ringside.

Two more women wrestlers ran out from the wings and jumped in the ring. Lula tossed one out and sat on the other. Animal jumped off the ropes at Lula, Lula let out a bloodcurdling shriek and went down in the mud with Animal.

Mary Maggie was back in the ring. The other wrestler was back in the ring. And some drunken guy climbed in. Now there were seven of us in the ring, rolling around, locked together. I was grabbing for anything I could find, trying to keep from smothering in the mud, and somehow I got a grip on Animal's G-string. And then everyone was hooting and cheering and the bouncers jumped into the ring and separated us.

"Hey," Lula said, still swinging, "I lost my shoe. Somebody better find my shoe or I'm never coming here again."

The stage manager had Lula by the arm. "Don't worry. We'll take care of it. Step this way. Right through the door."

And before we realized what was happening, we were out on the street. Lula with only one shoe and me with no shirt. The door opened again, and Valerie got tossed out along with our coats and purses.

"There was something wrong with that Animal person," Valerie said. "When you ripped her pants off she was *bald* down there!"

VALERIE DROPPED ME off at Morelli's house and waved good-bye.

Morelli opened the door and said the obvious. "You're covered with mud."

"It didn't work out exactly as planned."

"I like the no-shirt look. I could get used to it."

I stripped in the hall and Morelli took my clothes directly to the washer. I was still standing there when he returned. I was wearing the four-inch heels and mud and nothing more.

"I'd like to take a shower," I told him, "but if you'd rather I didn't track mud up the stairs you can just throw a bucket of water at me in the backyard."

"I know this is probably sick," Morelli said, "but I'm getting hard."

MORELLI LIVES IN a row house on Slater just a short distance from the Burg. He'd inherited the house from his Aunt Rose and he'd made it a home. Go figure that. The world is filled with mysteries. His house felt a lot like my parents' house, narrow and spare in luxuries, but filled with comforting smells and memories. In Morelli's case the smells were reheated pizza, dog, and fresh paint. Morelli was little by little working on window trim.

We were at his kitchen table . . . me, Morelli, and Bob. Morelli was eating a slice of raisin-cinnamon toast and drinking coffee. And Bob and I ate everything else in the refrigerator. Nothing like a big breakfast after a night of mud wrestling.

I was wearing one of Morelli's T-shirts, a borrowed pair of sweats, and I was barefoot since my shoes were still wet inside and out and would probably get tossed in the trash.

Morelli was dressed for work in his plain-clothes cop clothes.

"I don't get it," I said to Morelli. "This guy is riding around in a white Cadillac and the police aren't picking him up. Why is that?"

"Probably he's not riding around a lot. He's been spotted a couple times, but not by anyone who's been in a position to go after him. Once by Mickey Greene on bicycle patrol. Once by a blue-and-white stuck in traffic. And he's not a priority. It isn't like there's someone assigned full-time to finding him."

"He's a murderer. That's not a priority?"

"He's not exactly wanted for murder. Loretta Ricci died of a heart attack. At this point he's only wanted for questioning."

"I think he stole a pot roast from Dougie's freezer."

"Well, that ups the ante. That'll put him on the priority list for sure."

"Don't you think it's weird that he'd steal a pot roast?"

"When you've been a cop for as long as I have you don't think anything is weird."

Morelli finished his coffee, rinsed his cup, and put it in the dishwasher. "I have to go. Are you going to stay here?"

"No. I need a ride back to my apartment. I've got things to do and people to see." And I could use a pair of shoes.

Morelli dropped me at the door to my building. I walked in barefoot, wearing Morelli's clothes, carrying mine. Mr. Morganstern was in the lobby.

"Must have been some night," he said. "I'll give you ten dollars if you'll tell me the details."

"No way. You're too young."

"How about twenty? Only thing is you'll have to wait until the first of the month when I get my Social Security check."

Ten minutes later, I was dressed and out the door. I wanted to get to Melvin Baylor before he left for work. In honor of the Harley, I'd dressed in boots, jeans, T-shirt, and my Schotts leather jacket. I roared out of the parking lot and caught Melvin attempting to unlock his car. The lock had rusted and Melvin was having a hard time turning the key. Why he bothered locking it at all was beyond me. No one would want to steal this car. He was dressed in suit and tie and, with the exception of dark circles under his eyes, he looked much better.

"I hate to bother you," I said, "but you need to go to court and reschedule your date."

"What about work? I'm supposed to go to work."

Melvin Baylor was a very nice schnook. How he ever got the nerve to take a leak on the cake was a mystery.

"You'll have to go in late. I'll call Vinnie and have him meet us at the municipal building and hopefully it won't take long."

"I can't get my car open."

"Then you're in for a treat, because you get to ride on my bike."

"I hate this car," Melvin said. He stepped back and kicked the car in the door and a big piece of rusted metal fell off. He grabbed the side mirror and ripped it off and threw it onto the ground. "Fucking car," he said, kicking the mirror across the street.

"That's good," I said. "But maybe we should go now."

"I'm not done," Melvin said, trying his key on the trunk, having no luck there, either. *"Fuck!"* he yelled. He climbed up the bumper onto the trunk and jumped up and down. He climbed onto the roof and did more jumping.

"Melvin," I said, "you're a little out of control here."

"I hate my life. I hate my car. I hate this suit." He half fell, half jumped off the car and tried the trunk again. This time he got it open. He rummaged around in the trunk and came up with a baseball bat. "Ah-ha!" he said.

Oh boy.

Melvin hauled off and whacked the car with the bat. He whacked it again and again, working up a sweat. He whacked a side window, sending glass flying. He stepped back and looked at his hand. It had a big gash in it. Blood was everywhere.

Shit. I got off the bike and sat Melvin down on the curb. Every housewife on the block was standing on the street, watching the show. "I need a towel here," I said. Then I called Valerie and told her to bring the Buick to Melvin's house.

Valerie arrived a couple minutes later. Melvin had his hand wrapped in a towel, but his suit and shoes were spattered with blood. Valerie got out of the car, took one look at Melvin, and keeled over. Crash. Onto the Seligs' lawn. I left Valerie on the lawn and drove Melvin to the emergency room. I got him settled in and drove back to the Seligs'. I didn't have time to sit and wait for Melvin to get stitched up. Unless he went into shock from blood loss, he'd probably be there for hours before seeing a doctor.

Valerie was standing on the curb, looking confused.

"I didn't know what to do," she said. "I don't know how to drive a motorcycle."

"No problem. You can have the Buick back."

"What happened to Melvin?"

"Temper tantrum. He'll be fine."

A DROP-IN AT the office was next on my list. I thought I'd dressed for the day, but Lula made me look like an amateur. She was wearing boots from the Harley store, leather pants, leather vest, keys on a chain that clipped to her belt. And draped over her chair was a leather jacket with fringe running the length of the arm and a Harley emblem stitched across the back.

"Just in case we gotta go out on the bike," she said.

Fearsome leather-clad black biker chick causes havoc on highways. Traffic tied up for miles due to rubbernecking motorists.

"You'd better sit down so I can tell you about DeChooch," Connie said to me.

I looked to Lula. "Do you know about DeChooch?"

Lula's face broke into a smile. "Yeah, Connie told me when I came in this morning. And she's right, you better sit down."

"Only people in the family know about this," Connie said. "It's been kept real quiet so you have to keep it to yourself."

"What family are we talking about here?"

"*The* family."

"Gotcha."

"So here it is . . ."

Lula was already chuckling, unable to contain herself. "I'm sorry," she said. "It just cracks me up. Wait until you hear this, you'll fall off the chair."

"Eddie DeChooch set up a deal for contraband cigarettes," Connie said. "He figured it was a small operation and he could handle it himself. So he rented a truck and drove to Richmond to pick up the cartons of cigarettes. While he's there Louie D has a fatal heart attack. As you may know, Louie D is from Jersey. All his life he's lived in Jersey and then a couple years ago he relocated to Richmond to manage some business operations. So when Louie D goes toes-up DeChooch gets on the phone and immediately notifies the Jersey family.

"The first person DeChooch calls, of course, is Anthony Thumbs." Connie paused, leaned forward, and lowered her voice. "Do you know who I'm talking about when I say Anthony Thumbs?"

I nodded. Anthony Thumbs controls Trenton. Which I guess is a dubious honor, being that Trenton isn't exactly the center of the universe for mob activity. His real name is Anthony Thumbelli but everyone calls him Anthony Thumbs. Since Thumbelli isn't a common Italian name, I can only assume it was fabricated on Ellis Island and stuck, just as my Grandfather Plum's name was shortened from Plumerri by an overworked immigration clerk.

Connie went on. "Anthony Thumbs has never been especially fond of Louie D, but Louie D is related in some obscure way, and Anthony knows the family plot is in Trenton. So Anthony Thumbs does the right thing as head of the family and tells DeChooch to escort Louie D back to Jersey for burial. Only Anthony Thumbs, who's not known as being the world's most eloquent guy, says to Eddie DeChooch, who can't hear for anything, 'Bring the fart to me.' That's a direct quote. Anthony Thumbs says to Eddie DeChooch, '*Bring the fart to me.*'

"DeChooch knows there's no love lost between Louie D and Anthony Thumbs. And DeChooch thinks it's a vendetta thing and thinks Anthony Thumbs said, 'Bring the *heart* to me.'"

My mouth dropped open. "What?"

Connie was grinning and tears of laughter were streaming down Lula's cheeks.

"I love this part," Lula said. "I love this part."

"I swear to God," Connie said. "DeChooch thought Anthony Thumbs wanted Louie D's heart. So DeChooch breaks into the funeral home late at night and does a very nice job of slicing into Louie D and removing his heart. Had to crack a couple ribs to do it, apparently. The funeral director said . . ." Connie had to stop a minute to compose herself. "The funeral director said he'd never seen such a professional job."

Lula and Connie were laughing so hard they had to steady themselves with both hands on Connie's desk to keep from rolling on the floor.

I clapped a hand over my mouth, not knowing whether to join them laughing or go my own route and throw up.

Connie blew her nose and wiped the tears away with a clean tissue. "Okay, so De-Chooch puts the heart in an Igloo cooler with some ice and takes off for Trenton with the cigarettes and the heart. He brings the cooler to Anthony Thumbs, proud as any-thing, and tells him he's got Louie D's heart.

"Anthony goes nuts, of course, and tells DeChooch to take the fucking heart back to Richmond and have the undertaker return it to Louie D.

"Everyone's sworn to secrecy because this is not only embarrassing, it's danger-ously disrespectful between two family fac-tions that don't get along all that well during the best of times. And on top of that Louie D's wife, who is a very religious woman, is freaking because Louie's been desecrated. Sophia DeStephano has set herself up as the protector of Louie's immortal soul and is hell-bent to see Louie buried whole. And she's given DeChooch an ultimatum that ei-ther he gets Louie's heart back in Louie's body or DeChooch will be hamburger."

"Hamburger?"

"One of Louie's operations was a meat processing plant."

I gave an involuntary shiver.

"Now here's where it gets confusing. DeChooch somehow loses the heart."

It was so bizarre I wasn't sure if Connie was telling me the truth or if she and Lula had concocted the whole thing as a joke. "He lost the heart," I said. "How could he lose the heart?"

Connie did a palms-up. Like she couldn't totally believe it. "I got it all from my Aunt Flo, and that's as much as she knows."

"No wonder DeChooch is depressed."

"Fuckin' A," Lula said.

"Where does Loretta Ricci fit into this?"

Another palms-up from Connie. "Don't know."

"Mooner and Dougie?"

"Don't know that, either," Connie said.

"So DeChooch is looking for Louie D's heart."

Connie was still smiling. Connie really liked this. "Apparently."

I thought about it for a minute. "Somewhere along the way DeChooch decided Dougie had the heart. Then he decided Mooner had the heart."

"Yeah," Lula said, "and now he thinks *you* have the heart."

A bunch of black dots danced across my field of vision and bells started clanging in my head.

"Uh-oh," Lula said, "you don't look so good."

I put my head between my legs and tried to take a deep breath. "He thinks I have Louie D's heart!" I said. "He thinks I'm walking around with a heart. My God, what kind of a person walks around with a dead guy's heart?

"I thought we were talking about drugs. I thought I was trading some coke for Mooner. How am I ever going to pull off a swap for a heart?"

"Don't seem like anything you have to worry about," Lula said, "since DeChooch doesn't have Mooner or Dougie."

I told Connie and Lula about the limo and Mooner.

"Isn't that perfect," Lula said. "Some old lady kidnapped the Mooner. Maybe it was Louie D's wife trying to get Louie's heart back."

"You better hope it wasn't Louie D's wife," Connie said. "She makes Morelli's grandmother look sane. There's a story told about her that she thought a neighbor disrespected her, and the next day the woman was found dead with her tongue cut out."

"She made Louie kill the woman?"

"No," Connie said. "Louie wasn't home at the time. He was away on business."

"Omigod."

"Anyway, it's probably not Sophia because I hear she's been locked in her house ever since Louie died, lighting candles and praying and cursing DeChooch." Connie thought about it for a minute. "You know who else could have kidnapped Mooner? Louie D's sister, Estelle Colucci."

It wouldn't be difficult to kidnap Mooner, either. All you have to do is offer Mooner a joint and he'll happily follow you to the ends of the earth.

"Maybe we should go talk to Estelle Colucci," I said to Lula.

"I'm ready to roll," Lula said.

BENNY AND ESTELLE Colucci live in a nicely maintained duplex in the Burg. For that matter, just about every house in the Burg is nicely maintained. It's mandatory for survival. Decorating taste might vary, but windows damn well better be clean.

I parked the bike in front of the Colucci house, walked to the door, and knocked. No answer. Lula pushed into the bushes under the front windows and looked inside.

"Don't see anyone," Lula said. "No lights on. Television's not going."

We tried the club next. No Benny. I drove two blocks to Hamilton and recognized Benny's car at the corner of Hamilton and

Grand, parked in front of the Tip Top Sandwich Shop. Lula and I squinted in through
the plate-glass window. Benny and Ziggy
were inside having a late breakfast.

The Tip Top is a narrow hole-in-the-wall
café that serves homemade food for reasonable prices. The green-and-black linoleum
on the floor is cracked, the overhead light
fixtures are dim from grime, the Naugahyde
seats in the booths are patched with duct
tape. Mickey Spritz was an army cook during the Korean conflict. He opened the Tip
Top when he got out of the army thirty years
ago and he hasn't changed a thing since.
Not the flooring, the booth seats, the menu.
Mickey and his wife do all the cooking. And
a retarded man, Pookie Potter, buses the tables and washes the dishes.

Benny and Ziggy were concentrating on
eating their eggs when Lula and I approached.

"Jeez," Benny said, looking up from his
eggs, gaping at Lula in full leather. "Where
do you find these people?"

"We stopped by your house," I said to
Benny. "No one was home."

"Yeah. That's because I'm here."

"What about Estelle? Estelle wasn't home, either."

"We had a death in the family," Benny said. "Estelle is out of town for a couple days."

"I guess you're talking about Louie D," I said. "And the screw-up."

I had Benny and Ziggy's attention now.

"You know about the screw-up?" Benny asked.

"I know about the heart."

"Jesus H. Christ," Benny said. "I thought you were bluffing."

"Where's Mooner?"

"I'm telling you, I don't know where he is, but my wife is driving me fucking nuts over this heart thing. You gotta give me the heart. That's all I hear about . . . how I gotta get the heart. I'm only human, you know what I mean? I can't take it anymore."

"Benny isn't well himself," Ziggy said. "He has conditions, too. You should give him the heart so he can have some peace. It's the right thing to do."

"And just think about Louie D laying there without his heart," Benny said. "That's not nice. You should have your heart when they put you in the ground."

"When did Estelle leave for Richmond?"

"Monday."

"That's the day Mooner disappeared," I said.

Benny leaned forward. "What are you suggesting?"

"That Estelle snatched Mooner."

Benny and Ziggy looked at each other. They hadn't considered this possibility.

"Estelle doesn't do stuff like that," Benny said.

"How did she get to Richmond? Did she take a limo?"

"No. She drove. She was going to Richmond to visit Louie D's wife, Sophia, and then she was going to Norfolk. We got a daughter there."

"I don't suppose you have a picture of Estelle with you?"

Benny pulled his wallet out and showed me a picture of Estelle. She was a pleasant-looking woman with a round face and short gray hair.

"Well, I've got the heart, and now it's up to you to find out who has Mooner," I said to Benny.

And Lula and I left.

"Holy shit," Lula said when we were on the

bike. "You were so freaking cool in there. You actually had me thinking you knew what you were doing. Like, I was almost thinking you had the heart."

Lula and I went back to the office, and my cell phone buzzed just as I walked through the door.

"Is your grandmother with you?" my mother wanted to know. "She walked to the bakery early this morning to get some rolls and she hasn't come back."

"I haven't seen her."

"Your father went out to look for her but he couldn't find her. And I've called all her friends. She's been gone for hours."

"How many hours?"

"I don't know. A couple. It's just that it's not like her. She always comes right home from the bakery."

"Okay," I said, "I'll go look for Grandma. Give me a call if she turns up."

I disconnected and my phone immediately rang again.

It was Eddie DeChooch. "Do you still have the heart?" he wanted to know.

"Yes."

"Well, I've got something to trade."

I had a bad feeling in my stomach. "Mooner?"

"Guess again."

There was some scuffling and then Grandma came on the line.

"What's this business about a heart?" Grandma wanted to know.

"It's sort of complicated. Are you okay?"

"I've got a little arthritis in my knee today."

"No. I mean is Choochy treating you all right?"

I could hear Chooch in the background prompting Grandma. "Tell her you're kidnapped," he was saying. "Tell her I'm gonna blow your head off if she doesn't give me the heart."

"I'm not telling her that," Grandma said. "How would that sound? And don't get any funny ideas, either. Just because I'm kidnapped doesn't mean I'm easy. I'm not doing anything with you unless you take precautions. I'm not taking any chances getting one of them diseases."

DeChooch came back on the line. "Here's the deal. You take your cell phone and Louie D's heart to Quaker Bridge Mall and I'll call you at seven o'clock. Any cops come in on this and your granny's dead."

ELEVEN

"WHAT WAS THAT all about?" Lula wanted to know.

"DeChooch has Grandma Mazur. He wants to trade her for the heart. I'm supposed to take the heart to Quaker Bridge Mall, and he's going to call me at seven with further instructions. He said he'll kill her if I bring the police into it."

"Kidnappers always say that," Lula said. "It's in the kidnapper handbook."

"What are you going to do?" Connie wanted to know. "Do you have any idea who has the heart?"

"Hold up here," Lula said. "Louie D don't

have his name engraved on his heart. Why don't we just get another heart? How's Eddie DeChooch gonna know if it's Louie D's heart? I bet we could give Eddie De-Chooch a cow heart and he wouldn't know. We just go to a butcher and tell him we need a cow heart. We don't go to a butcher in the Burg because word might get around. We go to some other butcher. I know a couple over on Stark Street. Or we could try Price Chopper. They've got a real good meat department.

"I'm surprised DeChooch didn't come up with this. I mean, nobody has even seen Louie D's heart except for DeChooch. And DeChooch can't see for shit. DeChooch probably took that pot roast out of Dougie's freezer thinking it was the heart."

"Lula's come up with something here," Connie said. "It might work."

I picked my head up from between my legs. "It's creepy!"

"Yeah," Lula said. "That's the best part." She looked at the clock on the wall. "It's lunchtime. Let's go get a burger and then we'll get a heart."

I used Connie's phone to call my mother. "Don't worry about Grandma," I said. "I know where she is and I'm going to pick her up later tonight." Then I hung up before my mother could ask questions.

AFTER LUNCH LULA and I went to Price Chopper.

"We need a heart," Lula said to the butcher. "And it has to be in good condition."

"Sorry," he said, "we don't have any hearts. How about some other kind of organ meat. Like liver. We have some nice calf livers."

"Has to be a heart," Lula said. "You know where we can get a heart?"

"So far as I know, they all go to a dog food factory in Arkansas."

"We haven't got time to go to Arkansas," Lula said. "Thanks, anyway."

On the way out we stopped at a display of picnic necessities and bought a small red-and-white Igloo cooler.

"This'll be perfect," Lula said. "All we need now is the heart."

"Do you think we'll have better luck on Stark Street?"

"I know some butchers there that sell stuff you don't want to know about," Lula said. "If they don't got a heart they'll go get one, no questions asked."

There were parts to Stark Street that made Bosnia look good. Lula worked Stark Street when she was a ho. It was a long street of depressed businesses, depressed housing, and depressed people.

It took us close to a half hour to get there, rumbling through center city, enjoying the custom pipes and the attention a hog demands.

It was a sunny April day, but Stark Street looked dreary. Pages from a newspaper cartwheeled down the street and banked against curbs and the cement stoops of cheerless row houses. Gang slogans were spray-painted on brick fronts. An occasional building had been burned and gutted, the windows blackened and boarded. Small businesses squatted between the row houses. Andy's Bar & Grill, Stark Street Garage, Stan's Appliances, Omar's Meat Market.

"This is the place," Lula said. "Omar's Meat Market. If it's used for dog food then Omar's gonna be selling it for soup. We just want to make sure the heart isn't still beating when we get it."

"Is it safe to leave the bike parked here at the curb?"

"Hell no. Park it on the sidewalk next to the window so we can watch it."

There was a large black man behind the meat case. His hair was buzzed short and was shot with gray. His white butcher's apron was blood-smeared. He had a thick gold chain around his neck and he wore a single diamond stud. He smiled ear-to-ear when he saw us.

"Lula! Looking good. Never see you anymore since you stopped working the street. Like the leather."

"This here's Omar," Lula said to me. "He's about as rich as Bill Gates. He just runs this butcher shop because he likes sticking his hand up chicken butts."

Omar tipped his head back and laughed, and the sound was a lot like the Harley echoing off the Stark Street storefronts.

"What can I do for you?" Omar asked Lula.

"I need a heart."

Omar didn't blink an eye. Guess he got requests for hearts all the time. "Sure," he said, "what kind of a heart do you want?

What are you going to do with it? Make soup? Slice it and fry it?"

"I don't suppose you have any human hearts?"

"Not today. They're special order."

"What's the next closest thing, then?"

"Pig heart. Can't hardly tell the difference."

"Okay," Lula said, "I'll take one of those."

Omar went to the end case and pawed through a vat of organs. He picked one out and put it on the scale on a piece of waxed paper. "How's this?"

Lula and I looked around the scale at it.

"I don't know much about hearts," Lula said to Omar. "Maybe you could help us out here. We're looking for a heart that would fit a two-hundred-and-thirty-pound *pig* who just had a heart attack."

"How old is this pig?"

"Late sixties, maybe seventy."

"That's a pretty old pig," Omar said. He went back and picked out a second heart. "This one's been in the vat for a while. I don't know if the pig had a heart attack, but the heart don't look all that good." He poked it with his finger. "It's not that it's missing any parts, or anything, it just looks like it's been around the block, you know what I mean?"

"How much is it?" Lula asked.

"You're in luck. This one's on sale. I could let you have this one for half price."

Lula and I exchanged glances.

"Okay, we'll take it," I said.

Omar looked over the counter at the cooler in Lula's hand. "You want Porky wrapped up or do you want him packed in ice?"

ON THE WAY back to the office I pulled up for a light, and a guy on a Harley Fat Boy eased to a stop beside me.

"Nice bike," he said. "What have you got in the cooler?"

"A pig heart," Lula said.

And then the light changed and we both took off.

Five minutes later we were in the office, showing the heart to Connie.

"Boy, it looks like the real thing," Connie said.

Lula and I gave Connie some raised eyebrows.

"Not that I'd know," Connie said.

"This is gonna work good," Lula said. "All we have to do now is swap this for Granny."

Tendrils of fear curled in my stomach.

Nervous little flutterings that took my breath away. I didn't want anything bad to happen to Grandma.

Valerie and I used to fight all the time when we were kids. I always had some crazy idea and Valerie always snitched on me to my mother. Stephanie's up on the garage roof trying to fly, Valerie would scream to my mother, running into the kitchen. Or, Stephanie's in the backyard trying to tinkle standing up like a boy. After my mother yelled at me, when no one was looking, I'd give Valerie a really good smack on the head. *Whack!* And then we'd fight. And then my mother would yell at me again. And then I'd run away from home.

I always ran to Grandma Mazur's house. Grandma Mazur never passed judgment. Now I know why. Deep down inside Grandma Mazur was even crazier than I was.

Grandma Mazur would take me in without a word of admonishment. She'd haul her four kitchen chairs into the living room, arrange them in a square and drape a sheet over them. She'd give me a pillow and some books to read and send me into the tent she'd made. After a couple minutes a plate of cookies or a sandwich would get passed under the sheet.

At some point in the afternoon, before my grandfather came home from work, my mother would come fetch me and everything would be fine.

And now Grandma was with crazy Eddie DeChooch. And at seven I'd trade her for a pig heart. "Unh!" I said.

Lula and Connie glanced over at me.

"Thinking out loud," I told them. "Maybe I should call Joe or Ranger for backup."

"Joe's the police," Lula said. "And De-Chooch said no police."

"DeChooch wouldn't know Joe was there."

"Do you think he'll go along with the plan?"

That was the problem. I'd have to tell Joe I was trading Grandma for a pig heart. It was one thing to disclose something like that when it was all over and it had worked perfectly. At the moment it sounded a lot like the time I tried to fly off the garage.

"Maybe he'd come up with a better plan," I said.

"Only one thing DeChooch wants," Lula said. "And you've got it in that cooler."

"I have a *pig heart* in this cooler!"

"Well yeah, *technically* that's true," Lula said.

Probably Ranger was the better way to go. Ranger fit in with the nut cases of the world . . . like Lula and Grandma and me.

There was no answer on Ranger's cell phone, so I tried his pager and got a call back in less than a minute.

"There's a new problem with the De-Chooch thing," I said to Ranger. "He's got Grandma."

"A match made in heaven," Ranger said.

"This is serious! I let it be known that I had what DeChooch was after. Since he doesn't have Mooner he's kidnapped Grandma so he has something to trade. The swap is set for seven."

"What are you planning on giving De-Chooch?"

"A pig heart."

"That sounds fair," Ranger said.

"It's a long story."

"What can I do for you?"

"I could use backup in case something goes wrong." Then I told him the plan.

"Have Vinnie wire you," Ranger said. "I'll

stop by the office later this afternoon to get the receiver. Switch the wire on at six-thirty."

"Is the price the same?"

"This is a freebie."

AFTER I GOT wired, Lula and I decided to head for the mall. Lula needed shoes, and I needed to keep my mind off Grandma.

Quaker Bridge is a two-level mall just off Route 1, between Trenton and Princeton. It has all the typical mall stores plus a couple larger department stores anchoring each end with a Macy's in the middle. I parked the bike close to the Macy's door because Macy's was having a shoe sale.

"Look at this," Lula said to me in the Macy's shoe department. "We're the only people here with a picnic cooler."

Truth is, I had a death grip on the cooler, clutching it to my chest with both hands. Lula was still in full leather. I was in boots and jeans with my two black eyes and Igloo cooler. And people were crashing into display cases and mannequins, staring at us.

Bounty hunter rule number one . . . be inconspicuous.

My phone rang and I almost dropped the cooler.

It was Ranger. "What the hell are you doing? You're attracting so much attention you've got a security guard following you around. He probably thinks you've got a bomb in the cooler."

"I'm a little nervous."

"No shit."

And he disconnected.

"Listen," I said to Lula, "why don't we go have a piece of pizza and just chill until it's time."

"Sounds good to me," Lula said. "I don't see any shoes I like anyway."

At six-thirty I drained the ice melt out of the cooler and asked the kid at the pizza counter for some fresh ice.

He handed me a cupful.

"Actually I need it for the cooler," I said. "I need more than a cup."

He looked over the counter at the cooler. "I don't think I'm allowed to give you that much ice."

"You don't give us ice and our heart's gonna go bad," Lula said. "We gotta keep it cold."

The kid did another take on the cooler. "Your heart?"

Lula slid the top back and showed him the heart.

"Holy crap, lady," the kid said. "Take all the ice you want."

We filled the cooler half full, so that the heart looked nice and fresh on its bed of new ice. Then I went into the ladies' room and flipped the wire on.

"Testing," I said. "Can you hear me?"

A second later my phone rang. "I can hear you," Ranger said. "And I can hear the woman in the stall next to you."

I left Lula at the pizza place and walked to the middle of the mall, in front of Macy's. I sat on a bench with the cooler on my lap and my cell phone in my jacket pocket for easy access.

At exactly seven the phone rang.

"Are you ready for the instructions?" Eddie DeChooch asked.

"I'm ready."

"Drive to the first underpass going south on Route One . . ."

And at that moment I was tapped on the shoulder by the security guard.

"Excuse me, ma'am," he said, "but I'm going to have to ask to see the contents of that cooler."

"Who's there?" DeChooch wanted to know. "Who is that?"

"It's no one," I said to DeChooch. "Go ahead with the directions."

"I'm going to have to ask you to step away from the cooler," the guard said. *"Now."*

From the corner of my eye I could see another guard approaching.

"Listen," I said to DeChooch. "I've got a little problem here. Could you call me back in about ten minutes?"

"I don't like this," DeChooch said. "It's off. It's all off."

"No! Wait!"

He hung up.

Shit.

"What *is* the *deal* with you?" I said to the guard. "Couldn't you see I was talking on the phone? This is so important it couldn't wait two seconds? Don't they teach you anything in rent-a-cop school?"

He had his gun out now. "Just move away from the chest."

I knew Ranger was watching from somewhere, and he was probably having a hard time keeping from laughing.

I placed the chest on the bench and stepped away.

"Now reach out with your right hand and slide the top open so I can look inside," the guard said.

I did as I was asked.

The guard leaned forward and looked in the chest. "What the hell is that?"

"It's a heart. Is there a problem with that? Is it illegal to take a heart to the mall?"

There were two guards there now. They exchanged glances. The rent-a-cop handbook didn't cover this.

"Sorry to have disturbed you," the guard said. "It looked suspicious."

"Moron," I snapped.

Then I slid the top closed, took my cooler, and stormed back to Lula at the pizza stand.

"Uh-oh," Lula said. "How come you still got that cooler? You're supposed to have Granny."

"It got screwed up."

Ranger was waiting by my bike. "If I ever need to be ransomed, do me a favor and decline the job," he said. He reached under my shirt and turned the wire off. "Don't worry. He'll call back. How could he refuse a pig heart?" Ranger looked inside the chest and smiled. "It's really a pig heart."

"It's supposed to be Louie D's heart," I told

Ranger. "DeChooch removed it by mistake. And then somehow DeChooch managed to lose the heart while en route back to Richmond."

"And you were going to pawn a pig heart off on him," Ranger said.

"It was short notice," Lula said. "We tried to get a regular one, but they were special order."

"Nice bike," Ranger said to me. "Suits you."

And then he was in his car and gone.

Lula fanned herself. "That man is *so hot.*"

I CALLED MY mother when I got back to my apartment. "About Grandma," I said. "She's spending the night with her friend."

"Why didn't she call me?"

"I guess she figured it was enough to talk to me."

"That's very strange. Is this a man friend?"

"Yeah."

I heard the sound of a dish breaking and then my mother hung up.

I had the cooler sitting on the kitchen counter. I looked inside and wasn't happy with what I saw. The ice was melting and the heart wasn't looking all that good. There was only one thing to do. Freeze the damn thing.

I very carefully scooped it up and plopped it into a sandwich bag. I gagged a couple times, but I didn't blow chow so I was pretty pleased. Then I put the heart into the freezer.

There were two messages from Joe on my machine. Both of them said *call me.*

This wasn't something I wanted to do. He'd ask questions I didn't want to answer. Especially since the pig-heart swap had gotten snafued. There was an annoying voice in my head that kept whispering, *If the cops were involved it might have gone off better.*

And what about Grandma? She was still with Eddie DeChooch. Crazy, depressed Eddie DeChooch.

Crap. I dialed Joe. "I need you to help me," I said. "But you can't be a cop."

"Maybe you should spell that out for me."

"I'm going to tell you something, but you have to promise it stays between us and doesn't become official police business."

"I can't do that."

"You *have* to."

"What is it?"

"Eddie DeChooch has kidnapped Grandma."

"No offense, but DeChooch is lucky if he survives."

"I could use some company. Can you spend the night?"

A half hour later, Joe and Bob arrived. Bob ran through the apartment, snuffling chair seats, investigating waste baskets, and ended by clawing at the refrigerator door.

"He's on a diet," Morelli said. "He went to the vet today for shots and the vet says he's too fat." He clicked the television on and found the Rangers game. "You want to tell me about it?"

I burst into tears. "He's got Grandma and I screwed it up. And now I'm scared. I've haven't heard from him. What if he's killed Grandma?" I was sobbing. Unable to stop. Big, wracking, stupid sobs that made my nose run and my face get puffy and splotchy.

Morelli wrapped his arms around me. "How did you screw it up?"

"I had the heart in the cooler and the security guard stopped me and then De-Chooch called it off."

"The heart?"

I pointed to the kitchen. "It's in the freezer,"

Morelli broke loose and went to the freezer. I heard him open the freezer door. A moment passed. "You're right," he said. "There's a heart in here." And the freezer door squished shut.

"It's a pig heart," I told him.

"That's a relief."

I gave him the whole story.

The thing about Morelli is that he can be a tough person to read. He was a wise-ass kid and a wild teen. I guess he was living up to expectations. Morelli men have a certain reputation for hard living. But then somewhere in his twenties Morelli starting being his own man. So that now it's hard to tell where the new Morelli starts and the old Morelli stops.

I suspected the new Morelli would think foisting a pig heart off on Eddie DeChooch was a crackpot scheme. And I further suspected this would fan the flames of his fear that he was about to marry Lucy Ricardo of *I Love Lucy* fame.

"That was pretty clever of you to try a pig heart," Morelli said.

I almost fell off the couch.

"If you'd called me instead of Ranger I could have secured the area."

"Hindsight," I said. "I didn't want to do anything that would spook DeChooch."

We both jumped when the phone rang.

"I'm giving you another chance," De-Chooch said. "You screw this one up and your grandmother's gone."

"Is she okay?"

"She's driving me nuts."

"I want to talk to her."

"You can talk to her when you deliver the heart. Here's the new plan. Take the heart and your cell phone to the diner in Hamilton Township."

"The Silver Dollar?"

"Yeah. I'll call you tomorrow night at seven."

"Why can't we make the swap sooner?"

"Believe me, I'd love to make the swap sooner, but it don't work out for me. Is the heart still in good shape?"

"I've got it on ice."

"How much ice?"

"It's frozen."

"I figured you'd have to do that. Just make sure you don't chip a piece off. I was real careful taking it out. I don't want you messing it up."

He disconnected and my stomach felt sick.

"Ick."

Morelli put his arm around me. "Don't worry about your grandmother. She's like that '53 Buick. Frighteningly indestructible. Maybe even immortal."

I shook my head. "She's just an old lady."

"I'd feel a lot better if I honestly believed that," Morelli said. "But what I think we have here is a generation of women and cars that defy science and logic."

"You're thinking of your *own* grandmother."

"I've never admitted this to anyone before, but sometimes I worry she can actually give people the eye. Sometimes she scares the hell out of me."

I burst out laughing. I couldn't help it. Morelli had always been so casual about his grandmother's threats and predictions.

I slipped my number 35 jersey on over my T-shirt, and Morelli and I watched the Rangers game. After the game we walked Bob, and crawled into bed.

Crash. Scratch, scratch. *Crash.*

Morelli and I looked at each other. Bob was foraging, knocking dishes off the kitchen counter, looking for crumbs.

"He's hungry," Morelli said. "Maybe we should lock him in the bedroom with us so he doesn't eat a chair."

Morelli got out of bed and returned with Bob. Morelli locked the door and got back into bed. And Bob jumped into bed with us. Bob turned in a circle five or six times, scratched at the quilt, turned some more, looked confused.

"He's kind of cute," I said to Morelli. "In a prehistoric way."

Bob did a few more turns and then wedged himself between Morelli and me. He laid his big dog head on a corner of Morelli's pillow, gave a sigh of contentment, and instantly fell asleep.

"You need to get a bigger bed," Morelli said.

And I didn't have to worry about birth control, either.

MORELLI ROLLED OUT of bed at the crack of dawn.

I opened one eye. "What are you doing? It's barely light out."

"I can't sleep. Bob is hogging my side. Besides, I promised the vet I'd make sure Bob got some exercise, so we're going out running."

"That's nice."

"You, too," Morelli said.

"No way."

"You're the one who stuck me with this dog. You're going to get your ass out of there and run with us."

"No way!"

Morelli grabbed me by the ankle and dragged me out of bed. "Don't make me get rough," he said.

We both stood there looking at Bob. He was the only one left in bed. He still had his head on the pillow, but he looked worried. Bob wasn't an early morning sort of dog. And he wasn't much of an athlete.

"Get up," Morelli said to Bob.

Bob squeezed his eyes shut, pretending to sleep.

Morelli tried to drag Bob out of bed and Bob growled low in his throat like he meant business.

"Shit," Morelli said. "How do you do it? How do you get him to crap on Joyce's lawn so early in the morning?"

"You know about that?"

"Gordon Skyer lives across the street from Joyce. I play racquetball with Gordon."

"I bribe him with food."

Morelli went off to the kitchen and returned with a bag of carrots. "Look what I found," he said. "You have healthy food in your refrigerator. I'm impressed."

I didn't want to burst his bubble, but the carrots were for Rex. The only way I like carrots is if they're dipped in batter and deep-fat-fried or incorporated into carrot cake with lots of cream cheese frosting.

Morelli held a carrot out for Bob, and Bob gave him a *you've got to be kidding* look.

I was starting to feel sorry for Morelli. "Okay," I said, "let's just get dressed and go out into the kitchen and rattle some things around. Bob will cave."

Five minutes later we were suited up and Bob was collared and clipped to his leash.

"Hold on," I said. "We can't all go out and leave the heart home alone. People break into my apartment on a regular basis."

"What people?"

"Benny and Ziggy for starters."

"People can't just walk into your house. That's illegal. That's breaking and entering."

"It's no big deal," I said. "The first couple times it caught me by surprise, but you get used to it after a while." I took the heart out of the freezer. "I'll leave this with Mr. Morganstern. He's an early riser."

"My freezer is on the blink," I told Mr. Morganstern, "and I don't want this to defrost. Could you keep it for me until dinnertime?"

"Sure," he said. "It looks like a heart."

"It's a new diet. Once a week you have to eat a heart."

"No kidding. Maybe I should do that. I've been a little sluggish lately."

Morelli was waiting for me in the parking lot. He was jogging in place, and Bob was looking bright-eyed and smiley now that he was out in the fresh air.

"Is he empty?" I asked Morelli.

"All taken care of."

Morelli and Bob took off at a brisk pace, and I slogged along behind them. I can walk three miles in four-inch heels and I can shop Morelli into the ground, but I don't do running. Now if I was running to a sale on handbags, maybe.

Little by little, I fell farther and farther behind. When Morelli and Bob turned the corner and were lost from sight, I cut through a yard and came out at Ferarro's Bakery. I got an almond danish and leisurely walked home, eating my pastry. I was almost to my parking lot when I saw Joe and Bob loping down St. James. I immediately started jogging and gasping for air.

"Where were you guys?" I said. "I lost you."

Morelli shook his head in disgust. "That's so sad. You have powdered sugar on your shirt."

"Must have fallen from the sky."

"Pathetic," Morelli said.

We passed Benny and Ziggy in the hall when we returned.

"Looks like you were out jogging," Ziggy said. "That's very healthy. More people should do that."

Morelli put a hand to Ziggy's chest to detain him. "What are you doing here?"

"We came to see Ms. Plum, but no one was home."

"Well, here she is. Don't you want to talk to her?"

"Sure," Ziggy said. "Did you like the jelly?"

"The jelly is great. Thanks."

"You didn't break into her apartment just now, did you?" Morelli asked.

"We wouldn't do a thing like that," Benny said. "We got too much respect for her. Right, Ziggy?"

"Yeah, that's right," Ziggy said. "But I could if I wanted to. I still got the touch."

"Have you had a chance to talk to your wife?" I asked Benny. "Is she in Richmond?"

"I talked to her last night. And she's in Norfolk. She said things are as good as can be expected. I'm sure you understand this has been upsetting for all concerned."

"A tragedy. No other news from Richmond?"

"Sadly, no."

Benny and Ziggy trotted off to the elevator, and Morelli and I followed Bob into the kitchen.

"They were in here, weren't they?" Morelli said

"Yeah. Looking for the heart. Benny's wife is making his life a living hell until the heart is returned."

Morelli measured out a cup of food for Bob. Bob inhaled it and looked for more.

"Sorry, fella," Morelli said. "That's what happens when you get fat."

I sucked my stomach in, feeling guilty about the danish. Compared to Morelli I was a cow. Morelli had washboard abs. Morelli could actually do sit-ups. Lots of them. In my mind's eye I could do sit-ups, too. In real life, sit-ups ran a close second to the joy of jogging.

TWELVE

EDDIE DECHOOCH HAD Grandma stashed someplace. Probably not in the Burg because I would have heard something by now. Somewhere in the Trenton area. Both phone-in locations were local.

Joe had promised not to file a report, but I knew he'd work undercover. He'd ask questions and he'd have cops out there looking a lot harder for Eddie DeChooch. Connie and Vinnie and Lula were tapping their sources, too. I didn't expect anything to come of it. Eddie DeChooch was working alone. He might visit with Father Carolli once in a while. And he might be drawn to the occasional wake. But he was out there alone. I was convinced no one knew his lair. With the possible exception of Mary Maggie Mason.

For whatever reason, two days ago, DeChooch had come to call on Mary Maggie.

I picked Lula up at the office, and we motored off to Mary Maggie's condo building. It was midmorning and traffic was light. Clouds were coagulating overhead. Rain was expected later today. No one in Jersey gave a rat's ass. It was Thursday. Let it rain. In Jersey we cared about weekend weather.

The Low Rider rumbled in the underground garage, the vibrations bouncing off the cement ceiling and floor. We didn't see the white Cadillac, but the MMM-YUM silver Porsche was occupying its usual slot. I parked the Harley two lanes over.

Lula and I looked at each other. We didn't want to go upstairs.

"I feel funny about talking to Mary Maggie," I said. "That mud thing wasn't exactly a moment of shining glory for me."

"It was all her fault. She started it."

"I could have done better, but I was caught by surprise," I said.

"Yeah," Lula said. "I could tell that by the way you kept yelling *help*. I just hope she doesn't want to sue me for a broken back or something."

We got to Mary Maggie's door and we both turned quiet. I took a deep breath and rang the bell. Mary Maggie opened her door, and the instant she saw us she tried to slam the door closed. Bounty hunter rule number two—if a door opens, get your boot in there fast.

"Now what?" Mary Maggie said, struggling to get my boot out of the way.

"I want to talk to you."

"You've already talked to me."

"I need to talk to you again. Eddie De-Chooch kidnapped my grandmother."

Mary Maggie stopped struggling and looked out at me. "Are you serious?"

"I have something he wants. And now he has someone *I* want."

"I don't know what to say. I'm sorry."

"I was hoping you could help me find her."

Mary Maggie opened her door and Lula and I invited ourselves in. I didn't think I'd find Grandma tucked away in a closet, but I had to look anyway. The apartment was nice but not that large. Open floor plan living room and dining room and kitchen. One bedroom. Bath and a half. It was tastefully furnished with classic pieces. Soft colors. Grays and beiges. And of course there were books everywhere.

"I honestly don't know where he is," Mary Maggie said. "He asked to borrow my car. He's done it before. When the owner of the club asks to borrow something it's a good idea to loan it to him. And besides, he's a nice old man. After you were here I went to his nephew and told him I wanted my car back. Eddie was bringing it back when you and your friend ambushed him in my garage. I haven't heard from him since."

The bad news was that I believed her. The good news was that Ronald DeChooch communicates with his uncle.

"Sorry about your shoe," Mary Maggie said to Lula. "We looked for it, but we couldn't find it."

"Hunh," Lula said.

Lula and I didn't talk until we got to the garage.

"What do you think?" Lula asked.

"I think we need to visit Ronald De-Chooch."

I cranked the bike over, Lula climbed on,

and we tore through the garage like judgment day and headed for Ace Pavers.

"We're pretty lucky we got good jobs," Lula said when I pulled up to Ronald De-Chooch's brick office building. "We could be working at a place like this, smelling tar all day, always having chunks of black stuff stuck to the bottom of our shoes."

I got off the bike and removed my helmet. The smell of hot asphalt lay heavy in the air, and beyond the locked gate the blackened rollers and pitch trucks gave off shimmering waves of heat. There were no men in sight, but clearly the equipment had just come off a job.

"We're going to be professional but assertive," I said to Lula.

"You mean we're not taking any crap from that roody-poo jabroni Ronald DeChooch."

"You've been watching wrestling again," I said to Lula.

"I've got it on tape so I can do reruns of The Rock," Lula said.

Lula and I puffed ourselves up and marched in without knocking. We weren't going to be put off by a bunch of card-playing jerks. We were going to get answers. We were going to get respect.

We barreled through the small entrance hall and again without knocking went straight to the inside office. We whipped the doors open and came face-to-face with Ronald DeChooch playing hide-the-salami with the clerical help. Actually it wasn't face-to-face because DeChooch had his back to us. More correctly, he had his big hairy ass to us because he was doing the poor woman doggy-style. His pants were around his ankles and the woman was bent over the card table, holding on for all she was worth.

There was a moment of shocked silence, and then Lula started laughing.

"You should think about having your ass waxed," Lula said to DeChooch. "That is one *ugly* butt."

"Christ," DeChooch said, pulling his pants up. "A man can't even have relations in his own office."

The woman jumped up and adjusted her skirt and tried to stuff her boobs back into her bra. She scuttled away, looking mortally embarrassed, with her panties in her hand. I hoped she was being well compensated.

"Now what?" DeChooch said. "You have something special in mind, or you just come to see a show?"

"Your uncle kidnapped my grandmother."

"What?"

"He took her yesterday. He wants to ransom her for the heart."

The surprise in his eyes ratcheted up a notch. "You know about the heart?"

Lula and I exchanged glances.

"I . . . um, have the heart," I said.

"Jesus Christ. How the fuck did you get the heart?"

"It don't matter how she got it," Lula said.

"Right," I said. "What matters is that we get this all settled. First off, I want my grandmother back home. And then I want Mooner and Dougie."

"Your grandmother I might be able to arrange," Ronald said. "I don't know where my Uncle Eddie's hiding out, but I talk to him once in a while. He's got a cell phone. Those other two are something different. I don't know anything about them. So far as I can tell *nobody* knows anything about them."

"Eddie is supposed to call me tonight at seven. I don't want anything to go wrong. I'm going to give him the heart, and I want my grandmother back. If anything bad happens to my grandmother or she doesn't get swapped for the heart tonight, it's going to be ugly."

"I hear you."

Lula and I left. We closed two doors behind us, straddled the Harley, and took off. Two blocks later I had to pull over because we were laughing so hard I was afraid we were going to fall off the bike.

"That was the best," Lula said. "You want to get a man to pay attention, you just get him with his pants down."

"I've never seen anyone *doing it* before!" I said to Lula. My face was flaming under the laughter. "I've never even looked in a mirror."

"You never want to look in a mirror," Lula said. "Men love mirrors. They look at themselves doing the deed and they see Rex the Wonder Horse. Women look at themselves and think they need to renew their membership at the gym."

I was trying to get myself under control when my mother called on my cell phone.

"There's something funny going on," my mother said. "Where's your grandmother? Why hasn't she come home?"

"She'll be home tonight."

"You said that last night. Who is this man

she's with? I don't like this one bit. What will people say?"

"Don't worry. Grandma's being very discreet. She just had this *thing* to do." I didn't know what else to say so I made some crackling staticky sounds. "Uh-oh," I yelled, "I'm breaking up. I have to go."

Lula was staring over my shoulder. "I can see clear down the street," she said, "and there's a big black car just drove out of the lot by the paving company. And there's three men just came out the front door, and I could swear they're pointing at us."

I looked to see what was happening. From this distance it was impossible to see details, but one of them might have been pointing. The men got into the car and the car turned in our direction.

"Maybe Ronald forgot to tell us something," Lula said.

I had a weird feeling in my chest. "He could have called."

"My second thought is maybe you shouldn't have told him you have the heart."

Shit.

Lula and I jumped on the bike, but by now the car was only a block away and gaining.

"Hang on," I yelled. And we shot forward.

I accelerated to the corner and took it wide. I wasn't that good on the bike yet to take chances.

"Yow," Lula shouted in my ear, "they're right on your ass."

My peripheral vision caught the car coming up on my side. We were on a two-lane street with two blocks to go to Broad. These side streets were empty, but Broad would be busy at this time of day. If I could get to Broad I could lose them. The car eased past me, put some space between us, and then angled across the road, blocking my progress. The Lincoln's doors opened, all four men jumped out, and I slid to a stop. I felt Lula's arm rest on my shoulder and from the corner of my eye I got a glimpse of her Glock.

Everything came to a standstill.

Finally one of the men stepped forward. "Ronnie said I should give you his card in case you need to get in touch with him. It has his cell phone number on it."

"Thanks," I said, taking the card from him. "That was smart of Ronald to think of that."

"Yeah. He's a smart guy."

Then they all piled into the car and drove away.

Lula reset the safety on the gun. "I think I messed my pants," she said.

RANGER WAS IN the office when we got back.

"Seven o'clock tonight," I said to Ranger. "At the Silver Dollar Diner. Morelli knows about it, but he's promised no police action."

Ranger watched me. "Do you need me there, too?"

"Wouldn't hurt."

He got to his feet. "Wear the wire. Turn it on at six-thirty."

"How about me?" Lula asked. "Am I invited?"

"You're riding shotgun," I said. "I need someone to carry the cooler."

THE SILVER DOLLAR Diner is in Hamilton Township, just a short distance from the Burg, and an even shorter distance from my apartment. It's open twenty-four hours a day and has a menu that would take twelve hours to recite. You can get breakfast anytime and a nice greasy grilled cheese at two in the morning. It's surrounded by all of the ugliness that makes Jersey so great. Convenience stores, branch banks, warehouse grocery stores, video stores, strip malls, and dry cleaners. And neon signs and traffic lights as far as the eye can see.

Lula and I got there at six-thirty with the frozen heart clunking around in the Igloo cooler and my wire feeling uncomfortable and itchy under my plaid flannel shirt. We sat in a booth and ordered cheeseburgers and fries and looked out the window at the traffic streaming past.

I tested the wire and got the confirmation phone call back from Ranger. He was out there . . . somewhere. He was watching the diner. And he was invisible. Joe was there, too. Probably they'd communicated with each other. I've watched them work jobs together in the past. There were rules that men like Joe and Ranger used to dictate their roles. Rules I'd never understand. Rules that allowed two alpha males to co-exist for the common good.

The diner was still crowded with second-shift eaters. The first-shift eaters were the seniors who came for the early-bird special. By seven it would start to thin. This wasn't Manhattan, where people ate fashionably late at eight or nine. Trenton worked hard and much of it was asleep by ten.

My cell phone rang at seven and my heart

did a little tap dance when I heard De-Chooch's voice.

"Do you have the heart with you?" he asked.

"Yes. It's right here beside me in the cooler. How's Grandma? I want to talk to her."

There was some scuffling and mumbling and Grandma came on the line.

"Howdy," Grandma said.

"Are you okay?"

"I'm hunky-dory."

She sounded too happy. "Have you been drinking?"

"Eddie and me might have had a couple cocktails before dinner, but don't worry . . . I'm sharp as a tack."

Lula was sitting across the table from me and she was smiling and shaking her head. I knew Ranger would be doing the same.

Eddie came back on the line. "Are you ready for the instructions?"

"Yes."

"Do you know how to get to Nottingham Way?"

"Yes."

"Okay. Take Nottingham to Mulberry Street and turn right onto Cherry."

"Wait a minute. Ronald, your nephew, lives on Cherry."

"Yeah. You're taking the heart to Ronald. He's gonna see it gets back to Richmond."

Damn. I was going to get Grandma back, but I wasn't going to get Eddie DeChooch. I'd been hoping Ranger or Joe would snag him at the drop site.

"And what about Grandma?"

"As soon as I get a call from Ronald I'll turn your grandmother loose."

I slid my cell phone back into my jacket pocket and told Lula and Ranger the plan.

"He's pretty cagey for an old guy," Lula said. "That's not a bad plan."

I'd already paid for the food, so I dropped a tip on the table and Lula and I left. The black and green around my eyes had faded to yellow and the yellow was hidden behind dark glasses. Lula hadn't worn her leathers. She was dressed in boots and jeans and a T-shirt that had a lot of cows on it and advertised Ben & Jerry's ice cream. We were just two normal women out for a couple burgers at the diner. Even the cooler seemed innocuous. No reason to suspect it contained a heart to ransom my grandmother.

And these other people, scarfing down fries and cole slaw, ordering rice pudding for dessert. What were their secrets? Who was to say they weren't spies and thugs and jewel thieves? I looked around. For that matter, who was to say they were human?

I took my time getting to Cherry Street. I was worried about Grandma and nervous about giving Ronald a pig heart. So I drove very carefully. Crashing the bike would put a real crimp in my rescue effort. Anyway, it was a nice night to be on a Harley. No bugs and no rain. I could feel Lula behind me, holding tight to the cooler.

The porch light was on at Ronald's house. Guess he was waiting for me. Hope he had room in his freezer for an organ. I left Lula on the bike with her Glock in her hand, and I walked the cooler to the front door and rang the bell.

Ronald opened the door and looked out at me and then at Lula. "Do you two sleep together, too?"

"No," I said. "I sleep with Joe Morelli."

Ronald looked a little grim at that since Morelli is a vice cop and Ronald is a vice purveyor.

"Before I hand this over to you I want you to call and have Grandma released," I said.

"Sure. Come on in."

"I'll stay here. And I want to hear Grandma tell me she's okay."

Ronald shrugged. "Whatever. Let me see the heart."

I slid the top back and Ronald looked inside.

"Jesus," he said, "it's frozen."

I looked in the cooler, too. What I saw was a blechy-looking lump of maroon ice wrapped in plastic.

"Yeah," I said, "it was starting to look a little funky. You can't keep a heart around forever, you know. So I froze it."

"You saw it when it wasn't frozen, though, right? And it looked okay?"

"I'm not exactly an expert on this stuff."

Ronald disappeared and returned with a portable phone. "Here," he said, handing the phone over to me. "Here's your granny."

"I'm at Quaker Bridge with Eddie," Grandma said. "I saw a jacket I like at Macy's, but I have to wait for my Social Security check."

Eddie got on the line. "I'm going to leave

her at the pizza place here. You can pick her up anytime."

I repeated it for Ranger. "Okay, let me get this straight. You're going to leave Grandma at the pizza place at Quaker Bridge Mall."

"Yeah," Eddie said, "what are you, wearing a wire?"

"Who, me?"

I gave the phone back to Ronald and handed him the cooler. "If I were you I'd put the heart in the freezer for now and then maybe pack it in dry ice for the trip to Richmond."

He nodded. "I'll do that. Wouldn't want to give Louie D a heart full of maggots."

"Out of morbid curiosity," I said, "was it your idea for me to bring the heart here?"

"You said don't let anything go wrong."

When I got back to the bike I hauled my cell phone out and called Ranger.

"I'm on my way," Ranger said. "I'm about ten minutes from Quaker Bridge. I'll call when I have her."

I nodded my head and disconnected, unable to speak. There are times when life is just fucking overwhelming.

*   *   *

LULA LIVES IN a tiny apartment in a part of the ghetto that's pretty nice as far as ghettos go. I took Brunswick Avenue, wound around some, crossed over the train tracks, and found Lula's neighborhood. Streets were narrow and houses were small. Probably originally built for immigrants imported to work in the porcelain factories and steel mills. Lula lived in the middle of the block on the second floor of one of these houses.

My phone rang just as I cut the engine.

"I've got your grandmother with me, babe," Ranger said. "I'm taking her home. Do you want any pizza?"

"Pepperoni, extra cheese."

"That extra cheese will kill you," Ranger said and disconnected.

Lula got off the bike and looked at me. "You gonna be all right?"

"Yep. I'm fine."

She leaned forward and hugged me. "You're a good person."

I smiled back at her and blinked hard and wiped my nose on my sleeve. Lula was a good person, too.

"Uh-oh," Lula said. "Are you crying?"

"No. I think I inhaled a bug a couple blocks ago."

It took me ten more minutes to get to my parents' house. I parked one house down and cut my lights. No way was I going in ahead of Grandma. My mother was probably berserk by now. Better to explain Grandma was kidnapped after Grandma was there in the flesh.

I sat on the curb and used the down time to call Morelli. I got him on his cell phone.

"Grandma's safe," I told him. "She's with Ranger. He picked her up at the mall and he's bringing her home."

"I heard. I was behind you at Ronald's. I stayed there until I got the word from Ranger that he had your grandmother. I'm on my way home now."

Morelli asked me to spend the night at his house, but I declined. I had things to do. I got Grandma back, but Mooner and Dougie were still out there.

After a while headlights flashed at the end of the street and Ranger's gleaming black Mercedes eased to a stop in front of my parents' house. Ranger helped Grandma out and smiled at me. "Your grandmother ate your pizza. Guess you work up an appetite being a hostage."

"Are you coming in with me?"

"You'd have to kill me first."

"I need to talk to you. This won't take long. Will you wait for me?"

Our eyes held and the silence stretched between us.

I mentally licked my lips and fanned myself. Yep. He'd wait.

I turned to go into the house and he pulled me back. His hands slid under my shirt and my breath caught.

"The wire," he said, removing the tape, his fingertips warm against my skin, skimming the swell of breast not covered by my bra.

Grandma was already through the door when I caught up with her.

"Boy, I can't wait to go to the beauty parlor tomorrow and tell everyone about this one."

My father looked up from his paper, and my mother gave an involuntary shudder.

"Who's laid out?" Grandma asked my father. "I haven't seen a paper in a couple days. Did I miss anything?"

My mother narrowed her eyes. "Where were you?"

"Danged if I know," Grandma said. "I had a bag over my head when I went in and out."

"She was kidnapped," I told my mother.

"What do you mean . . . kidnapped?"

"I happened to have something that Eddie DeChooch wanted, and so he kidnapped Grandma and held her for ransom."

"Thank God," my mother said. "I thought she was shacked up with a man."

My father went back to reading his paper. Just another day in the life of the Plum family.

"Did you learn anything from Choochy?" I asked Grandma. "Do you have any idea where Mooner and Dougie have gone?"

"Eddie doesn't know anything about them. He'd like to find them, too. He says Dougie's the one who started it all. He says Dougie stole his heart. I could never figure out what that heart business was about, though."

"And you don't have any idea where you were kept?"

"He had a bag over my head when we went in and out. At first I didn't realize I was kidnapped. I thought it was some kinky sex thing. What I know is we did some driving around and then we went into a garage. I know because I heard the garage door open and close. And then we went into the downstairs part of a house. It was like the garage opened into the cellar except the cellar was fixed up. There was a television room and two bedrooms and a little kitchen down there. And another room with the furnace and the washer and dryer. And I couldn't see out because there were only those little basement windows and they were closed up with shutters on the outside." Grandma yawned. "Well, I'm going to bed. I'm pooped and I've got a big day tomorrow. I've got to make the most of this kidnapping. I've got a lot of people to tell."

"Just don't say anything about the heart," I told Grandma. "The heart is a secret."

"Fine by me since I don't know what to say about it, anyway."

"Are you going to press charges?"

Grandma looked surprised. "Against Choochy? Heck no. What would people think?"

Ranger was leaning against his car, waiting for me. He was dressed in black. Black dress slacks, expensive-looking black loafers, black T-shirt, black cashmere jacket. I knew the jacket wasn't for warmth. The jacket covered the gun. Not that it made any difference. The jacket was handsome.

"Ronald is probably going to take the heart to Richmond tomorrow," I said to

Ranger. "And I'm worried they'll discover it doesn't belong to Louie D."

"And?"

"And I'm afraid they might want to send a message by doing something terrible to Mooner or Dougie."

"And?"

"And I think Mooner and Dougie are in Richmond. I think Louie D's wife and sister are secretly working together. And I think they have Mooner and Dougie."

"And you'd like to rescue them."

"Yes."

Ranger smiled. "Might be fun."

Ranger has an odd sense of fun.

"I got Louie D's home address from Connie. Louie D's wife has supposedly been locked up there since Louie died. Estelle Colucci, Louie's sister, is down there, too. She left for Richmond the same day Mooner disappeared. I think somehow the women kidnapped Mooner and took him to Richmond. And I bet Dougie's also in Richmond. Maybe Estelle and Sophia got fed up with Benny and Ziggy bumbling around and decided to take matters into their own hands." Unfortunately, my theory got a lot fuzzier from there on out. One of the reasons for the fuzziness was that Estelle Colucci didn't fit the description of the crazy-eyed woman. In fact, she didn't even fit the description of the woman in the limo.

"Do you want to stop home first for anything?" Ranger asked. "Or do you want to leave now?"

I looked back at the bike. I had to stash the bike somewhere. Probably it wasn't a good idea to tell my mother I was going to Richmond with Ranger. And I didn't feel entirely comfortable just leaving the bike in my parking lot. The seniors in my building tend to run over objects smaller than a Cadillac. God knows, I didn't want to leave it with Morelli. Morelli would insist on going to Richmond. Morelli was as competent at this sort of operation as Ranger. In fact, Morelli might even be better than Ranger because Morelli wasn't as crazy. Problem was, this wasn't a police operation. This was a bounty hunter operation.

"I need to do something with the bike," I told Ranger. "I don't want to leave it here."

"Don't worry about it. I'll have Tank take care of it until we get back."

"He needs the key."

Ranger looked at me like I was a very dim bulb.

"Right," I said. "What was I thinking?" Tank didn't need a key. Tank was one of Ranger's merry men and Ranger's merry men had better fingers than Ziggy.

We left the Burg and headed south, picking the turnpike up at Bordentown. The rain started a few minutes later, a fine mist at first, growing more steady as the miles flew by. The Mercedes hummed along, following the ribbon of road. The night enveloped us, the darkness broken only by the lights on the dash.

All the comforts of a womb with the technology of a jet airplane cockpit. Ranger pushed a button on the CD player and classical music filled the car. A symphony. Not Godsmack, but nice anyway.

By my calculations it was about a five-hour trip. Ranger wasn't the sort to make small talk. Ranger kept his life and his thoughts to himself. So I reclined my seat and closed my eyes. "If you get tired and want me to drive just let me know," I said.

I relaxed back into the seat and wondered about Ranger. When we first met he was all muscle and street swagger. He talked the talk and walked the walk of the Hispanic end of the ghetto, dressing in fatigues and SWAT black. Now suddenly he was dressed in cashmere, listening to classical music, sounding more like Harvard Law and less like Coolio.

"You don't by any chance have a twin brother, do you?" I asked.

"No," he said softly. "There's only one of me."

THIRTEEN

I WOKE UP when the car stopped moving. It was no longer raining, but it was very dark. I looked at the digital clock on the dash. It was almost three. Ranger was studying the large brick colonial on the opposite side of the street.

"Louie D's house?" I asked.

Ranger nodded.

It was a large house on a small lot. The houses around it were similar. They were all relatively new houses. No mature trees or shrubs. In twenty years it would be a lovely neighborhood. Right now it seemed a little too new, too bare. There were no lights shining in Louie D's house. No cars parked at the curb. Cars were kept in garages or driveways in this neighborhood.

"Stay here," Ranger said. "I need to look around."

I watched him cross the street and disappear into the house shadows. I cracked the window and strained to hear sounds but heard nothing. Ranger had been Special Forces in another life, and he's lost none of his skills. He moves like a large lethal cat. I, on the other hand, move like a water buffalo. Which I suppose was why I was waiting in the car.

He emerged from the far side of the house and sauntered back to the Mercedes. He slid behind the wheel and turned the key in the ignition.

"It's locked up tight," he said. "The alarm is on and most of the windows have heavy drapes drawn. Not much to see. If I knew more about the house and its routine I'd go in and look around. I'm reluctant to do that not knowing how many people are inside." He pulled away from the curb and rolled down the street. "We're fifteen minutes away from a business district. The computer tells me there's a strip mall, some fast-food places, and a motel. I had Tank get us rooms. You can have a couple hours to sleep and get freshened up. My suggestion is to knock on Mrs. D's door at nine and finesse ourselves into the house."

"Works for me."

Tank had gotten rooms in a classic two-story chain motel. Not luxurious but not awful, either. Both rooms were on the second floor. Ranger opened my door and hit the light, giving the room a quick scan. Everything looked in order. No mad man lurking in darkened corners.

"I'll come for you at eight-thirty," he said. "We can get breakfast and then say hello to the ladies."

"I'll be ready."

He pulled me toward him, lowered his mouth to mine, and kissed me. The kiss was slow and deep. His hands were firm on my back. I grasped his shirt and leaned into him. And I felt his body respond.

A vision of myself in the wedding gown popped into my head. "Shit!" I said.

"That's not the usual reaction I get when I kiss a woman," Ranger said.

"Okay, here's the truth. I'd really like to

sleep with you, but I have this stupid wedding gown . . ."

Ranger's lips swept along my jawline to my ear. "I could make you forget the gown."

"You could. But that would create really terrible problems."

"You have a moral dilemma."

"Yes."

He kissed me again. Lightly this time. He stepped back and a small humorless smile pulled at the corners of his mouth. "I don't want to put any pressure on you and your moral dilemma, but you better hope you can bring Eddie DeChooch in all by yourself because if I help you I'll collect my fee."

And then he left. He closed the door behind him, and I could hear him walk partway down the hall and enter his own room.

Yikes.

I stretched out on the bed, fully clothed, lights on, eyes wide. When my heart stopped hammering in my chest and my nipples started to relax I got up and splashed water on my face. I set the alarm for eight. Yippee, four hours to sleep. I turned the light out and crawled into bed. Couldn't sleep. Too many clothes. I got up and stripped down to my panties and crawled into bed. Nope, couldn't sleep that way, either. Not enough clothes. I put my shirt back on, crawled back under the covers, and instantly clonked off to dreamland.

WHEN RANGER KNOCKED on my door at eight-thirty I was as ready as I was going to get. I'd taken a shower and done the best I could with my hair in the absence of gel. I carry a lot of stuff in my bag. Who would have thought I'd need gel.

Ranger had coffee and fruit and a whole-grain bagel for breakfast. I had an Egg McMuffin, a chocolate shake, and breakfast fries. Plus Ranger was treating so I got a Disney action figure.

It was warmer in Richmond than it had been in Jersey. Some of the trees and early azaleas were flowering. The sky was clear and struggling to be blue. It was going to be a good day for bullying a couple old ladies.

Traffic was heavy on the major roads but disappeared the instant we entered Louie D's neighborhood. School buses had come and gone, and the adult inhabitants were off to yoga class, the gourmet market, the tennis club, Gymboree, and work. The neighborhood had a lived-in, get-up-and-go feel this morning. With the exception of Louie D's house. Louie D's house looked exactly as it had at 3:00 A.M. Dark and still.

Ranger called Tank and was told Ronald left his house at eight with the cooler. Tank had followed him south to Whitehorse and then turned back once he was certain Ronald was on his way to Richmond.

"So what do you think of the house?" I asked Ranger.

"I think it looks like it has a secret."

We both got out of the car and walked to the door. Ranger rang the bell. After a moment the door was opened by a woman in her early sixties. Her brown hair was cut short and framed a long, narrow face dominated by thick black eyebrows. She was dressed in black. Black shirtwaist dress on her small, wiry frame, black cardigan sweater, black loafers, and dark stockings. She wore no makeup or jewelry other than a simple silver cross around her neck. Her eyes were dark-rimmed and dull, as if she hadn't slept for a very long time.

"Yes?" she said without animation. No smile on her thin, colorless lips.

"I'm looking for Estelle Colucci," I said.

"Estelle isn't here."

"Her husband said she would be visiting."

"Her husband was wrong."

Ranger moved forward and the woman blocked his way.

"Are you Mrs. DeStefano?" Ranger asked.

"I'm Christina Gallone. Sophia DeStefano is my sister."

"We need to speak to Mrs. DeStefano," Ranger said.

"She's not seeing visitors."

Ranger pushed her back into the room. "I think she is."

"No!" Christina said, pulling at Ranger. "She's not well. You have to leave!"

A second woman stepped out of the kitchen, into the foyer. She was older than Christina, but the resemblance was there. She wore the same black dress and shoes and simple silver cross. She was the taller of the two, her short brown hair shot with gray. Her face was more animated than her sister's, but her eyes were eerily empty, sucking light in and giving nothing out. My first impression was that she was medicated. My second guess would be that she was insane. And I was pretty sure I was looking at the crazy-eyed woman who shot Mooner.

"What's going on?" she asked.

"Mrs. DeStefano?" Ranger asked.

"Yes."

"We'd like to speak to you about the disappearance of two young men."

The sisters looked at each other and the nape of my neck prickled. The living room was to my left. It was dark and forbidding, formally furnished with polished mahogany tables and heavy brocade upholstery. The drapes were closed, allowing no sunlight to penetrate the interior. A small study opened to my right. The door was partially open, revealing a cluttered desk. Again, curtains were drawn in the study.

"What would you like to know," Sophia said.

"Their names are Walter Dunphy and Douglas Kruper, and we'd like to know if you've seen them."

"I don't know either of them."

"Douglas Kruper is in violation of his bail bond," Ranger said. "We have reason to believe he's here in this house, and as apprehension agents for Vincent Plum we're authorized to conduct a search."

"You'll do no such thing. You will leave immediately or I'll call the police."

"If you'd feel more comfortable having the police present while we search, by all means place the call."

Again, the exchange of silent communication between the sisters, Christina twisting her skirt in her fingers now.

"I don't appreciate this intrusion," Sophia said. "It's disrespectful."

Uh-oh, I thought. There goes my tongue . . . just like Sophia's poor dead neighbor.

Ranger stepped to the side and opened the door to the coat closet. He had his gun in his hand, at his side.

"Stop that," Sophia said. "You have no right to search this house. Do you know who I am? Do you realize I'm the widow of Louis DeStefano?"

Ranger opened another door. Powder room.

"I command you to stop or suffer the consequences," Sophia said.

Ranger opened the door to the study and flipped the light on, watching the women while investigating the house.

I followed his lead and walked through the living room and dining room, turning the lights on. I walked through the kitchen. There was a locked door in a hallway just off the kitchen. Pantry or cellar probably. I was reluctant to investigate. I didn't have a gun. And even if I had a gun, I wouldn't be much good at using it.

Sophia suddenly came after me in the kitchen. "Out of there!" she shouted, grabbing me by the wrist, yanking me forward. "You will get out of my kitchen."

I jerked away from her. And in a motion I can only describe as reptilian, Sophia reached into a kitchen drawer and came out with a gun. She turned and aimed and shot Ranger. And then she turned on me.

Without thinking, acting totally from blind fear, I lunged at her and took her down to the floor. The gun skidded away and I scuttled after it. Ranger got to it before I did. He calmly picked it up and put it in his pocket.

I was on my feet, not sure what to do. The sleeve of Ranger's cashmere jacket was soaked with blood. "Should I call for help?" I asked Ranger.

He shrugged out of the jacket and looked at his arm. "It's not bad," he said. "Get me a towel for now." He reached behind him and brought out cuffs. "Cuff them together."

"Don't touch me," Sophia said. "You touch me and I'll kill you. I'll scratch your eyes out."

I closed a bracelet on Christina's wrist and tugged her toward Sophia. "Hold your hand out," I said to Sophia.

"Never," she said. And she spit at me.

Ranger moved closer. "Hold your hand out or I'll shoot your sister."

"Louie, do you hear me, Louie?" Sophia shouted, looking up, presumably beyond the ceiling. "Do you see what's happening? Do you see the disgrace? Jesus, God," she wailed. "Jesus, God."

"Where are they?" Ranger asked. "Where are the two men?"

"They're mine," Sophia said. "I won't give them up. Not until I get what I want. That moron DeChooch, hiring his fence to drive the heart back to Richmond. Too lazy, too ashamed to bring the heart back himself. And do you know what that little pisser brought me? An empty cooler. Thought he could get away with it. Him and his friend."

"Where are they?" Ranger asked again.

"They're where they should be. In hell. And they're going to stay there until they tell me what they did with the heart. I want to know who has the heart."

"Ronald DeChooch has the heart," I said. "He's on his way here."

Sophia's eyes narrowed. "Ronald De-Chooch." She spit on her floor. "That's what I think of Ronald DeChooch. I'll believe he's got Louie's heart when I see it."

Obviously she hadn't been told the full story with my involvement.

"You have to let my sister go," Christina begged. "You can see she's not well."

"Do you have cuffs on you?" Ranger asked me.

I dug around in my bag and came up with cuffs.

"Cuff them to the refrigerator," Ranger said, "and then see if you can find a first-aid kit."

We both had previous personal experience with gunshot wounds, so we had the drill down pretty good. I found some first-aid supplies in the upstairs bathroom, got a sterile compress on Ranger's arm, and bound it with gauze and tape.

Ranger tried the locked room off the kitchen.

"Where's the key?" he asked.

"Rot in hell," Sophia said, her snake eyes narrowed.

Ranger put his foot to the door and the door crashed open. There was a small landing and steps leading down to the cellar. It was inky black. Ranger flipped the light on and went down the stairs, gun drawn. It was an unfinished basement with the usual assortment of cartons and tools and articles too good to throw away but of no practical use. A couple pieces of outdoor furniture partially covered with discarded sheets. One corner devoted to furnace and water heater. One corner devoted to laundry. And one corner had been walled off floor-to-ceiling with cinder blocks, forming a small enclosed room, maybe nine by nine. The door was metal and padlocked.

I looked at Ranger. "Bomb shelter? Root cellar? Cold storage?"

"Hell," Ranger said. He motioned me back and fired off two rounds, destroying the lock.

We pulled the door open and staggered back from the stench of fear and excretion. The small room was unlit but eyes looked out at us from the far corner. Mooner and Dougie were huddled together. They were naked and filthy, their hair matted, their arms dotted with open sores. They were handcuffed to a metal table that was attached to the wall. Empty plastic water bottles and bread bags littered the floor.

"Dude," Mooner said.

I felt my legs go and sank down to one knee.

Ranger pulled me up with a hand under my armpit. "Not now," he said. "Get the sheets off the furniture."

A couple more gunshots. Ranger was freeing them from the table.

Mooner was in better shape than Dougie. Dougie had been in the room longer. He'd lost weight and his arms were scarred with burn marks.

"I thought I was going to die here," Dougie said.

Ranger and I exchanged glances. If we hadn't intervened they most likely would have. Sophia wouldn't have turned them loose after kidnapping and torturing them.

We wrapped them in the sheets and got them upstairs. I went to the kitchen to call for police and couldn't believe what I was seeing. A pair of cuffs hung from the refrigerator. The refrigerator door was smeared with blood. The women were gone.

Ranger stood behind me. "Probably gnawed her hand off," he said.

I dialed 911 and ten minutes later a patrol

car angled into the curb. It was followed by a second car and EMS.

We didn't leave Richmond until early evening. Mooner and Dougie were hydrated and dosed with antibiotics. Ranger's arm was sutured and dressed. We'd spent a lot of time with the police. Difficult to explain some of the story. We neglected to mention the pig heart en route from Trenton. And we hadn't muddied the waters with Grandma's kidnapping. Dougie's 'Vette was found locked in Sophia's garage. It would be shipped back to Trenton later in the week.

Ranger gave me the keys to the Mercedes when we left the hospital. "Don't attract attention," he said. "Wouldn't want the police to look too closely at this car."

Dougie and Mooner, dressed in new sweats and sneakers, were bundled into the backseat, looking clean and relieved to be out of the cellar.

The ride back was quiet. Dougie and Mooner instantly fell asleep. Ranger went into his zone. If I'd been more alert I might have used the time to sort through my life. As it was I had to concentrate on the road, working not to drift off to autopilot.

I opened my apartment door half expecting to find Benny and Ziggy. Instead I found quiet. Blissful quiet. I locked the door behind me and collapsed on the couch.

I woke up three hours later and stumbled out to the kitchen. I dropped a cracker and a grape into Rex's cage and apologized. Not only was I a slut lusting after two men, I was a bad hamster mother.

My answering machine was furiously blinking. Most of the messages were from my mother. Two were from Morelli. One was from Tina's Bridal Shoppe telling me my gown was in. A message from Ranger telling me Tank had left my bike in my lot, advising me to be careful. Sophia and Christina were out there somewhere.

The last message was from Vinnie. "Congratulations, you got your grandmother back. And now I hear you got Mooner and Dougie back. Do you know who's missing? Eddie DeChooch. Remember him? He's the guy *I* want you to get back. He's the guy who's gonna bankrupt me if you don't drag his decrepit ass back to jail. He's old, for crissake. He's blind. He can't hear. He can't take a piss without help. And you can't catch him. What's the problem here?"

Crap. Eddie DeChooch. I'd actually forgotten about him. He was staying in a house somewhere. It had a garage that opened to a basement. And from the number of rooms Grandma had described it was a pretty big house. Nothing you'd find in the Burg. Nothing you'd find in Ronald's neighborhood, either. What else did I have. Zero. I had no idea how to find Eddie DeChooch. To tell the truth, I didn't even *want* to find Eddie De-Chooch.

It was 4:00 A.M. and I was exhausted. I turned the ringer off on my phone, shuffled into my bedroom, crawled under the covers, and didn't wake up until two in the afternoon.

I HAD A movie in the VCR and a bowl of popcorn on my lap when my pager buzzed.

"Where are you?" Vinnie asked. "I called your house and nobody answered."

"I have the ringer turned off on my phone. I need a day off."

"Your day off is over. I just picked a call up on the police scanner," Vinnie said. "A freight train coming out of Philly rammed a white Cadillac on the Deeter Street crossing. Only happened a few minutes ago. Sounds like the car's squash city. I want you to get down there pronto. With any luck there'll be something identifiable left from what used to be DeChooch."

I looked at the clock in the kitchen. It was almost seven. Twenty-four hours ago I was in Richmond, getting ready to drive home. It was like a bad dream. Hard to believe.

I grabbed my bag and the bike keys and shoved what was left of a sandwich into my mouth. DeChooch wasn't my favorite person but I didn't necessarily want him run over by a train. On the other hand, it would make my life better. I rolled my eyes as I barreled through the lobby. I was going straight to hell for thinking a thought like that.

It took me twenty minutes to get to Deeter Street. Much of the area was blocked off by police cars and emergency vehicles. I parked three blocks away and walked the rest. Crime-scene tape was going up as I approached. Not so much to preserve the scene as to keep the gawkers back. I scanned the crowd for a familiar face, searching out someone who could get me inside. I spotted Carl Costanza, standing with several uniformed cops. They'd responded to the call and now were one step above the gawkers, looking at the wreck, shaking their heads. Chief Joe Juniak was with them.

I pushed my way through to Carl and Juniak, trying not to look too closely at the smashed car, not wanting to see severed limbs lying about.

"Hey," Carl said when he saw me. "I've been expecting you. It's a white Cadillac. Used to be, anyway."

"Has it been identified?"

"No. The plates aren't visible."

"Anybody in the car?"

"Hard to tell. The car's only about two feet high. Got flipped over and compacted. The fire department has their infrared out, trying to detect body heat."

I gave an involuntary shiver. "Ick."

"Yeah. I know what you mean. I was the second on the scene. I took one look at the Cadillac and my nuts went north."

I couldn't see much of the car from where I was standing. That was fine by me now that I knew the extent of the destruction. It had been hit by a freight train and the train didn't look like it had sustained any damage. From what I could see it hadn't derailed.

"Has anyone called Mary Maggie Mason?" I asked. "If this is the car Eddie

DeChooch was driving, Mary Maggie is the owner."

"I doubt anyone's called her," Costanza said. "I don't think we're that organized yet."

Somewhere in my possession was Mary Maggie's address and phone number. I pawed through the loose change, gum wrappers, nail file, breath mints, and other assorted flotsam that collects in the bottom of my bag and finally found what I was looking for.

Mary Maggie answered on the second ring.

"It's Stephanie Plum," I told her. "Have you gotten your car back yet?"

"No."

"There's been a train crash involving a white Cadillac. I thought you might want to get down here and see if you can ID the car."

"Was anyone injured?"

"It's too early to tell. They're working on the wreckage now."

I gave her the location and told her I'd look for her.

"I hear you and Mary Maggie are buddies," Costanza said. "I hear you roll around in the mud together."

"Yeah," I said, "I'm thinking of making a career change."

"Better rethink that. I'm told The Snake Pit is closing down. The word is that it's been in the red for two years."

"That's impossible. It was packed."

"A place like that makes its money on the booze, and people aren't drinking enough. They come in and buy the cover and that's it. They know if they drink too much they're going to get tagged and maybe lose their license. That's why Pinwheel Soba got out. He opened an operation in South Beach where he has a walk-in crowd. Dave Vincent doesn't care. This was a lark for him. He makes his money on stuff you don't want to know about."

"So Eddie DeChooch isn't making any money on his investment?"

"Don't know. These guys skim off the top, but my guess is DeChooch isn't getting a lot."

Tom Bell was the primary on the Loretta Ricci case, and it looked like he pulled this one, too. He was one of several plainclothes cops milling around the car and the train engine. He turned and walked toward us.

"Anyone in the car?" I asked.

"Can't tell. There's so much heat from the train engine we can't get a good read from the heat-seeker. We're going to have to wait until the engine cools or we get the car off the track and opened up. And that's going to take a while. Part of it's caught under the engine. We're waiting for equipment to get here. What we know is there's no one *alive* in the car. And to answer your next question, we haven't been able to read the plate, so we don't know if it's the car DeChooch was driving."

Being Morelli's girlfriend has its rewards. I'm afforded special courtesies, like sometimes getting my questions answered.

The Deeter Street crossing has bells and a gate. We were standing about an eighth of a mile away because that's how far the car got pushed. The train was long and stretched beyond Deeter Street. I could see from where I stood that the gates were still down. I suppose it's possible that they malfunctioned and came down after the accident. My better guess is that the car was stopped on the tracks deliberately and was waiting for the train to hit.

I caught a glimpse of Mary Maggie on the far side of the street and waved to her. She worked her way through the curious and joined me. She got her first distant look at the car and her face went pale.

"Omigod," she said, eyes wide, the shock obvious on her face.

I introduced Tom to Mary Maggie and explained her possible ownership.

"If we bring you closer do you think you might be able to tell if it's your car?" Tom asked.

"Is there anyone in it?"

"We don't know. We can't see anyone. It's possible that it's empty. But we just don't know."

"I'm going to be sick," Mary Maggie said.

Everyone mobilized. Water, ammonia capsules, paper bag. I don't know where it all came from. Cops can move fast when faced with a nauseous mud wrestler.

After Mary Maggie stopped sweating and she got some color back to her face, Bell walked her closer to the car. Costanza and I followed a couple paces behind. I didn't especially want to see the carnage, but I didn't want to miss anything, either.

We all stopped about ten feet from the wreck. The train engine was still but Bell was right, the engine was radiating a lot of heat. The sheer mass of the engine was intimidating even at rest.

Mary Maggie stared at what was left of the Cadillac and swayed in place. "It's my car," she said. "I think."

"How can you tell?" Bell asked.

"I can see some of the upholstery fabric. My uncle had the car seats reupholstered in blue. It wasn't the normal upholstery fabric."

"Anything else?"

Mary Maggie shook her head. "I don't think so. There's not much left to see."

We all walked back and huddled again. Some trucks pulled up with heavy rescue equipment and started to work on the Cadillac. They had a jaws of life standing by, but they were using acetylene torches to cut the car away from the train. It was getting dark, and portable spots had been brought to light the scene, giving it an eerie, movie-lot feel.

I felt a tug on my sleeve and turned to find Grandma Mazur standing on tiptoe trying to get a better view of the accident. Mabel Pritchet was with her.

"Have you ever seen such a thing?" Grandma said. "I heard on the radio that a train hit a white Cadillac, and I got Mabel to drive me over. Is it Chooch's car?"

"We don't know for sure, but we think it might be."

I introduced Grandma to Mary Maggie.

"It's a real pleasure," Grandma said. "I'm a big admirer of wrestling." She looked back at the Cadillac. "Be a shame if DeChooch is in there. He's such a cutie." Grandma leaned across me to Mary Maggie. "Did you know I was kidnapped? I had a bag over my head and everything."

"It must have been scary," Mary Maggie said.

"Well, in the beginning I thought Choochy was just trying something kinky. He has this problem with his penis, you know. It don't do nothing. Just lays there like it was dead. But then it turned out I was kidnapped. Isn't that something? First off we drove around some. And then I could hear us going into a garage that had an automatic door. And the garage was attached to one of those finished-off basements with a couple bedrooms and a television room. And the television room had chairs that were done in leopard print."

"I know that house," Mary Maggie said. "I went to a party there once. There's a little kitchen downstairs, too, right? And the downstairs bathroom has wallpaper that's tropical birds."

"That's right," Grandma said. "It was all jungle motif. Chooch said Elvis used to have a jungle room, too."

I couldn't believe I was hearing this. Mary Maggie knew DeChooch's secret hideout. And now I probably didn't need it.

"Who owns the house?" I asked.

"Pinwheel Soba."

"I thought he moved to Florida."

"He did, but he kept the house. They have relatives here, so they spend part of the year in Florida and part of the year in Trenton."

There was the sound of tearing metal, and the Cadillac was separated from the train. We watched in silence for several tense minutes while the top was peeled back. Tom Bell stood close to the car. After a moment he turned and looked at me and mouthed the word *empty*.

"He's not in there," I said. And we all choked on tears of relief. I'm not sure why. Eddie DeChooch wasn't such a great person. But then maybe no one is bad enough to deserve getting made into a pizza by a train.

* * *

I CALLED MORELLI when I got home. "Did you hear about DeChooch?"

"Yeah, Tom Bell called."

"This was really strange. I think De-Chooch just left the car there to get run over."

"Tom thought that, too."

"Why would DeChooch do that?"

"Because he's crazy?"

I didn't think DeChooch was crazy. You want to see crazy? Take a look at Sophia. DeChooch had problems, physical and emotional. And his life was snowballing out of control. A few things went wrong and he tried to fix them and it just kept getting worse instead of better. I could see how everything was related now with the exception of Loretta Ricci and the Cadillac on the train tracks.

"One good thing happened tonight," I said. "Grandma showed up and started talking to Mary Maggie, telling her about the kidnapping. Grandma described the house De-Chooch took her to. And Mary Maggie said it sounded like Pinwheel Soba's house."

"Soba lived in Ewing, off Olden Avenue. We have a file on him."

"That makes sense. I've seen DeChooch

in that area. I always assumed Ronald was the draw, but maybe he was going to Soba's house. Can you get me the address?"

"No."

"What do you mean, no?"

"I don't want you going over there, prowling around. DeChooch is unstable."

"It's my job."

"Don't get me started on your job."

"You didn't think my job was so bad when we first got together."

"That was different. It wasn't like you were going to be the mother of my children."

"I don't know if I even want children."

"Christ," Morelli said. "Don't ever say that to my mother or my grandmother. They'll put a contract out on you."

"You're really not going to give me the address?"

"No."

"I'll get it some other way."

"Fine," Morelli said. "I want no part of this."

"You're going to tell Tom Bell, aren't you?"

"Yes. Leave this to the police."

"This is war," I said to Morelli.

"Oh boy," he said. "War again."

FOURTEEN

I HUNG UP on Morelli and got the address from Mary Maggie. Now I had a problem. I had no one to partner with me. It was Saturday night and Lula was out on a date. Ranger would respond, but I didn't want to impose on him so soon after the shooting. And besides, there was the price to pay. I got heart palpitations thinking about it. When I was close to him and the body chemistry was working I wanted him bad. When there was distance between us the possibility of sleeping with Ranger scared the hell out of me.

If I waited until tomorrow I'd be one step

behind the police. There was one person left, but the thought of working a case with him made me break out in a cold sweat. That person was Vinnie. When Vinnie had started the agency he'd done all his own apprehensions. As the business grew he'd added staff and put himself behind the desk. He still does the occasional apprehension, but it isn't his favorite thing. Vinnie is a good bail bondsman, but it's rumored that Vinnie isn't the world's most ethical bounty hunter.

I looked at the clock. I had to make a decision. I didn't want to procrastinate so long that I had to roust Vinnie out of bed.

I took a deep breath and dialed.

"I've got a lead on DeChooch," I told Vinnie. "I'd like to check it out but I haven't got anyone to do backup for me."

"Meet me at the office in a half hour."

I PARKED THE bike in the back, next to Vinnie's midnight blue Cadillac. Lights were on inside and the back door was open. Vinnie was strapping a gun to his leg when I strolled in. He was in requisite bounty hunter black, complete with Kevlar vest. I, on the other hand, was dressed in jeans and olive-drab T-shirt with a navy flannel shirt worn jacket-style. My gun was home in the cookie jar. I hoped Vinnie didn't ask about the gun. I hate the gun.

He tossed a vest at me, and I shrugged into it.

"I swear," he said, looking at me, "I don't know how you ever make a capture."

"Luck," I told him.

I handed him the address and followed him to the car. I'd never gone out with Vinnie before, and it was a strange sensation. Our relationship has always been adversarial. We know too much about each other to ever be friends. And we know we would both be willing to use that knowledge in ruthless ways if pushed too far. Okay, the truth is I'm not all that ruthless. But I can deliver a good threat. Maybe the same is true of Vinnie.

Soba's house was in a neighborhood that had probably originated in the seventies. Lots were large and trees had matured. The houses were classic split foyer with two-car garages and fenced backyards to corral dogs and kids. Most houses had lights on, and I imagined adults were sleeping in front of televisions and kids were in bedrooms doing homework or surfing the Net.

Vinnie idled across from Soba's house.

"You're sure this is the place?" Vinnie asked.

"Mary Maggie said she'd been to a party here and it matched the description Grandma gave."

"Oh boy," Vinnie said, "I'm going to break into a house on the say-so of a mud wrestler. Not just any house, either. Pinwheel Soba's house." He drove halfway around the block and parked. We got out and walked back to the house. We stood for a moment on the sidewalk, looking at the surrounding houses, listening for sounds that might indicate people outdoors.

"There are black shutters on the small downstairs windows," I said to Vinnie. "They're closed shut just as Grandma described."

"Okay," Vinnie said, "we're going in, and here are the possibilities. We could have the wrong house, in which case we're in trouble for scaring the shit out of some innocent dumb-ass family. Or we could have the right house and crazy DeChooch shoots at us."

"I'm glad you listed it out for me. I feel much better now."

"Do you have a plan?" Vinnie wanted to know.

"Yeah. How about if you go up and ring the doorbell and see if anyone's home. I'll wait here and do backup."

"I've got a better idea. How about if you bend over and I'll *show* you *my* plan."

"There aren't any lights on in this house," I said. "I don't think anyone's in there."

"They could be asleep."

"They could be dead."

"Now that would be a good thing," Vinnie said. "Dead people don't shoot at you."

I started across the grass. "Let's see if there are any lights on in back."

"Remind me not to take any more bonds out on old guys. You can't count on them. They don't think normal. They skip a couple pills and next thing they're stashing stiffs in their shed and kidnapping old ladies."

"No lights on in the back, either," I said. "Now what? Are you any good at breaking and entering?"

Vinnie took a couple pairs of disposable rubber gloves from his pocket and we both snapped them on.

"I've had some experience with breaking and entering," he said. He walked to the back door and tried the handle. Locked. He turned and looked at me and smiled. "Piece of cake."

"You can pick the lock?"

"No, I can stick my hand through the hole where a pane of glass used to be."

I moved up close behind Vinnie. Sure enough, one of the windows on the door had been removed.

"Guess DeChooch lost his key," Vinnie said.

Yeah. Like he ever had it. Pretty clever of him to think to use Soba's vacant house.

Vinnie turned the doorknob from the inside and opened the door. "Show time," he whispered.

I had my flashlight in hand and my heart was beating faster than normal. Not exactly racing yet, but definitely jogging.

We did a quick search of the upstairs by penlight and decided the upstairs hadn't been inhabited by DeChooch. The kitchen was unused, the refrigerator turned off and propped open. The bedrooms, living room, and dining room were undisturbed, every pillow in place, crystal vases on tables waiting for flowers. Pinwheel Soba lived well.

Between the outside shutters and heavy interior curtains we were able to turn the lights on downstairs. It was exactly as Grandma and Maggie had described. Tarzan country. Leopard-spotted and zebra-striped upholstered furniture. And then just to confuse things, wallpaper with birds found only in South and Central America.

The refrigerator was shut off and empty but still cool inside. Closets were empty. Drawers were empty. The sponge in the dish drain stored under the sink was still damp.

"We just missed him," Vinnie said. "He's gone and it looks to me like he's not coming back."

We shut the lights off, and we were about to leave when we heard the automatic garage door roll up. We were in the finished part of the basement. A short hallway and a foyer with stairs going up stood between us and the garage. The door leading to the garage was closed. A bar of light appeared under the closed door.

"Oh shit!" Vinnie whispered.

The door to the garage opened and DeChooch stood outlined in the light. He moved into the foyer and flipped the lights on at the base of the stairs and stared directly at us. We were all frozen like deer in headlights. It lasted for several seconds before he flipped the lights off and ran up the stairs. I assumed he was going for the first-floor front door, but he ran past it and into the kitchen, making pretty good time for an old guy.

Vinnie and I lunged up the stairs after him, knocking into each other in the dark. We reached the top of the stairs and off to my right I saw the flash of gunfire and *BLAM*, DeChooch took a potshot at us. I shrieked and dropped to the ground and scuttled for cover.

"Bond enforcement," Vinnie yelled. "Drop the gun, DeChooch, you dumb old fuck!"

DeChooch answered with another shot. I heard something crash and Vinnie did more swearing. And then Vinnie opened fire.

I was behind the couch with my hands over my head. Vinnie and DeChooch were doing blind-man's buff target practice in the dark. Vinnie carried a Glock holding fourteen rounds. I don't know what DeChooch had, but between the two of them it sounded like machine-gun fire. There was a pause and then I heard Vinnie's clip fall to the floor and a new clip get shoved into place. At least I thought it was Vinnie. Hard to tell since I was still cowering behind the couch.

The silence felt even more deafening than the gunfire. I poked my head out and squinted into the smoky blackness. "Hello?"

"I've lost DeChooch," Vinnie whispered.

"Maybe you killed him."

"Wait a minute. What's that noise?"

It was the automatic garage door opening.

"Fuck!" Vinnie yelled. He ran for the stairs, slipped on the first step in the dark, and went head over ass to the landing. He scrambled to his feet, threw the front door open, and aimed. I could hear wheels squeal and Vinnie slammed the door shut. *"Damn, piss, shit, fuck!"* Vinnie said, stamping around the foyer, stomping upstairs. "I don't believe he got away! He slipped past me when I was reloading. *Fuck, fuck, fuck!"*

The *fucks* being said with such vehemence, I was afraid he was going to pop a vein in his head.

He flicked a light on and we both looked around. Lamps were smashed, walls and ceilings were cratered, upholstery had been torn apart by bullet holes.

"Holy crap," Vinnie said. "This looks like a war zone."

Sirens wailed in the distance. Police.

"I'm out of here," Vinnie said.

"I don't know if it's a good idea to run from the police."

"I'm not running from the police," Vinnie said, taking the stairs two at a time. "I'm running from Pinwheel Soba. I think it'd be a real good idea for us to keep this to ourselves."

Good point.

We streaked across the darkest part of the yard and cut through the property behind Soba's house. Porch lights were going on up and down the block. Dogs were barking. And Vinnie and I were gasping for air, sprinting between bushes. When the car was just a front yard away we emerged from the shadows and sedately walked the distance. All activity was halfway around the block in front of Soba's house.

"This is why you never park in front of the house you're going to hit," Vinnie said.

Something to remember.

We got in the car. Vinnie calmly turned the key in the ignition, and we drove off like two respectable, responsible citizens. We got to the corner and Vinnie looked down.

"Jesus," he said, "I've got a boner."

* * *

SUNLIGHT WAS PEEKING from between my bedroom curtains and I was thinking about getting up when someone knocked on my door. It took me a minute to find my clothes, and in the meantime the knocking turned to yelling.

"Hey Steph, are you there? It's Mooner and Dougie."

I opened the door to them and they reminded me of Bob, all happy-faced and filled with goofy energy.

"We brought you doughnuts," Dougie said, handing me a big white bag. "And we have something to tell you."

"Yeah," Mooner said, "wait until you hear this. This is so cool. Dougie and me were like, talking. And we figured out what happened to the heart."

I put the doughnut bag on the kitchen counter and we all helped ourselves.

"It was the dog," Mooner said. "Mrs. Belski's dog, Spotty, ate Louie D's heart."

I froze with a doughnut halfway to my mouth.

"See, DeChooch made a deal with the Dougster to take the heart to Richmond," Mooner said. "But DeChooch didn't tell the

Dougster anything except that the cooler
had to be delivered to Mrs. D. So the Dougster put the cooler on the front seat of the
Batmobile, figuring he'd take off first thing in
the morning. Only problem was my roommate Huey and me got to wanting some Ben
& Jerry's Cherry Garcia at about midnight
and borrowed the Batmobile for our quest.
Since the Batmobile only has two seats I put
the cooler on the back stoop."

Dougie was grinning. "This is so excellent," he said.

"So anyway, Huey and me brought the car
back super early the next morning because
Huey had to be at work at Shoppers Warehouse. I dropped Huey off, and when I
parked the car in Dougie's yard the cooler
was tipped over and Spotty was chewing on
something. I didn't think much. I mean,
Spotty's always in the garbage. So I put the
cooler back in the car and went home to
watch some morning television. Katie Couric
is like, so cute."

"And then I took the empty cooler to Richmond," Dougie said.

"Spotty ate Louie D's heart," I said.

"That's it," Mooner said. He finished his

doughnut and wiped his hands on his shirt. "Well, we've got to go. Things to do."

"Thanks for the doughnuts."

"Hey, no problemo."

I stood in the kitchen for ten minutes, trying to come to terms with this new information, wondering if it meant something in the larger scheme of things. Is this what happens when you irreparably screw up your karma? A dog eats your heart? I couldn't reach any conclusions, so I decided to take a shower and see if that helped.

I locked the door and shuffled off to the bathroom. I got as far as the living room when there was another knock, and before I could get to the door it was opened with enough force to make the security chain *kaching* into place and then break loose from its moorings. This was followed by cussing, which I recognized as coming from Morelli.

"Good morning," I said, eyeing the chain, which was dangling uselessly.

"Not by any stretch of the imagination is it a good morning," Morelli said. His eyes were dark and narrowed and his mouth set tight. "You didn't go over to Pinwheel Soba's house last night, did you?"

"No," I said, shaking my head. "Not me."

"Good. That's what I thought . . . because some idiot went in there and destroyed it. Shot the shit out of it. In fact, it's suspected there were two people having the gunfight of the century in there. And I knew you wouldn't be that fucking stupid."

"Got that right," I said.

"Jesus Christ, Stephanie," he yelled, "what were you thinking? What the hell was going on over there?"

"Wasn't me, remember?"

"Oh yeah. I forgot. Well then, what do you suppose *someone else* was doing in Soba's house?"

"I imagine they were looking for De-Chooch. And then maybe they found De-Chooch and an altercation arose."

"And DeChooch escaped?"

"That would be my guess."

"Good thing no prints were found other than DeChooch, because otherwise *whoever* was fucking stupid enough to shoot up Soba's house would not only be in trouble with the police but would answer to Soba."

I was starting to get annoyed that he was still yelling at me. "Good thing," I said with my PMS voice. "Anything else?"

"Yes, there's something else. I ran into Dougie and Mooner in the parking lot. They told me you and Ranger rescued them."

"So?"

"In Richmond."

"So?"

"And Ranger got shot?"

"Flesh wound."

Morelli pressed his lips tighter together. "Jesus."

"I was worried the pig heart would be discovered and revenge would be taken out on Mooner and Dougie."

"Very admirable, but it doesn't make me feel any better. Christ, I'm getting an ulcer. You've got me drinking bottles of Maalox. I hate this. I hate going through the day wondering what harebrained scheme you're involved in, wondering who's shooting at you."

"That's so hypocritical. You're a cop."

"I *never* get shot at. The only time I have to worry about getting shot is when I'm with you."

"So what are you saying?"

"I'm saying you're going to have to choose between me or the job."

"Well, guess what, I'm not spending the

rest of my life with someone who gives me ultimatums."

"Fine."

"Fine."

And he left, slamming the door behind him. I like to think I'm a pretty stable person, but this was too much. I cried until I was totally cried out and then I ate three dough-nuts and took a shower. I toweled off and still felt overwhelmed so I decided to bleach my hair blond. Change is good, right?

"I WANT IT blond," I told Mr. Arnold, the only hairdresser I could find open on a Sunday. "Platinum blond. I want to look like Marilyn."

"Darling," Arnold said, "with your hair you won't look like Marilyn. You'll look like Art Garfunkel."

"Just do it."

MR. MORGANSTERN WAS in the lobby when I got back. "Whoa," he said, "you look like that singer . . . what's the name?"

"Garfunkel?"

"No. The one with the breasts like ice-cream cones."

"Madonna."

"Yep. That's the one."

I let myself into my apartment and went straight to the bathroom and looked at my hair in the mirror. I liked it. It was different. Classy in a slutty sort of way.

I had a stack of mail on the kitchen counter that I'd been avoiding. I got a beer to celebrate my new hair, and I sorted through the mail. Bills, bills, bills. I thumbed through my checkbook. Not enough money. I needed to capture DeChooch.

My guess was DeChooch had a money problem, too. No vig coming in anymore. No money from the cigarette fiasco. Little to no money from The Snake Pit. And now he had no car and no place to live. Correction, he didn't have the Cadillac. He drove away in something. I didn't get a good look at it.

There were four messages on my machine. I hadn't checked them because I was afraid they were from Joe. I suspect the truth is that neither of us is ready to get married. And instead of facing the real issue we're finding ways to sabotage the relationship. We don't talk about important things like kids and jobs. We each take a stand and yell at each other.

Maybe it's just not the right time for us to be married. I don't want to be a bounty hunter for the rest of my life, but I certainly don't want to be a housewife right now. And I really don't want to be married to someone who gives me ultimatums.

And maybe Joe needs to examine what he wants from a wife. He was raised in a traditional Italian household with a stay-at-home mother and domineering father. If he wants a wife who will fit into that mold, I'm not for him. I might be a stay-at-home mother someday, but I'll always be trying to fly off the garage roof. That's just who I am.

So let's see some guts, Blondie, I told myself. This is the new and improved Stephanie. Check out those messages. Be fearless.

I pulled up the first one and it was from my mother.

"Stephanie? This is your mother. I have a nice roast for tonight. And cupcakes for dessert. With sprinkles. The girls like cupcakes."

The second was another reminder from the bridal shop that my gown was in.

The third was from Ranger with an update on Sophia and Christina. Christina had turned up at the hospital with every bone in her hand broken. Her sister had smashed it with a meat mallet to get it out of the cuff.

Unable to stand the pain, Christina turned herself in, but Sophia was still at large.

The fourth message was from Vinnie. The charges had been dropped against Melvin Baylor, and Melvin had bought himself a one-way ticket to Arizona. Apparently his ex-wife had witnessed Melvin's berserk attack on his car and had gotten frightened. If Melvin would do that to his car, there was no telling what Melvin might do next. So she had her mother drop the charges, and she made a cash settlement with Melvin. Sometimes crazy is good.

Those were the messages. None from Morelli. Funny thing how a woman's mind works. Now I was bummed because Morelli hadn't called.

I told my mother I'd be there for dinner. And then I told Tina I'd decided not to take the gown. I hung up from Tina and felt twenty pounds lighter. Mooner and Dougie were okay. Grandma was okay. I was a blonde and I didn't have a wedding gown. Overlooking my problems with Morelli, life couldn't get much better.

I took a short nap before heading for my parents' house. When I woke up my hair was doing strange things so I took a shower.

After washing and drying my hair I looked like Art Garfunkel. But more. It was as if my hair had exploded.

"I don't care," I said to my reflection in the mirror. "I'm the new and improved Stephanie." It was a lie, of course. Jersey girls care.

I put on a pair of new black jeans, black boots, and a short-sleeved ribbed red sweater. I walked into the living room and found Benny and Ziggy sitting on the couch.

"We heard the shower going so we didn't want to disturb you," Benny said.

"Yeah," Ziggy said, "and you should get your security chain fixed. No telling who might come in."

"We just came back from Louie D's funeral and we heard all about how you found the fruity little guy and his friend. That was a terrible thing Sophia did."

"Even when Louie was alive she was crazy," Ziggy said. "You'd never want to turn your back on her. She doesn't think right."

"And you should tell Ranger he has our best wishes. We hope his arm isn't too bad."

"Was Louie D buried with his heart?"

"Ronald took it straight to the undertaker and they put it in and sewed him up good as new. And then Ronald followed the hearse back here to Trenton for burial today."

"No Sophia?"

"There were flowers on the grave, but she didn't come to the ceremony." He shook his head. "Lots of police in attendance. It ruined the privacy."

"I guess you're still looking for Choochy," Benny said. "You should be careful of him. He's a little . . ." Benny made a circling motion against his head with his index finger to denote *screw loose*. "Not like Sophia, though. Chooch is an okay person at heart."

"It's the stroke and the stress," Ziggy said. "Stress shouldn't be underestimated. If you need help with Choochy you should call us. Maybe we could do something."

Benny nodded his head. I should call them.

"Your hair looks nice," Ziggy said. "You got a perm, right?"

They stood and Benny gave me a box. "I got some peanut brittle for you. Estelle brought it back from Virginia."

"You can't buy peanut brittle up here like they got in Virginia," Ziggy said.

I thanked them for the peanut brittle and

closed the door behind them. I gave them five minutes to clear the building, and then I grabbed my black leather jacket and bag and locked up.

MY MOTHER LOOKED past me when she came to the door. "Where's Joe? Where's your car?"

"I traded my car in for the bike."

"That bike at the curb?"

I nodded.

"It looks like one of those Hell's Angels bikes."

"It's a Harley."

That's when it hit her. The hair. Her eyes opened wide and her mouth dropped open. "Your hair," she whispered.

"I thought I'd try something new."

"My God, you look like that singer . . ."

"Madonna?"

"Art Garfunkel."

I left my helmet, jacket, and bag in the hall closet and took my seat at the table.

"You got here right in time," Grandma said. "Holy cats! Look at you. You look just like that singer."

"I know," I snapped. *"I know."*

"Where's Joseph?" my mother said. "I thought he was coming to dinner."

"We've sort of . . . broken up."

Everyone stopped eating, except for my father. My father used the opportunity to take more potatoes.

"That's impossible," my mother said. "You have a gown."

"I canceled the gown."

"Does Joseph know this?"

"Yep." I tried to act casual, digging in to my meal, asking my sister to pass the green beans. I can get through this, I thought. I'm a blonde. I can do anything.

"It's the hair, isn't it?" my mother asked. "He called the wedding off because of the hair."

"*I* called the wedding off. And I don't want to talk about it."

The doorbell rang and Valerie jumped up. "That's for me. I have a date."

"A date!" my mother said. "That's wonderful. You've been here such a short time and already you have a date."

I did some mental eye rolling. My sister is clueless. This is what happens when you grow up as the good girl. You never learn the value of lies and deceit. I *never* brought my dates home. You meet dates at the mall so you don't give your parents a stroke when your date shows up with tattoos and tongue studs. Or, in this case, is a lesbian.

"This is Janeane," Valerie said, introducing a short, dark-haired woman. "I met her when I interviewed at the bank. I didn't get the job but Janeane asked me out."

"She's a woman," my mother said.

"Yes, we're lesbians," Valerie said.

My mother fainted. *Crash*. Flat out on the floor.

Everyone jumped up and ran to my mother.

She opened her eyes but didn't move a muscle for a good thirty seconds. Then she yelled out, "A lesbian! Mother of God. Frank, your daughter's a lesbian."

My father squinted at Valerie. "Is that my tie you've got on?"

"You have a lot of nerve," my mother said, still on her back on the floor. "All those years when you were normal and had a husband, you lived in California. And now that you're here you turn into a lesbian. Isn't it enough your sister shoots people? What kind of a family is this?"

"I hardly ever shoot anyone," I said.

"I bet there are lots of good things to being a lesbian," Grandma said. "If you marry a lesbian you never have to worry about someone leaving the toilet seat up."

I got under one arm and Valerie got under the other and we got my mother to her feet.

"There you go," Valerie said, all chipper. "Feeling better?"

"Better?" my mother said. "Better?"

"Well, we're going now," Valerie said, retreating to the foyer. "Don't wait up. I've got a key."

My mother excused herself, went to the kitchen, and smashed another plate.

"I've never known her to smash plates," I said to Grandma.

"I'm going to lock up all the knives tonight, just to be safe," Grandma said.

I followed my mother into the kitchen and helped pick up the pieces.

"It slipped out of my hand," my mother said.

"That's what I thought."

Nothing ever seems to change in my parents' house. The kitchen feels just as it did when I was a little girl. The walls get repainted and the curtains replaced. New linoleum was laid down last year. Appliances get swapped out as they became unrepairable. That's the extent of the renovation. My mother has been cooking potatoes in the same pot for thirty-five years. The smells are the same, too. Cabbage, applesauce, chocolate pudding, roast lamb. And the rituals are the same. Sitting at the small kitchen table for lunch.

Valerie and I did our homework on the kitchen table, under my mother's watchful eye. And now I imagine Angie and Mary Alice keep my mother company in the kitchen.

It's hard to feel like a grown-up when nothing ever changes in your mother's kitchen. It's like time stands still. I come into the kitchen and I want my sandwiches cut into triangles.

"Do you ever get tired of your life?" I asked my mother. "Is there ever a time when you'd like to do something new?"

"You mean like get in the car and just keep driving until I get to the Pacific Ocean? Or take a wrecking ball to this kitchen? Or divorce your father and marry Tom Jones? No, I never think about those things." She took the top off the cake plate and looked at her cupcakes. Half chocolate with white icing and half yellow with chocolate icing. Multicolored spinkles on the white icing. She mumbled something that sounded a little like *fucking cupcakes.*

"What?" I asked. "I couldn't hear you."

"I didn't say anything. Just go in and sit down."

"I was hoping you could give me a ride to the funeral parlor tonight," Grandma said to me. "Rusty Kuharchek is laid out at Stiva's. I went to school with Rusty. It's going to be a real good viewing."

It wasn't like I had anything else to do. "Sure," I said, "but you'll have to wear slacks. I've got the Harley."

"A Harley? Since when do you have a Harley?" Grandma wanted to know.

"There was a problem with my car, so Vinnie loaned me a motorcycle."

"You are *not* taking your grandmother on a motorcycle," my mother said. "She'll fall off and kill herself."

My father very wisely didn't say anything.

"She'll be okay," I said. "I've got an extra helmet."

"You're responsible," my mother said. "If anything happens to her, *you're* the one who's going to be visiting her in the nursing home."

"Maybe I could get a motorcycle," Grandma said. "When they take away your car driving license does that include motorcycles?"

"*Yes!*" we all said in unison. No one wanted Grandma Mazur back on the road.

Mary Alice had been eating her dinner with her face down on her plate because horses don't have hands. When she picked her face up it was covered with smashed potatoes and gravy. "What's a lesbian?" she asked.

We all sat frozen.

"It's when girls have girlfriends instead of boyfriends," Grandma said.

Angie reached for her milk. "Homosexuality is thought to be the result of an aberrant chromosome."

"I was going to say that next," Grandma said.

"What about horses?" Mary Alice asked. "Are there lesbian horses?"

We all looked at one another. We were stumped.

I stood at my seat. "Who wants a cupcake?"

FIFTEEN

GRANDMA USUALLY GETS dressed up for an evening viewing. She has a preference for black patent pumps and swirly skirts just in case there's some beefcake present. As a concession to the motorcycle, she was wearing slacks and tennis shoes tonight.

"I need some biker clothes," she said. "I just got my Social Security check, and first thing tomorrow I'm going shopping, now that I know you've got this Harley."

I straddled the bike. And my father helped Grandma get on behind me. I turned the key in the ignition, revved the engine, and the vibrations rumbled through the pipes.

"Ready?" I yelled at Grandma.

"Ready," she yelled back.

I went straight up Roosevelt Street to Hamilton Avenue, and in a short time we were at Stiva's, parked in the lot.

I helped Grandma off and removed her helmet. She stepped away from the bike and straightened her clothes. "I can see why people like these Harleys," she said. "They really wake you up *down there*, don't they?"

Rusty Kuharchek was in Slumber Room number three, the positioning of Rusty indicating that his relatives had cheaped out on his casket. Horrific deaths and those purchasing the top-of-the-line hand-carved, lead-lined, mahogany eternity vessel got laid out in room number one.

I left Grandma with Rusty and told her I'd be back at Stiva's in an hour and I'd meet her by the cookie table.

It was a nice night, and I wanted to walk. I wandered down Hamilton and cut into the Burg. It wasn't quite dark. In another month people would be sitting on porches at this time of night. I told myself I was walking to relax, maybe to think about things. But before long I found myself standing in front of Eddie DeChooch's house, and I wasn't feeling relaxed at all. I was feeling annoyed that I hadn't made my capture.

The DeChooch half looked utterly abandoned. The Marguchi half was blasting out a game show. I marched up to Mrs. Marguchi's door and knocked.

"What a nice surprise," she said when she saw me. "I've been wondering how things are going with you and Chooch."

"He's still out there," I said.

Angela made a *tsch* sound. "He's a wily one."

"Have you seen him? Have you heard any activity next door?"

"It's like he dropped off the face of the earth. I never even hear the phone ringing."

"Maybe I'll just poke around a little."

I walked around the perimeter of the house, looked in the garage, paused at the shed. I had Chooch's house key with me, so I let myself in. There was no sign that DeChooch had visited. A stack of unopened mail sprawled across the kitchen counter.

I knocked on Angela's door again. "Are you taking DeChooch's mail in?"

"Yes. I bring the mail in each day and make sure everything's okay over there. I don't know what else to do. I thought Ronald might have come around to get the mail, but I haven't seen him."

When I got back to Stiva's, Grandma was at the cookie table talking to Mooner and Dougie.

"Dude," Mooner said.

"Are you here to see someone?" I asked.

"Negative. We're here for the cookies."

"The hour just zipped by," Grandma said. "There's lots of people here I didn't get to visit with. Are you in a rush to get home?" she asked me.

"We could take you home," Dougie said to Grandma. "We never leave before nine because that's when Stiva puts out the cookies with the chocolate inside."

I was torn. I didn't want to stay, but I didn't know if I could entrust Grandma to Dougie and Mooner.

I took Dougie aside. "I don't want anybody smoking pot."

"No pot," Dougie said.

"And I don't want Grandma going to strip bars."

"No strip bars."

"I don't want her involved in any hijackings, either."

"Hey, I'm a reformed man," Dougie said.

"Okay," I said, "I'm counting on you."

AT TEN O'CLOCK I got a phone call from my mother.

"Where's your grandmother?" she wanted to know. "And why aren't you with her?"

"She was supposed to go home with friends."

"What friends? Have you lost your grand-mother again?"

Damn. "I'll get back to you."

I hung up and another call came in. It was Grandma.

"I've got him!" she said.

"Who?"

"Eddie DeChooch. All of a sudden at the funeral parlor I had this brainstorm, and I knew where Choochy would be tonight."

"Where?"

"Picking up his Social Security check. Everybody in the Burg gets their check on the same day. And it was yesterday, only yesterday DeChooch was busy wrecking his car. So I said to myself he's going to wait until it gets dark, and then he's going to ride by and get his check today. And sure enough that's just what he did."

"Where is he now?"

"Well, that's the complicated part. He went into his house to get his mail and when we tried to arrest him he got a gun and we all got scared and ran away. Except Mooner didn't run fast enough and now he has Mooner."

I thunked my head down on the kitchen counter. I thought it might feel good to just keep banging it like that. *Thunk, thunk, thunk* with my head against the kitchen counter.

"Have you called the police?" I asked.

"We didn't know if that was such a good thing to do, being that Mooner might have some controlled substances on him. I think Dougie mentioned something about a certain package in Mooner's shoe."

Great. "I'll be right there," I said. "Don't do *anything* until I get there."

I grabbed my bag, ran down the hall and the stairs, out the door, and jumped on the bike. I skidded to a stop in Angela Marguchi's driveway and looked around for Grandma, spotting her and Dougie hiding behind a car on the opposite side of the street. They were wearing Super Suits and they had bath towels pinned around their necks like capes.

"Nice touch with the towels," I said.

"We're crime-fighters," Grandma said.

"Are they still in there?" I asked.

"Yes. I've been talking to Chooch on Dougie's cell phone," Grandma said. "He said he'll only release Mooner if we get him a helicopter and then have a plane waiting at Newark to take him to South America. I think he might be drinking."

I punched his number into my cell phone.

"I want to talk to you," I said.

"Never. Not until I get my helicopter."

"You're not going to get a helicopter with Mooner as hostage. Nobody cares if you shoot him. If you let Mooner go, I'll come in and take his place. I'd be a better hostage for a helicopter."

"Okay," DeChooch said. "That makes sense."

As if *any* of this made sense.

Mooner came out dressed in his Super Suit and bath towel. DeChooch kept a gun to his head until I stepped onto the porch.

"This is like, embarrassing," Mooner said. "I mean, how does it look for a superhero crime-fighter to get snatched by an old dude." He looked at DeChooch. "Nothing personal, man."

"Take Grandma home," I said to Mooner. "My mother is worried about her."

"You mean like now?"

"Yes. Now."

Grandma was still across the street and I didn't want to shout at her, so I called her on the cell phone. "I'm going to work this out with Eddie," I said. "You and Mooner and Dougie should go home."

"That doesn't sound like a good idea to me," Grandma said. "I think I should stay."

"Thanks, but this will be easier if I do it myself."

"Should I call the police?"

I looked at DeChooch. He didn't look crazy or angry. He looked tired. If I brought the police in DeChooch might go into defense mode and do something dumb, like shoot me. If I got some quiet talk time with him I might be able to persuade him to come in. "Negative on that," I said.

I disconnected and DeChooch and I remained on the porch until Grandma and Mooner and Dougie left.

"Is she going to call the police?" De-Chooch asked.

"No."

"Think you can bring me in all by your-self?"

"I don't want anyone to get hurt. Me included." I followed him into the house. "You don't really expect a helicopter, do you?"

He made a disgusted gesture with his hand and shuffled into the kitchen. "I just said that to impress Edna. I had to say something. She thinks I'm a big-shot fugitive." He opened the refrigerator. "There's nothing to eat. When my wife was alive there was always something to eat."

I filled the coffeemaker with water and spooned coffee into the filter. I looked through the cupboards and found a box of cookies. I put some cookies on a plate and sat down at the kitchen table with Eddie DeChooch.

"You look tired," I said.

He nodded his head. "I didn't have any place to sleep last night. I was going to pick up my Social Security check tonight and get a hotel room somewhere, but Edna showed up with the two clowns. Nothing goes right for me." He picked at a cookie. "I can't even kill myself. Fucking prostate. I pulled the Cadillac across the tracks. I'm sitting there waiting to die and what happens? I've gotta take a piss. I've *always* gotta take a piss. So I get out and go over to a bush to take a leak and the train comes. What are the chances of that happening? And then I didn't know what to do and I chickened out. Ran away like a fucking coward."

"It was a terrific crash."

"Yeah, I saw it. Boy, he must have pushed that Cadillac a quarter mile."

"Where did you get the new car?"

"Boosted it."

"So you're still good at some things."

"The only things that work on me are my fingers. I can't see. I can't hear. I can't piss."

"You can fix those things."

He pushed the cookie around. "There's some things I can't fix."

"Grandma told me."

He looked up, surprised. "She told you? Aw jeez. Christ. I'm telling you, women are such blabbermouths."

I poured out two cups of coffee and handed one to DeChooch. "Have you seen a doctor about it?"

"I'm not talking to a doctor. Before you know it they're poking around and telling you to get one of them implants. I'm not getting a goddamn penile implant." He shook his head. "I can't believe I'm talking to you about this. Why am I talking to you?"

I smiled at him. "I'm easy to talk to." And also, he had hundred-proof breath. De-Chooch was doing a lot of drinking. "While we're talking, why don't you tell me about Loretta Ricci?"

"Cripes, she was a hot one. She came to bring me one of them Meals-on-Wheels and she was all over me. I kept telling her I wasn't any good for that anymore, but she wouldn't listen. She said she could get any-one to . . . you know, do it. So I figured, what the hell, what have I got to lose, right? Next thing I know she's down there and she's having some luck with it. And then just when I'm thinking it's going to happen she keels over and dies. I guess she gave herself a heart attack from working so hard. I tried to revive her, but she was goddamn dead. I was so pissed off I shot her."

"You could use some anger-management skills," I said.

"Yeah, people tell me that."

"There wasn't any blood anywhere. No bullet holes."

"What do I look like, an amateur?" His

face crinkled and a tear slid down his cheek. "I'm real depressed," he said.

"I bet I know something that'll cheer you up."

He looked like he didn't believe it.

"You know Louie D's heart?"

"Yeah."

"It wasn't his heart."

"Are you kidding me?"

"Swear to God."

"Whose heart was it?"

"It was a pig heart. I bought it at a butcher shop."

DeChooch smiled. "They put a pig heart back into Louie D and buried him?"

I nodded my head yes.

He started to chuckle. "Then where's Louie D's real heart?"

"A dog ate it."

DeChooch burst out laughing. He laughed until he had a coughing fit. When he got himself under control and he stopped coughing and laughing, he looked down at himself. "Jeezus, I've got an erection."

Men get erections at the strangest times.

"Look at it," he said. *"Look at it!* It's a beauty. It's hard as a rock."

I looked over at it. It was a pretty decent erection.

"Who would have thought," I said. "Go figure."

DeChooch was beaming. "Guess I'm not so old after all."

He's going to jail. He can't see. He can't hear. He can't take a leak that lasts under fifteen minutes. But he has an erection and all the other problems are small change. Next time around I'm coming back as a man. Priorities are so clearly defined. Life is so simple.

DeChooch's refrigerator caught my eye. "Did you by any chance take a pot roast out of Dougie's freezer?"

"Yeah. At first I thought it was the heart. It was all wrapped up in plastic wrap and it was dark in the kitchen. But then I realized it was too big, and when I took a closer look I saw it was a pot roast. I figured they'd never miss it, and it might be nice to have a pot roast. Only I never got to cook it."

"I hate to bring this up," I said to De-Chooch, "but you should let me bring you in."

"I can't do that," DeChooch said. "Think

about it. How's it going to look . . . Eddie DeChooch brought in by a girl."

"It happens all the time."

"Not in my profession. I'd never live it down. I'd be disgraced. I'm a man. I need to be brought in by somebody tough, like Ranger."

"No. Not Ranger. He's not available. He's not feeling good."

"Well, that's what I want. I want Ranger. I'm not going if it's not Ranger."

"I liked you better before you had an erection."

DeChooch smiled. "Yeah, I'm back in the saddle, chickie."

"How about if you turn yourself in?"

"Guys like me don't turn themselves in. Maybe the young guys do. But my generation has rules. We have a code." His gun had been lying on the table in front of him. He picked the gun up and chambered a round. "Do you want to be responsible for my suicide?"

Oh brother.

There was a table lamp lit in the living room, and the overhead light had been switched on in the kitchen. The rest of the house was dark. DeChooch sat with his back to a doorway leading to the dark dining room. Like a ghost from horrors past, with only a slight rustle of clothing, Sophia appeared in the doorway. She stood there for a moment, swaying slightly, and I thought she might truly be an apparition, a figment of my overactive imagination. She held a gun at waist level. She stared straight at me, aimed, and before I could react, she fired. *POW!*

DeChooch's gun flew from his hand, blood spurted from the side of his head, and he slumped to the floor.

Someone screamed. I think it was me.

Sophia laughed softly, her pupils shrunk to pinpoints. "Surprised the two of you, didn't I? I've been watching through the window. You and Chooch, sitting here having cookies."

I didn't say anything. I was afraid if I opened my mouth I'd stutter and dribble or maybe just make unintelligible guttural sounds.

"They put Louie into the ground today," Sophia said. "I couldn't be at graveside because of you. You ruined everything. You and Chooch. He's the one who started it all, and he's going to pay. I couldn't take care of him until I got the heart back, but now it's his time. An eye for an eye." More soft laughter. "And you're going to be the one to help me. You do a good enough job, maybe I'll let you go. Would you like that?"

I think I might have nodded, but I'm not sure. She would never let me go. We both knew that.

"An eye for an eye," Sophia said. "It's the word of God."

My stomach sickened.

She smiled. "I can see on your face that you know what must be done. It's the only way, isn't it. If we don't do this we'll be forever damned, forever shamed."

"You need a doctor," I whispered. "You've been under a lot of stress. You're not thinking right."

"What do you know about thinking right? Do you talk to God? Are you guided by His words?"

I stared at her, feeling my pulse pounding in my throat and at my temple.

"I talk to God," she said. "I do what He tells me to do. I am His instrument."

"Well yeah, but God's a good guy," I said. "He wouldn't want you to do bad things."

"I do what's right," Sophia said. "I cut evil

out at its source. My soul is that of an avenging angel."

"How do you know this?'

"God told me."

A terrible new thought popped into my head. "Did Louie know you talked to God? That you're God's instrument?"

Sophia froze.

"That room in the cellar . . . the cement room where you kept Mooner and Dougie. Did Louie ever lock you in that room?"

The gun was shaking in her hand, and her eyes glittered under the light. "It's always difficult for the faithful. The martyrs. The saints. You're trying to distract me, but it won't work. I know what I must do. And you're going to help me now. I want you to get down on your knees and unbutton his shirt."

"No way!"

"You *will*. You'll do it now, or I'll shoot you. I'll shoot you in first one foot and then the other. And then I'll shoot you in the knee. And I'll continue to shoot you until you either do as I tell you or you die."

She took aim and I knew she was telling the truth. She'd shoot me without a moment's regret. And she'd continue to shoot me until I was dead. I stood, using the table for support. I walked wooden-legged to DeChooch and knelt beside him.

"Do it," she said. "Unbutton his shirt."

I put my hand to his chest and felt his warmth, felt him take a shallow breath. "He's still alive!"

"Even better," Sophia said.

I gave an involuntary shudder and began unbuttoning his shirt. One button at a time. Slowly. Buying time. My fingers feeling stupid and clumsy. Barely able to manage the task.

When I had the shirt unbuttoned, Sophia reached behind her and got a butcher knife from the wooden block on the kitchen counter. She tossed the knife on the floor beside DeChooch. "Cut his undershirt away."

I took the knife in hand, feeling the weight of it. If this was television, in one swift move I'd have the knife plunged into Sophia. But this was real life, and I had no idea how to throw a knife or how to move fast enough to beat the bullet.

I put the knife to the white undershirt. My mind was scrambling. My hands were shaking and sweat prickled at my underarms and scalp. I made the initial stab and then ran the knife the length of the shirt, exposing DeChooch's knobby chest. My own chest feeling hot as fire and painfully constricted.

"Now cut his heart out," Sophia said, her voice quiet and steady.

I looked up at her and her face was serene . . . except for the terrifying eyes. She was confident that she was doing the right thing. Probably had voices in her head reassuring her even as I knelt over DeChooch.

Something dripped onto DeChooch's chest. Either I was drooling or else my nose was running. I was too scared to tell which it was. "I don't know how to do this," I said. "I don't know how to get at the heart."

"You'll find a way."

"I can't."

"You *will*!"

I shook my head.

"Would you like to pray before you die?" she asked.

"The room in the cellar . . . did he put you in it often? Did you pray there?"

The serenity left her. "He said I was crazy, but *he* was the one who was crazy. He didn't have faith. God didn't speak to *him*."

"He shouldn't have locked you in the room," I said, feeling a rush of anger at the man who put his schizophrenic wife in a cement cell rather than get her medical attention.

"It's time," Sophia said, leveling the gun at me.

I glanced down at DeChooch, wondering if I could kill him to save myself. How strong was my sense of survival? I glanced over at the cellar door. "I have an idea," I said. "DeChooch has some power tools in the cellar. I might be able to get through his ribs if I had a power saw."

"That's ridiculous."

I jumped up. "No. It's exactly what I need. I saw this on television. On one of those doctor shows. I'll be right back."

"Stop!"

I was at the cellar door. "This will only take a minute." I opened the door, turned the light on, and moved onto the first step.

She was several paces behind me with the gun. "Not so fast," she said. "I'm going down with you."

We took the steps together, going slowly, not wanting to misstep. I crossed the cellar and grabbed a portable power saw that was sitting on DeChooch's tool bench. Women want babies. Men want power tools.

"Back upstairs," she said, agitated at being in the cellar, looking anxious to leave.

I took the stairs slowly again, dragging my feet, knowing she was antsy behind me. I could feel the gun at my back. She was too close. Taking chances because she wanted to get out of the cellar. I got to the top stair and I whirled around, catching her at mid-chest with the power saw.

She gave a small exclamation, and there was a gunshot that went wild, and then she was tumbling down the stairs. I didn't wait to see the outcome. I jumped through the door, slammed it and locked it, and ran out of the house. I ran through the front door I'd carelessly left unlocked when I'd followed De-Chooch into the kitchen.

I pounded on Angela Marguchi's door, yelling for her to open it. The door opened and I almost knocked Angela over in my rush to get in. "Lock the door," I said. "Lock all the doors and get me your mother's shotgun." Then I ran to the phone and called 911.

The police arrived before I got enough control over myself to go back into the house. No point going in if my hands were shaking so badly I couldn't hold the shotgun.

Two uniforms entered DeChooch's half of the house and minutes later gave the all-clear for the paramedics to enter. Sophia was still in the cellar. She'd broken her hip and probably had some cracked ribs. I thought the cracked ribs were chillingly ironic.

I followed the EMS crew and stopped in my tracks when I got to the kitchen. De-Chooch wasn't on the floor.

Billy Kwiatkowski had been the first uniform in. "Where's DeChooch?" I asked him. "I left him on the floor by the table."

"The kitchen was empty when I entered," he said.

We both looked at the trail of blood leading to the back door. Kwiatkowski switched his flashlight on and walked into the yard. He returned moments later.

"Hard to follow the trail through the grass in the dark, but there's some blood in the alley behind the garage. It looks to me like he had a car back there and drove off."

Unbelievable. Fucking unbelievable. The man was like a roach . . . turn the light on and he disappears.

I gave my statement and slipped away. I was worried about Grandma. I wanted to make sure she was safe at home. And I wanted to sit in my mother's kitchen. And most of all, I wanted a cupcake.

LIGHTS WERE BLAZING when I pulled up to my parents' house. Everyone was in the front room watching the news. And if I knew my family, everyone was waiting up for Valerie.

Grandma jumped off the couch when I walked in. "Did you get him? Did you get DeChooch?"

I shook my head. "He got away." I didn't feel like going into a big explanation.

"He's a pip," Grandma said, sinking back into the couch.

I went into the kitchen to get a cupcake. I heard the front door open and close and Valerie drooped into the kitchen and slumped into a chair at the table. She had her hair slicked back behind her ears and sort of plumped up on top. Blond lesbian impersonator does Elvis.

I put the plate of cupcakes in front of her and took a seat. "Well? How was your date?"

"It was a disaster. She's not my type."

"What's your type?"

"Not women, apparently." She peeled the

paper wrapper off a chocolate cupcake. "Janeane kissed me and nothing happened. Then she kissed me again and she was sort of . . . passionate."

"How passionate?"

Valerie turned scarlet. "She Frenched me!"

"And?"

"Weird. It was really weird."

"So you're not a lesbian?"

"That would be my guess."

"Hey, you gave it a try. Nothing ventured, nothing gained," I said.

"I thought it could be an acquired taste. Like, you know how when we were kids and I hated asparagus? And now I love asparagus."

"Maybe you need to stick with it longer. Took you twenty years to get to like asparagus."

Valerie thought about that while she ate her cupcake.

Grandma came in. "What's going on here? Am I missing something?"

"We're eating cupcakes," I said.

Grandma took a cupcake and sat down. "Have you been on Stephanie's motorcycle yet?" she asked Valerie. "I rode on it tonight and it made my privates tingle."

Valerie almost choked on her cupcake.

"Maybe you want to give up on being a lesbian and get a Harley," I said to Valerie.

My mother came into the kitchen. She looked at the cupcake plate and sighed. "They were supposed to be for the girls."

"We're girls," Grandma said.

My mother sat down and took a cupcake. She chose the vanilla with the colorful spinkles. We all stared in shock at this. My mother almost never ate a perfect cupcake with sprinkles. My mother ate leftover halves and cupcakes with ruined icing. She ate the broken cookies and pancakes that got burned on one side.

"Wow," I said to her, "you're eating a whole cupcake."

"I deserve it," my mother said.

"I bet you've been watching Oprah again," Grandma said to my mother. "I always know when you've been watching Oprah."

My mother fiddled with the wrapper. "There's something else . . ."

We all stopped eating and stared at my mother.

"I'm going back to school," she said. "I applied to Trenton State, and I just got word I'm accepted. I'm going part-time. They have night courses."

I let out a whoosh of air in relief. I'd been afraid she was going to announce she was getting a tongue stud or maybe a tattoo. Or maybe that she was running away from home and joining the circus. "That's great," I said. "What kind of a program are you in?"

"It's just general right now," my mother said. "But someday I'd like to be a nurse. I always thought I'd make a good nurse."

IT WAS ALMOST twelve when I got back to my apartment. The adrenaline high was gone, replaced by exhaustion. I was full of cupcakes and milk and I was ready to crawl into bed and sleep for a week. I took the elevator and when the doors opened on my floor I stepped out and stood statue still, barely believing my eyes. Down the hall, in front of my door, sat Eddie DeChooch.

DeChooch had a huge wad of towel held to his head with his belt, the buckle jauntily placed at his temple. He looked up when I walked toward him, but he didn't get to his feet and he didn't smile or shoot me or say hello. He just sat there staring.

"You must have a beaut of a headache," I said.

"I could use an aspirin."

"Why didn't you just let yourself in? Everyone else does."

"No tools. You need tools to do that."

I pulled him to his feet and helped him into my apartment. I sat him down in my comfy living room chair and hauled out the half-empty bottle of hooch Grandma had left hidden in my closet from an overnight stay.

DeChooch chugged three fingers and got some color back into his face.

"Christ, I thought you were gonna carve me up like a Sunday goose," he said.

"It was close. When did you come around?"

"When you were talking about getting through the ribs. Jesus. Makes my balls crawl just remembering it." He took another hit on the bottle. "I got out of there as soon as the two of you went down the stairs."

I had to smile. I booked through the kitchen so fast I didn't even notice De-Chooch was gone. "So what's up now?"

He slouched back into the chair. "I rode around for a while. I was gonna take off, but my head hurts. She shot half the ear away.

And I'm tired. Jeez, I'm tired. But you know what? I'm not so depressed. So I figure, what the hell, let's see what my lawyer can do for me."

"You want me to bring you in."

DeChooch opened his eyes. "Hell no! I want Ranger to bring me in. I just don't know how to get in touch with him."

"After all I've been through, I at least deserve the collar."

"Hey, what about me? I only got half an ear!"

I did a large sigh and called Ranger.

"I need help," I said. "But it's a little strange."

"It always is."

"I'm here with Eddie DeChooch, and he doesn't want to be brought in by a girl."

I could hear Ranger laughing softly at the other end.

"It's not funny," I said.

"It's perfect."

"Are you going to help me out here, or what?"

"Where are you?"

"My apartment."

This wasn't the sort of help I'd anticipated, and it didn't seem to me the bargain should hold. Still, you never knew with Ranger. For that matter, I wasn't entirely sure he'd ever been serious about the price for aid.

Twenty minutes later, Ranger was at the door. He was dressed in black fatigues, with a full utility belt. God only knows what I'd dragged him away from. He looked at me and grinned. "Blond?"

"It was one of those impulse things."

"Any other surprises?"

"Nothing I want to tell you about right now."

He walked farther into the apartment and raised an eyebrow at DeChooch.

"I didn't do it," I said.

"How bad is it?"

"I'll live," DeChooch said, "but it hurts like hell."

"Sophia showed up and shot his ear off," I told Ranger.

"And she's where now?"

"Police custody."

Ranger got an arm under DeChooch and pulled him to his feet. "I have Tank in the SUV outside. We'll take Chooch to the emergency room and have him admitted overnight. He'll be more comfortable there than in jail. They can lock him down at the hospital."

DeChooch had been smart to hold out for Ranger. Ranger had ways of accomplishing the impossible.

I closed the door after Ranger and locked it. I zapped the television on and flipped through the channels. No wrestling or hockey. No movies of interest. Fifty-eight channels and nothing to watch.

I had a lot of things on my mind, and I didn't want to think about any of them. I prowled through the house, annoyed and at the same time relieved that Morelli hadn't called.

I had nothing on my slate. I'd found everyone. I had no open cases. On Monday I'd collect my finder's fee from Vinnie, and I'd be able to pay another month's worth of bills. My CR-V was in the shop. I hadn't gotten the estimate on that yet. With any luck the insurance would cover it.

I took a long hot shower, and when I came out I wondered who the blond person was in the mirror. Not me, I thought. Probably next week I'd go to the mall and have my hair dyed back to its original color. One blonde in the family is enough.

The air coming through my open bedroom window smelled like summer, so I decided on undies and a T-shirt for bed. No more flannel nightgowns until next November. I dropped a white shirt over my head and crawled under the quilt. I shut the light out and lay there for a long time in the dark, feeling alone.

I have two men in my life and I don't know what to think of either of them. Strange how things turn out. Morelli has been in and out of my life since I was six years old. He's like a comet that once every ten years gets sucked into my gravitational pull, furiously circles me, and then rockets back out into space. Our needs never seem to be in total alignment.

Ranger is new to my life. He's an un-known quantity, starting as mentor and progressing to . . . what? Hard to assess exactly what Ranger wants from me. Or what I want from him. Sexual satisfaction. Beyond that I'm not sure. I gave an invol-untary shiver at the thought of a sexual en-counter with Ranger. I know so little about him that in some ways it would be like mak-ing love blindfolded . . . pure sensation and physical exploration. And trust. There is a quality to Ranger that instills trust.

The blue numbers of my digital clock floated in blackness across the room. It was one o'clock. I couldn't sleep. An image of Sophia popped into my mind. I closed my eyes tight against it and willed it to go away. More sleepless minutes ticked by. The blue numbers said 1:30.

And then in the silent apartment I heard the distant *click* of a lock turning. And the soft scrape of my broken security chain as it swung across the wood door. My heart stopped dead in my chest. When it restarted it banged so hard against my rib cage my vision blurred. Someone was in my apartment.

The footsteps were light. Not cautious. Not pausing periodically to listen, to look around the dark apartment. I tried to control my breathing, to steady my heart. I suspected I knew the intruder's identity, but that did little to lessen the panic.

He stepped into the doorway to my bedroom and knocked softly on the jamb. "Are you awake?"

"I am now. You scared the hell out of me."

It was Ranger.

"I want to see you," he said. "Do you have a night-light?"

"In the bathroom."

He got the light from the bathroom and plugged it into a baseboard outlet in my bedroom. It didn't give off much light, but it was enough to see him clearly.

"So," I said, mentally cracking my knuckles. "What's going on? Is DeChooch okay?"

Ranger removed his gun belt and dropped it on the floor. "DeChooch is fine, but *we* have unfinished business."